THE GRACEKEEPERS

Also by Kirsty Logan

The Rental Heart and Other Fairytales

The
Grackeepers

KIRSTY LOGAN

HarperCollins*PublishersLtd*

Published by HarperCollins Publishers Ltd

First Canadian edition

HarperCollins books may be purchased for educational, business,
or sales promotional use through our Special Markets Department.

HarperCollins Publishers Ltd
2 Bloor Street East, 20th Floor
Toronto, Ontario, Canada
M4W 1A8

www.harpercollins.ca

Library and Archives Canada Cataloguing in Publication
information is available upon request

ISBN 978-1-44343-793-6

Printed and bound in the United States of America
RRD 9 8 7 6 5 4 3 2 1

to Annie Bee,
my first and last reader

I'm not afraid of storms, for I'm learning how to sail my ship.
LOUISA MAY ALCOTT

Before

The first Callanish knew of the Circus Excalibur was the striped silk of their sails against the grey sky. They approached her tiny island in convoy: the main boat with its bobbing trail of canvas-covered coracles following like ducklings, chained in an obedient line. Ships arrived a dozen a day in the archipelagos, and Callanish knew that the circus folk would have to fight for their place on her island. Tomorrow the dock would be needed for a messenger boat, or a crime crew, or a medic. In a world that is almost entirely sea, placing your feet on land was a privilege that must be earned.

As dusk fell, Callanish loitered at the blackshore, her slippered feet restless on the wooden slats. She watched as the circus crew spilled ashore: a red-faced barrel of a man, trailed by a bird-delicate boy; a trio of tattooed ladies, hair bright as petals; two gleaming horses left to gum at the seaweed. To a chorus of shouts - *hoist! hoist! hoist!* - the crew pulled ropes in unison, their limbs slick with saltwater.

Callanish tugged at her white gloves as she watched the circus unfold. She saw how the boat's sails would become the striped ceiling of the big top; how the wide, flat deck would be the stage. With each billow of sail or tightening of ropes, she inched further off the dock and on to the shore. It was only when the sun dipped below the horizon that she felt the damp chill in her toes and saw how her slippers had darkened with seawater. Oh, she would be in trouble now.

She ran home doing giant steps, leaping high into the air like a circus acrobat, hoping the wind would dry her slippers before her mother saw.

That night Callanish huddled under the striped canopy, mouth open as she gazed up, gloved hands gripped between her knees. Not all the landlockers on her island found the circus a glad sight: there were enough people on the island to crowd out the big top twice over, but it was only half full. Still, Callanish was excited enough for every single landlocker in the whole archipelago.

Her mother had scrubbed and scrubbed at the white silk slippers, muttering that Callanish would have to skip the performance. Callanish had shut herself in the wooden chest, hiding among the sealskins, until her mother relented. She promised that she would not fiddle with her gloves and slippers, and she would be silent and good and unnoticed, and it would all be worth it for the circus.

'We shouldn't welcome damplings like this,' murmured Callanish's mother, folding her bare hands on her lap. 'And at night-time, too, when good people should be tucked up safe in their houses! What are those circus folk hiding in the dark, hmm?' She patted Callanish's hands, making sure the gloves were on. 'Some islands don't even let damplings come above the blackshore. If they want to perform, they can do it in the daytime with waves lapping at their ankles like they're meant. Those people belong in the water. They're dirtying the land.'

But Callanish knew that would never work. The circus would not look good in the bland, bright day: its colours would fade against the clouds, spitty rain would threaten the fire-breather, the acrobats' sodden feet would make them shiver so much they missed their catches. What would be the point of an imperfect circus?

The red-faced barrel-man strode onstage, dressed in a ringmaster's costume of an elaborate hat, black trousers, and a shirt covered in rows of paper ruffles. Even Callanish's mother gasped at that: so much paper must have cost a fortune.

At the ringmaster's urging the circus burst into colours, lights, the death-mocking glory of twists and catches and bright gleams of skin. To Callanish it felt more daring than secrets, more vivid than memory, and her eyes opened wide as eggs. After each act – acrobats! horses! fire-breathers! – the landlockers rushed to fill the ringmaster's hat with lumps of gold and coal and quartz and copper. By the time he was introducing the final act, he had to drag his treasure-filled hat offstage.

On to the stage stepped a family: a man and a woman with a girl of about Callanish's age. They were all dark-haired and draped in fabric, pure white and shimmering. The woman held one end of a golden chain, the other end hidden behind a curtain. They bowed to the crowd, then the woman tugged the chain. An enormous shadow lumbered towards her.

'A bear!' cried out Callanish. 'From the storybook! A bear and a baby bear!' And sure enough, padding unsteadily in the big bear's wake, came a bear no bigger than Callanish.

Offstage, a needle whined on to a record. Violins swooped around the big top. The man and woman began to dance. They waltzed around the golden-chained bear as it reached its heavy paws out for them, at first in play, then in frustration. The song eased into another rhythm, and the woman slipped away from the man and into the bear's grasp. The crowd gasped, shrieked, stood as if to run – but the bear was turning and stepping gracefully, its paws clasping the woman's hands. They were dancing. After a moment, the little girl and the little bear joined hands and danced too, a mirror in miniature. Callanish clapped with glee, and even her mother seemed charmed.

In the years that followed, Callanish tried many times to remember exactly what happened next. It did not help that as soon as the big bear roared, her mother wrapped her arms around Callanish's head and pulled her close, the world instantly reduced to the earthy, floral smell of her mother's skin and the scratchy wool of her dress. But Callanish could still hear the screams, the roars, the chaos of running feet. She felt herself lifted as her mother hefted her on to her hip and ran.

Jolting with movement, Callanish fought to peer back over her mother's shoulder. She saw landlockers scrambling to the exits. She saw the dropped bodies of the man and woman, their white clothing stained dark, their skin sheened red. She saw the bright gleam of a blade in the woman's motionless hand. She saw the big bear, belly sliced open, a shadow heaving its final breaths.

And in the centre of it all she saw two figures: one draped in white, one furred black; both with eyes open moon-round and empty. A small girl and a small bear, hands and paws still linked.

1
North

Behindcurtains, North and her bear waited. Their cue wouldn't come for a while yet. The air back here was still chilly, though the smell of sweat and soil was getting stronger. North never felt comfortable with her feet touching land. She didn't trust its steadiness, its refusal to move or change in the honest way of the sea. The landlockers hadn't given the circus much room on their island – it was small, north-west, not a capital – and behindcurtains was a narrow space.

The damp hem of the curtains huddled around her ankles as she pressed her face to her bear's chest, breathing in his musty smell, hearing the beginnings of a growl within him. She reached her hand to his nose and tapped it, as a warning for him to stay silent. Their show today would be uncomplicated: North and her bear would dance, they would kiss, they would bow to the crowd. Simple. Or as simple as anything can be in a circus.

Out on stage, the rest of the circus folk were performing the maypole, everything wrapped in ribbons: the pole, their hair, their bodies, all wrapped tight so the crowd couldn't tell which were girls and which were boys, so they were all girlboygirls. The ribbons were dyed bright with ground-up shells and seaweed, streaking colour on to their bare skin.

North's bear was not bright. He was brown as wood and he was patterned a little like wood too, whorls of lighter fur amongst the dark. To match his fur, North's dark hair was tied up in loops and her pale body was draped in brown fabric. She had to match his golden chains, too, so she had dyed strands of her hair gold and woven them into braids. North stroked her hands along her bear's broad neck in swoops, keeping rhythm with his breath. It was important to calm him before a perform-ance, to show him that she was on his side, to get him used to his chains all over again. Bears are harder to train than dogs or horses or any other animals, because they're vicious and have faulty memories. North was like that too, or at least that's what Avalon, the ringmaster's wife, said.

As if summoned by the thought, Avalon slid out from behind a wedge of curtain. She had a sprig of apple blossom tucked behind her ear, its petals velvety as her cheek. North had never seen fresh flowers before Avalon started wearing them in her hair.

'Darling urchin,' she purred. She tossed an object from hand to hand as she spoke, smooth as juggling. 'Is your mangy beast ready to terrify the children?'

But North did not hear a word. She stared, hypnotised, at the object passing between Avalon's hands. The apple was a perfect sphere, green speckled with red, shiny as a bird's eye. Avalon pulled a silver knife from her dress pocket and cut the apple's softening flesh into quarters, exposing the pips tenderly. Its scent exploded in the air: sweetly souring, past its best but still with a sheen of juice. She didn't know how much apples cost, but it was certainly worth weeks of the circus crew's dinners. North inhaled as deeply as she could.

Avalon ate a slice from the knife's blade, pips and stem and all. Then another. Then she raised a third to her mouth, and, noticing North's gaze, paused.

'Oh, little wraith. You only have to ask, you know. Would you like a piece?'

6

North tried to speak, but she'd spent all afternoon murmuring to the bear and her throat had tightened. She coughed.

'What was that?'

'Yes.' North had to clench her jaw and swallow hard before she could force herself to add – 'Please.'

Avalon sighed, and someone who didn't know her might think that her regret was genuine. North knew better, and wished she hadn't said *please*.

'I am sorry, urchin. It's for the baby.' Avalon cupped her belly maternally and chewed the third quarter of the apple. For the baby, for the baby. In the few months since Avalon had announced her pregnancy, everything that happened in the circus was for the baby. North couldn't wait for the damned thing to be born – though Red Gold already had one pampered son, and he certainly didn't need another.

As Avalon swallowed, she smiled. With a flick of her little silver knife, she tossed the last quarter of the apple under the curtain, where it disappeared in the dust and shadow. North bit down a mewl of dismay. As if sensing her mood, North's bear began growling, low and thick.

Avalon narrowed her eyes at the bear as if he had offended her, but North could see that his growls made her nervous. She wanted to command her bear, to anger him, to prod him into swiping his half-moon claws through the air in front of Avalon's smug face. Perhaps the threat of the bear was enough for a moment's peace. Instead North swooped her hand down her bear's neck, soothing his growl to silence.

From the stage, the ringmaster was announcing THE CLIMAX OF THE MAYPOLE, MORE SENSUAL AND DRAMATIC THAN ANYTHING YOU HAVE EVER SEEN, and without a backward glance Avalon stalked away, tucking her silver knife back into her dress pocket, BUT WAIT, DO NOT LEAVE YOUR SEATS, FOR OUR SEDUCTIVE PERFORMERS WILL ENTER YOUR RANKS, and left North still gaping at the shadow that hid the tiny, perfect quarter of apple, an item she had not tasted or even seen for months, FOR NOW YOU CAN BUY YOUR OWN RIBBON AND LEARN THE MYSTIC ART OF MAYPOLE TO THE DELIGHT OF YOUR LOVER.

She was still motionless, the bear's fur growing hot under her hand, when the maypole dancers paraded offstage. The *Excalibur*'s crew numbered thirteen, including North, and their faces were more familiar to her than her own. Even in the gloom she recognised the angular jaws of Melia and Whitby, the acrobats, though bandaged in their ribbons it was tricky to tell which was which. Sometimes they said they were siblings, sometimes a long-married couple. North didn't know the truth about their lives before they bought their way on to the *Excalibur*: of all the tales they'd told, one must be true, but it was impossible to pick it out of the made-up ones. The acrobats both had monkey-small feet and hips, with shoulders as big as a bull's: perfect for rolling up ropes and swinging out over the heads of the crowd. Their ribbons covered the shining remnants of old injuries criss-crossing their limbs. All the circus crew bore their scars, but the acrobats' were enough to make even North flinch. Whichever circus they'd been in before, it couldn't have had safety nets either.

Melia and Whitby sniffed the air, dragging their faces into sneers in imitation of Avalon, then pressed North into the embrace of the curtain so the other performers could file past. They huddled together, placing their wide hands on the bear's back as if to bring him into the conversation. The curtains and overhead of the big top were made of the schooner's four sails, and the fabric felt rough with saltwater.

'I hear,' stage-whispered one acrobat, 'that Avalon, our beloved ringmaster's wife, has had quite enough of circus life. She wishes to abandon us all to the jaws of the sea.'

'But how could she ever tire of us, pray tell?' said the other in mock shock.

'It's sad news indeed, sweet sister,' said Whitby. 'Avalon scorns the sea and wishes only for land. A house, a garden, a piece of ground that doesn't move.'

'Just think on it! All that gold, taken straight from our ringmaster's pockets and funnelled into a teensy piece of land, without any of it touching our dinner table. For shame, my darling husband.'

North hunched her shoulders, sure that if she looked up she'd see the ringmaster's reddened, glittered cheeks looming towards her. The stage make-up irritated his skin so he plastered on more to cover it, which irritated it more until it cracked and bled. North had seen the pinkish gleam of the bowl after Red Gold had washed; his veins must hold as much glitter as blood.

'Land? How very dull, brother! What a yawnful sort of life!'

'So true – the exact same sky and the exact same ground, every single day! You'd barely be able to breathe for all the yawning!'

'Hush now,' said North, as from the stage came the boom of Red Gold introducing THE WONDROUS BEAR-GIRL, FEARLESS AND FIERCE. She shrugged her shoulders out from under the acrobats' arms, then made a show of fussing with her bear's collar until she felt them leave. Her bear always went onstage shackled, though if he decided to use his strength, the fine gold chains would snap like strands of hair. The chains were decorative, meant only for the eyes of the crowd. Spectacle is grounded in the illusion of control. The crowd think they want safety, but what they really crave is the trick gone wrong: the fall from a trapeze, the uncovering of bone.

Earlier, when the *Excalibur* had docked, North had spied on the landlockers from under the canvas top of her coracle. They all seemed haggard and hunched in their hard-won finery, as if even the crust of soil they'd allowed the circus was too much. It didn't matter that damplings outnumbered landlockers ten to one; they had land, and land meant food, and food meant power, and no one was allowed to forget that.

For their act, North and her bear would mime a courtship: her kisses on his sharp teeth, the two of them in a clumsy waltz, then a musty-furred swoon in his arms and the slight lifting of her dress as the applause swept them offstage. It was always a crowd-pleaser: the female side of the big top loved the romance, the male side appreciated the reveal of flesh, and everyone was thrilled by the danger of the bear. North could still do her act. She would let out her costume when she needed to.

From the stage Red Gold's voice grew even louder, HERE TO TAME THE TERRIFYING BEAST WITH TEETH SHARPER THAN RAZOR-SHELLS, CHILDREN AVERT YOUR INNOCENT EYES, and North darted her hand under the curtain and groped around in the dust for the apple slice. She ate it in one bite, sucking her lips inward so she wouldn't miss any of its juice. As she wrapped her bear's chain around her fist and stepped out from behind the curtain, she let her tongue prod at the shreds of appleskin between her teeth, and swallowed them too. She had to. For the baby.

With the crowd's shouts and claps still echoing in her ears, North settled the bear in the shell of their boat. After a performance he needed to be groomed, fed, soothed. She'd worked hard to get him used to the golden chains, but he knew they weren't natural and shuddered back from them every time. North had never hurt him, and never would. Other animals could learn by cruelty: jewelled whips for ponies, kicks and slaps for dogs. But that would not work on bears. They learned steadily, through rapport, a dialogue built up over years. The problem was that her bear seemed hardly to remember her from day to day. She believed that he loved her, but he sometimes looked at her as if she were a stranger.

Faulty memory, like everyone said, and that's why North's job was so hard, but also why she had a place in the circus at all. There were many circus boats – all of them less decrepit than the *Excalibur* – but none of the others had a bear-girl. In a world with so little land, mammals were rare outside the landlocker farms. Because North's bear was a rarity, that meant that North was a rarity too.

Before she could begin his grooming, he would have to eat. There was no point in grooming him first, as bears are not known for being tidy eaters.

The main circus boat had been pulled ashore, as with various unfurlings the mast became the centre of the big top, the striped sails became the canvas, the deck the stage. Some circuses left their ships in the water and performed up on the dock. North shuddered at the thought. She found it hard enough to walk on the islands. She could never find the balance and concentration to perform there.

Luckily, the brightly painted coracles where the crew lived didn't need to touch land. They had only to tighten the chains between them and the convoy became one long, snaking raft. North used the salt-crusty chains as a handhold to giant-step between the coracles. The swaying chains and bobbing decks felt steadier to her than walking on ground.

She managed to collect dinner from the mess boat without getting dragged into conversation with any of the *Excalibur*'s crew. She brought the food back to her boat and ate with her bear: stewed hock, baked potatoes, a cup of milk. Neither of them had drunk milk for weeks, so the crowd must have paid well. North hoped there would be eggs for the morning. Their bowls were not quite full enough for their bellies, but it took the edge off their gnaw of hunger.

After they had licked their bowls clean, North drained the water from the filter into a washbucket. She ensured that her bear was watching, then put the gold chains in a box and tucked them under her berth. He grumbled a roar, but it seemed involuntary, like indigestion, and he settled to his grooming without fuss. It took a long time: many of the women landlockers seemed to have taken a fancy to him, and had thrown perfumed leaves that caught in his fur. The perfume was waxy and ratted the fur into clumps, resisting North's damp fingers. She was probably supposed to do something noble with the leaves, like burn them or bury them, but she didn't care about the land-lockers' superstitions. She pulled back the coracle's canvas top and threw the leaves into the water. She hoped that their waxy coating would make them float back to shore, so those fancy ladies could see what she thought of their gifts.

By the time she was finished, she could barely muster the energy to comb her own hair. All circus folk kept their hair long, dyed bright with whatever coloured things they could scavenge. It helped with the illusion of their performance; their tightrope-walk between the genders. Once a preacher from a revival boat had picketed the circus show with signs proclaiming THE SINS OF GLAMOUR, shouting about how the words glamour and grammar meant the same, and every word spoken by a beautiful woman was a spell cast over the god-fearing man. Red Gold loved the publicity; the performance that night was packed. And ever since, the three crewmembers on the beauty boat had been called the glamours.

North's hair was currently dark, except for her scatter of gold braids. She combed it through with her fingers, then retied the braids. The dyed hair felt rougher than the rest, but still sturdy enough. She hadn't asked the glamours how they'd made the golden colour; once they had made silver-blue dye from eels, and it damaged everyone's hair so much that it crumbled in their hands.

She went to close the canvas, then pushed it back instead, letting the night's chill soothe her tired eyes. The wind was strong enough to cover all other sounds: the chatter from the coracles, the lazy slap of waves on hulls, the distant whisper of leaves from the centre of the island.

Above her, the stars outshone the meagre lights on the land. All the answers lay up there to those who could see. Without knowledge of the sky, no one would know where to find safe port, when to sail hard and when to seek anchor. North gave her prayers to the stars and the tides, just as she did every night. They deserved worship for being the only reliable things in the world. Except, perhaps, for one other.

North fastened the canvas and slid under her bear's warm frontpaw. His heart beat a thud-a-thud against her back as she let the waves rock them both to sleep. She was good at looking after her bear, and she clung to that thought. Soon there would be another person on their boat, but it would be okay, because North already knew how to care for a creature that needed her. She could still be the bear-girl. In time, her child could earn its own place in the circus. She could look after them both, baby and bear. She could keep them safe from the world – and from each other.

North was awoken by the sound of knuckles on metal. Dreams were still caught on the insides of her eyelids - birthing a demon, an eight-tentacled monster that strangled her while still inside her - and she had to choke back a scream. Her lungs vibrated with the roar that was beginning in her bear's chest, and she twisted round in his arms to tap on his nose.

'No,' she whispered, and felt the growl sink back down. She struggled out of his embrace and pulled on an old shirt, worn to softness.

'Knock knock!' called Red Gold, which seemed pointless to North as he was already knocking. She heard him unclip the edge of the canvas cover, and his berry-red cheeks appeared over the coracle's edge. 'North child, why are you hiding from me?'

'Don't be silly, Jarrow. I slept in, that's all. Is it late?' Behind Red Gold's head the sky was dark blue threaded with pink. The sun wasn't up, and North knew it would be a while until breakfast. She was soothed by the slow breath of waves and the scrape of the coracles shifting: the lullaby of the sleeping circus.

'No, no, don't worry about that. Just ready yourself and come out here. I have a surprise.'

North tied her hair in a knot and began gathering her bear's things. If she had to be woken so early, she might as well make the most of it. 'I'm sorry, I can't. We'll be moving pitch soon, and I should let the bear get some exercise in the shallows while we're here, so if you don't mind –'

'Come out here. I'm not asking.' Red Gold's head disappeared from the lip of the coracle. In the gap left, North saw that the streaks of pink in the sky were burning to red.

She leaned over the bunk to settle her bear. Her toe bumped against the box containing the golden chains, and she did consider them; she rarely left her bear alone, and if he woke without her there he might be frightened or angry. But no – the chains would make him angrier still, and even a bear on the rampage was not as scary as Red Gold when disobeyed. She pulled on trousers and a knitted jumper. It took her a moment to find her bell – all damplings had to wear a tiny brass bell on their clothes when on land, in case they were mistaken for landlockers – and another moment to attach it to the laces of her soft leather shoes. Usually she went barefoot, and the soles of her feet felt as thick as her coracle's hull. But no matter how tough it was, she would not let her bare skin touch land. She stretched her jumper, making sure it hung loose over her middle, and climbed out of the coracle.

Red Gold had already made it to the dock and stood with his arm around his son, chest thrust forward. North's boat was midway along the line, and she took as long as she dared to make her way along the chains. In the brightening light, she could not ignore the peeling paint and rusted metal of the coracles. In places, the reds and greens and purples had flaked off entirely, leaving patches of dull grey. Saltwater and paint did not mix well.

Ainsel had clearly paid a visit to the Island of Maidens – Whitby and Melia's scathing nickname for the glamours' boat. His hair was braided with feathers and the contours of his face were subtly shaded to match his clothing. Blue under his cheekbones, green along his brows, a merging of the two at the corners of his eyes. He looked as vain and haughty as his horse.

'Good morning, North,' he said as she stepped on to the dock where the *Excalibur* was moored.

'Good morning, Ainsel. I trust you slept well.'

'Such a fine day for an adventure, isn't it, my little ones?' cooed Red Gold. He hooked his arms into North's and Ainsel's elbows. He managed a few steps like this, but their different heights made it impossible, so he settled for striding along between them. 'The sky – glorious! This land – glorious! The joy of being with my two most favourite young lovers – most glorious of all!'

North offered up a tight smile. It was taking all her concentration to make sure that Red Gold stayed in the middle. More than anything, she did not want Ainsel to reach for her hand. She'd have to let him take it, and his skin would be as smooth as satin slippers, and she'd be forced to run back to her coracle and tie shut the canvas and never come out again.

Red Gold carried on a steady stream of exclamations as the three of them followed the gangway up from the port, their leather shoes soft on the wooden slats. The tin-sided towers looked more ramshackle than ever, the waves slapping at their bases. North could not understand why anyone would choose to live there. The crew called the landlockers 'clams' for their brainless need to cling to the shore. Was the desire to be near land so overwhelming that people would accept these shoddy homes, hoping that over the years they could creep gradually closer to the centre of the island? Soil was dirty, and it smelled; North wanted nothing more than to be away from it.

They were past the tower blocks and on to the reclaimed land, where the houses became lower and larger. These houses were not impossible to buy – reclaimed land was cheaper, not worshipped like the real earth. As they walked, North kept one ear to Red Gold's stream of exclamations, while the other listened out for early-rising landlockers. If spotted, she could either make excuses or run. From experience, North knew it was better to run.

Ainsel's attention seemed to be wandering. He kept glancing back at the port, to where the line of circus coracles sat sleeping. His turning affected his stride, losing the rhythm of his steps and making his toes drag. If he didn't keep his eyes down, the unsteady, too-steady path would trip him. And then he'd stumble, and he'd fall, and his bare hands would have to touch – ugh. As much as she didn't want his hands in hers, North would catch him to save him from touching the ground.

Red Gold must have noticed Ainsel's distraction: he picked up the pace, talking faster and louder, and before North knew it their steps changed to the steadier thud of real land. It felt too solid under her feet, and it made her knees judder. The houses here were not much taller than she was, and there were no tower blocks. Rich people wanted to live as low to the old ground as possible.

Past the houses, closer still to the island's centre, lay farmland. Red Gold glanced over his shoulder as they climbed the stile; it wasn't technically illegal for damplings to walk through the farmland, but if a farmer 'accidentally' shot them the punishment would be light. North put her sleeve over her mouth. It stank here: mud and plants and the faint reek of animal shit.

Red Gold paused on top of the stile, spreading his arms to North and Ainsel as if they were his big-top crowd. He spoke in a stage whisper.

'Now listen, my little ones. Be sure and stick to the paths. The last thing I need is to have to bribe you off a prison boat.' He stepped down from the stile, landing with a thud and striding off down the path.

'Jarrow, if you don't mind – if I can ask –' she called after him. 'Why are we doing this?'

Red Gold winced at her volume, glancing theatrically across the fields to the farmhouse. He mimed something that North could not translate, then turned and carried on walking.

'It's about the wedding,' said Ainsel in an undertone.

Everything in North jolted to her throat. 'Haven't you spoken to him yet?'

'Not yet.' Ainsel fussed with his hair and glanced back at the coracles, although they were lost behind the houses. 'Look, I will. But I have to choose the moment properly. I know my father, and I'll know the right time. Just wait.'

North wondered what that was like – to know your father. Ainsel was the only one on the *Excalibur* with a parent still alive. He didn't seem to realise how special it was.

'You have to tell him, Ainsel. If I say I won't marry you, he'll make me leave the *Excalibur*. But he won't kick out his own son. I just want to stay in the circus with my bear and my – with the crew.'

'I don't want to get married any more than you do, North. But if he thinks we're going against him, he'll just dig his heels in further.'

'But you have to tell him before –'

'I'll tell him! Just shut up about it.'

Ainsel was lingering, picking at the notches in the wood, and North was thinking scathing thoughts about how he was so prettily useless he couldn't even climb a stile, when she realised that he was waiting for her to go first.

'Oh,' she said. 'Thanks.' She climbed over it as fast as she could. Her jumper hung loose, but she didn't want Ainsel to look too closely.

They remained silent as they walked through the farmland. The only sound was the wind in the trees and the tinny jingle of bells from their clothing. Ainsel was ungrateful and dull, but North had known him her whole life; she should try to think of something to say, anything to break the awkward silence, but she couldn't. Never mind friendship or familiarity. It was too early to think straight.

At the edge of the trees, they paused. North had never been inside a copse before, and she could guess from the look on Ainsel's face that he hadn't either. The woods were old – some of the trees were prehistoric, people said – and they'd all heard stories about the awful things that landlockers did in there. She bent and peered into the copse. The ground was clear, but above that the trees twisted together, interlocking black shapes too dense for them to see far. Scraps of coloured fabric were tied around some of the branches. There were little piles of things at the base of several trees: shiny objects, scraps of paper, soft-looking moss. A shrine? An offering? North looked over her shoulder to see Ainsel reach out his hand to touch a twig, then think better of it.

'Jarrow?' hissed North into the dimness beneath the trees. In answer, the shush of leaves. She tried to edge her body in sideways, but it was too overgrown. She reached up and took hold of a thin branch, ready to snap it off and make room to slide through.

'North! No!' Red Gold came tearing around the edge of the trees, arms outstretched as if to catch her. 'You mustn't!'

She stepped back on to the path. 'It's okay. There's no one around to see.'

Red Gold slapped her hands away from the trees, even though

she'd already stepped back from them. Her skin burned. 'That doesn't matter. Don't you know that the trees are sacred?' He elbowed past her and examined the branch she'd touched, as if she'd left dirty fingerprints on it.

'Oh come on, you can't believe in -' North stopped at the look on Red Gold's face. As a dampling he did not need to worship the gods of the land, but apparently he did anyway.

'This is where we're from, child,' he said.

'But I'm not -'

He sucked his teeth and made a tutting sound. 'Not you, North! Me and my boy. We're landlockers, you know. The land is where we're from, and the land is where we'll return.' North looked away so that Red Gold wouldn't see her expression of disgust. 'And when you're married,' continued Red Gold, 'it will be on land.'

'But when did you decide this?' Ainsel seemed to be struggling not to shout. He swallowed hard and lowered his voice. 'How long do we have until - when is the happy day?'

North tried to keep her face neutral. Bad enough to go on to land, and bad enough to have to marry Ainsel - now Red Gold wanted to combine the two? But it would be fine. Ainsel would tell him. There would be no wedding, on land or at sea.

The ringmaster brought his great paw down on his son's shoulder. 'I decided, and that's all that matters. You and our north child will be married when we get to the North-East 19 archipelago. The capital, by the World Tree. It's not usually allowed for landlockers who aren't - well, who don't currently live on land. But I've bought special permission. Because you are special, my boy. You're special because you're mine.'

North's heart began to beat in double-time. It would take four months to get to North-East 19, give or take a day, if they didn't get stuck in the doldrums crossing the equator.

'Jarrow,' said Ainsel, his voice uncertain. 'Father. I have to tell you something. North and I, we – and don't blame North for this, it's nothing to do with her, she's always happy with your decisions. It's entirely my choice, although she does agree with me about it, though she agrees with you too, of course, and –'

'Yes, yes.' Red Gold pulled Ainsel closer, then reached out his other arm for North. 'I'm listening. But first, I must tell you that I have a most special surprise for you. That's why I brought you out here, my darlings. I know there has been talk amongst the crew about this, but I want to tell you and North officially. I have scrimped and plotted and gathered my resources, and I plan to buy, just for you –' He paused, as if waiting for trumpets to sound. 'A house! On land!' He released Ainsel and North in a *ta-da!* gesture. 'Now, it can't be on old land, I must tell you, only reclaimed. For damplings like you, North, it's tricky. But in time, with lots of landlocker children between you – well, people might forget where you're from. Eventually, North, you could be one of us. Not a true landlocker, but close enough to pass.'

North could not speak. Four months. By then all the sewing in the world wouldn't make her performance dress hide it, and Ainsel would know, and Red Gold would know, and there would be no use at all in lying. And the house! It was true, what Melia and Whitby had said – all that wealth really was going on a house. But not for Avalon. For North.

'Now, my little ones,' went on Red Gold, 'I know that your silence is simply because you're too overwhelmed to speak. I've put everything I have into this house. But it's worth it, my loves. It's worth it to ensure my son's happiness and to get our family back on to land. To ensure that the Stirling legacy is restored to glory.' He beamed at his son, who offered nothing in return. Ainsel seemed distracted, staring at his feet as he scuffed the ground, lost in thought. 'And you will be happy, and you will be glorious,' said Red Gold. 'You will be glorious because I want you to be.'

The morning light had turned buttery and North had to raise a hand to shield her eyes. Ainsel was not looking at her; he'd lifted his head to look back the way they had come.

'Ainsel,' she said. She tried not to let her voice shake. But he would not look at her. She turned instead to Red Gold.

'I want to make you happy, Jarrow,' she said. 'I do, I promise, but Ainsel and I, we don't...'

'Yes? Do consider, before you speak, that I have built the Excalibur up from nothing, and both of you with it. And do consider all the things that the whole crew has gone without to save for this house. This is not about making me happy. It's about much more than that.' Jarrow kept his voice treacle-sweet, but with each passing moment his smile stretched wider. North knew this was not a good sign.

'I mean,' she stumbled on, 'I want to be happy. For you. The way you want. I want to be glorious. But landlockers, and babies, and I don't know if I can...'

'Yes, north child? Spit it out. Don't keep us waiting.' Jarrow's smile was now so wide and tight that the skin began to crack. Tiny dots of blood gleamed on his reddened cheeks.

Why wasn't Ainsel saying anything? North resisted the urge to punch him right in his pretty face. 'Ainsel wants to tell you something.'

Red Gold turned to his son.

'Yes.' Ainsel finally spoke. 'Yes. I want to tell you that I am glad. I can think of nothing more glorious than having a house on land, and raising my child as a true Stirling, and living with...' He trailed off.

'With North,' prompted Red Gold. 'With your wife.'

'With... uh, yes, with –'

From a farmhouse, the slam of a door. All three heads snapped up.

Red Gold took their hands and gripped hard. 'Now. We're going to walk back, calm and quick. Don't touch anything. Don't put even your littlest toe off the path. Got it? Go.'

Along the path with their heads down and over the stile in single file and past the low houses and past the higher houses, trying not to panic, trying not to run, and there was the blackshore, and North remembered how to breathe because there were the tin-sided towers, and there was the shush of their shoes on the gangplank, and there was her coracle chained in its row. She walked the chains and ducked under the canvas without a word. It wasn't until she slid under her bear's sleeping paw that she felt her heart slow.

2
Callanish

Callanish could always predict the weather, because the graces told her. Under clear skies they stayed silent in their cages, their movement slowing as they starved. But when storms were due they couldn't be at rest. They'd pweet and muss, shuddering their wings so that the murky green-blue feathers stuck out at defensive angles. Callanish couldn't help but feel their disquiet.

The morning slipped by in silence, broken only by the shift and coo of the graces. Callanish sat on the front porch of the house, perched at the edge, feet tucked under so they wouldn't touch the water. In the distance ships passed, tiny as toys. The sea here was busy with fish, but Callanish would not catch them. She knew that fish had to eat something, and all living things grew from dead things, and there was no point being squeamish about it. But it was different when you had seen the bodies, when you knew their names, when you had laid them to rest with your own hands. In eating the fish, Callanish would have felt that she was eating the bodies. Sometimes, she could almost laugh: surrounded by a fish-rich sea, she had enough food and water to last her a lifetime, but she could have none of it.

A Resting was due that afternoon, so after her morning of silence Callanish went inside to prepare. The grace was ready; when she entered the house he was huddled in the corner of his cage, head under his wing, speckled feathers puffling around the metal bars. He knew that a storm would come soon, but that there was nothing he could do to get away from it.

'I know the feeling,' said Callanish to the grace, and she dropped five sunflower seeds into the cage. She wasn't supposed to feed the graces, but she believed that some people deserved a longer remembrance. She'd already met some of the crew who were coming for the Resting, and her stomach clenched to think of the quickness in their smiles, their relief when they saw that the grace was so small. She wished she'd chosen a bigger grace for the dead man, but it was too late. All she could do now was sneak it some food to make it live longer. Real grief, and Callanish didn't feed the grace. Those people didn't need the grace's death to tell them when mourning was over. Ships rarely came back to check anyway; the birds were bred to be tiny and they could not live long, caged without food or fresh water. Callanish didn't feel bad about feeding the graces. It was such a small crime.

She checked that her white dress was dry, then pulled it off the line and over her head. It was hardened with salt and she stretched out her shoulders to loosen the fabric; her filter wasn't working properly, and she hadn't wanted to waste drinking water on laundry. She roped her silver-blonde hair at the back of her head, looping it low over her ears to hide her scars, and added a spray of white flowers – fake, but no one could expect them to be real. White silk gloves, white silk slippers; both sewn by her mother and re-stitched over the years. She couldn't trade for these. They had been specially made to disguise the webbing between her fingers and toes.

Callanish was kept busy as a gracekeeper: at least two Restings a week, always. People liked a gracekeeper who looked young. Innocent. Unthinkably far from her own death.

For lunch she ate rye bread and honey, drank a bone cup of milk about to turn. Only eating landlocker food meant that quantities were small, and there was never quite enough of anything. She wouldn't mind dampling food, but worried about her reputation as a grace-keeper if she requested it. Callanish could not remember how it felt to be full. More supplies would arrive with the Resting group: a large parcel of body, along with a small parcel of soap and eggs and gold. Graceyards were not a destination. Lined up along the equator as they were, deep in the doldrums, they were places for passing through. Perfect for the dead. Perfect for Callanish.

She hoped that the Resting party would arrive before the weather turned; the graces had been restless all morning, but the sky stayed pale. Callanish strained her eyes in every direction, but she couldn't see any storm clouds. What she could see, though, was the approach of a small tin rowing boat. The Resting party was on its way, and Callanish was ready to perform.

After the service, before Callanish could grasp the oars to row back to the dock, the widow grabbed her wrists. Callanish tensed all her muscles. If the widow's hands moved down from Callanish's wrists, if the gloves were to slip – then they would see her hands, and they would know, and they would tell.

Callanish already knew what she would do if she was revealed. It would be so easy to tip herself off the side of the boat and into the water. Then she would straighten her body like a dart and sink right down to the bottom of the sea. It was the only way.

But the widow, it seemed, only wanted to thank her. She gripped Callanish's exposed wrists as she spoke, and her hands felt damp and swollen, the palms soft with fresh blisters from the boat's oars.

'He was…' said the widow, then trailed off. She spoke in fummels and haffs as if she could not get enough breath to speak proper words.

'I know,' said Callanish, doing her best expression of sympathy, trying not to let her panic show. It was a fine line: she had to stay noble and restrained, as a gracekeeper should, but she did not want to be unkind. She took the widow's hands in her own, noticing how her wedding ring dug into her finger, making the flesh bulge out at either side. Callanish wondered whether she would wear it until it was engulfed in her own flesh, forming a secret totem. She had a flash of the dead man's hands; the way she'd tied them in fists before wrapping him in the netting so that his fingers wouldn't poke through. She kept her own fingers pressed tight together.

Callanish placed the widow's hands back in her lap and let go, pretending that she was checking the grace's cage. It was one of the finer ones, and she had made sure to polish its bars to a shine. The effect wouldn't last long in the saltwater, but that didn't matter as long as it looked good for the Resting.

She regretted feeding the grace. The others on the man's ship might be eager to finish mourning him, but she saw now that his wife wouldn't be back to check on the grace – not because she didn't care, but because she would remember her husband no matter when the grace died. Callanish pulled on the oars to draw the rowing boat back to the dock.

No matter what she felt, the show must go on. She said the words, she performed the actions, she took her payment. But she only mimed grief. She didn't mean it. How could she? She didn't know this man, beyond his stitched-shut face and his wife's too-tight wedding ring.

Sometimes she pretended that she was saying the words of the service about her mother. This helped, and on the darkest days she'd had to leave long pauses for fear that her voice would crack. After those Restings she'd sit down to write a letter to her mother, but she rarely finished them and never sent them.

'Farewell,' said Callanish in a soothing sort of voice, as the crew climbed back into their boat.

'Farewell,' they chorused solemnly, and she knew that they were really saying it to the man they'd lost. Everyone played a role at a Resting.

Legally, all dead damplings had to be interred in a graceyard. But Callanish knew that didn't always happen. If someone died in the far north or south, could a crew really be expected to keep the body on board for the months it took to reach the equator? And so it would be tied in canvas and tipped overboard, and the family would decide their own time of mourning, and the dead would end up as a meal for the fishes just as they would in a graceyard. Such small crimes.

As the little boat sailed away, back to the main ship anchored at the edge of the graceyard, Callanish felt that one end of a fine thread was tied to the boat's stern and the other to her ribs. With every beat of the oars she felt something over her heart stretch, and stretch, until it might break. A string like the one between a body and its grace. But all threads broke eventually. It was for the best. For Callanish, being alone was safer.

She turned away from the retreating boat and went back into the house, carrying the parcel of supplies with her. For one adult Resting she was paid a mix of food, supplies and tradable goods: ten eggs, a thick wedge of bacon, a hank of fabric for letter-writing, a lump of copper the size of her thumbnail. It was fine. It was enough. What else could she need? She would eat tonight, and that was all that mattered.

She stacked the items on the shelf, and found herself humming so loudly that her throat burned. It reminded her that she was still there. She could eat and she could breathe. She lived.

She would write a letter to her mother tomorrow.

When it started to get dark, Callanish sat out on the porch, her feet tucked up, a cup of milk in her hand. To keep her white dress clean, she'd exchanged it for a grey one. She was alone, and so she did not need her gloves or her slippers. The sea reflected the sky in a mass of fire. Sunset is fast at the equator; blink in the day, open your eyes to the night.

As a child, Callanish had imagined chunks of land floating on a globe of sea, held by thick chains fastened to anchors the size of castles. She had asked her mother what would happen if the chains were to rust away, if the countries were to bump and jostle one another. Would they become attached? Would bridges be built where only sea had been before? Or would the edge of one country tip under another, upending it like a toy tug carrying too many pebbles at one end?

'Your brain is upside-down,' her mother had said. 'Land does not float on sea; the earth is a solid mass like a rubber ball, and oceans sit in cups carved out of land. No matter how deep the sea, there is always land at the bottom of it. Land decides water, not the other way around.'

It was only when she'd been left at her new home in the graceyard that Callanish realised her mother was wrong. Land would never choose this. Water had decided the shape of the world. She sipped her milk and watched the sea roll out in every direction, mirror-flat.

There was nothing, nothing, nothing – and then there was something. A shadow on the horizon, moving closer.

There was no Resting due, no meeting with a bereaved family, and Callanish swithered on the porch, not sure whether she should change back into her white dress. She squinted her eyes until she was sure that there was only one person in the rowing boat. One person, no bundle of body. She put on her gloves and slippers then sat back down on the porch, finished her cup of milk, and waited.

'Ahoy,' gasped the stranger, still a few boat-lengths away from the dock. Callanish couldn't help smiling at the old-fashioned term.

'Ahoy,' she replied, and stood to help the stranger climb out of the rowing boat. Except that the stranger was not exactly a stranger. 'I know you,' she said. 'Odell, is it?'

She waited for him to catch his breath. It was a fair distance to row.

'Well remembered,' he finally said. 'It's been a while – a year or so, I think. When I first arrived, with that little tour to the neighbours. I forget the name of the fellow on the other side. Time acts funny round here and I lose track sometimes.' Odell stood on the dock, shifting from one foot to the other. 'It's nice to see you again.'

'My name is Callanish.'

'Right! Right. You know what it's like out here, I just…' He slapped his forehead. 'Callanish. I'll remember that now.'

Callanish couldn't think of a polite way to say *what do you want?* She should invite him in, she should get him a cup of milk. Instead she stood awkwardly on the porch.

Odell reached down to his rowing boat and pulled out a bottle, tilting his head as a question. Callanish went into the house and got her bowl. Odell would just have to be happy drinking from it, as she didn't have another cup. Gracekeepers were given one cup, one plate, one bowl, one spoon. They were not expected to entertain visitors. Odell filled the bowl from the bottle without comment, then went to tip some into Callanish's empty cup.

She shook her head. 'I can't –'

'Yes you can.'

She let him fill the cup. They sat on the porch together, and Odell tugged off his shoes and let his feet dangle in the water. Fish clustered around his toes, gulping at the surface of the water. Callanish suppressed a shudder.

The sun had tipped below the horizon, leaving the sky inky and a chill in the air.

'You've been doing this longer than me. Does it get easier?'

She shrugged. The liquid in the cup burned her throat as she drank.

'I thought so,' he said.

The only sound was the tick of the fishes' mouths against the water. Callanish was sure she could hear Odell's heart beating.

'It was my choice to do this,' he said, as if she'd asked a question. 'My wife, she got into religion. Clapping and chanting – like on those revival boats, you know? All burning and swooning. And I tried to get her back – spoke to the preacher, all gentleman-like, but he was having none of it. Got heated, like it does, and maybe things went too far. It was a matter of the heart, you know? Anyway, I won.'

So Odell had hit a man, beaten a man, maybe killed a man. It made no difference to Callanish. But if he was determined to tell her, she'd let him talk.

'I won, but Roche still wouldn't come back to me. She told the island council, and they gave me a choice, and – well, you know how it goes.' He motioned to Callanish's house, to the rows of grace-cages, to the endless sea. 'Of course you know. It was my choice, really. I thought – I can be one better than a preacher. I can be holy. I can be a hermit, you know?'

He refilled his bowl and glanced at Callanish. There was nothing to see on the horizon, but she kept her gaze on it anyway, so she wouldn't have to look at Odell.

'I told Roche that it wasn't all about her, that I had my own life too, and I had to leave the island because I didn't want to see her face every single day, you know? So I did it. I left. I chose to become holy.'

His tone dared Callanish to argue. She didn't argue.

'I didn't do anything wrong. I really didn't. And it's not even a punishment really, when you think about it. It's more of a step up, you know? Your very own island.' He drained his bowl and made a sound somewhere between a cough and a laugh. 'Well, it's not a boat, so it must be an island. At least it doesn't move. Want some more?'

Callanish tipped her cup towards him. He refilled it, and then his bowl. She felt goosebumps rise along her arms from the cooling air;

she drank again to feel the warmth of it. Her limbs began to relax, her feet dipping closer to the water.

'It's not right that we're stuck out here, you know?' went on Odell. 'I should be able to leave whenever I want.'

The silence stretched. Callanish felt her throat close around all the words she did not want to say. 'You make your own choices,' she said.

'I know. But do we have to live with them for the rest of our lives?'

'Just leave. Your island council won't even know you've gone until the deliveryman comes by. They can't hurt you if they can't find you.'

'And where am I supposed to go? I can't ever go back to my island.'

'There's more to the world than islands.'

'You mean boats?' asked Odell.

Callanish shrugged. Islands or boats, it was all the same. She didn't care. She wanted to drink, and slip into the water, and live in the sea for ever.

'Come on, I can't live on a boat. I'm not a dampling. It was bad enough coming here on that big ship. First time my feet left land, you know? Now look at me. Toes wet and no islands for miles.' He made an *ugh* sound, a snort, and shifted his feet in the water. The fish scattered. 'Going out in the rowing boat makes me sick, but at least it's temporary. Life at sea – that's no life at all.'

He fiddled with his bowl, turning it between his palms, and his movements were jerky, as if he was annoyed, as if Callanish had not fulfilled some promise she didn't recall making.

This was not the first time that she had heard a confession. With some Restings, people did not play their proper roles. They thought that Callanish was something she was not. After the body had sunk, after the grace was settled, they'd turn to her. Hunched in the boat's prow, or speaking in a monotone while staring at the horizon, they'd confess to her. They'd lied or hurt or killed, and they wanted her to make it all better. She couldn't fix anything, but she could listen and stay quiet, and that had always been enough. Eventually tears were dried, spines were straightened, and Callanish would pull the boat back to the dock.

'That's the choice,' she said to Odell. 'Here or there. Dampling or landlocker. Sea or land. Man or woman. But this is something different. Don't you see? We made our homes on the sea and on the land. We can stay here in the graceyards and be nothing. I mean, be neither.'

Odell was not listening. The bottle was empty now and he had started talking again, his words merging. It was as if Callanish had never spoken. She glanced up and the world spun, the grace-cages doubling. She blinked them straight again.

'I don't know if I can do it,' Odell said. 'This type of life – it's impossible. How can anyone? Why should anyone? It's a punishment, but we haven't done anything wrong. Not really. It can be forgiven.'

If he thought that gracekeepers were holy, then she'd be holy for him. She'd hear his confession, and then he'd go back to his graceyard, and he'd never come back, and everything would be fine. He'd stay and do his job, or he'd buy his way on to a boat and do something else, and she'd never even know. But she would not give him a confession in return.

'I don't want to fall in the sea and drown,' he said. 'They haven't told us about that. If I die, will they leave me there, or will they dive down and get my body? Will you Rest me? If you die, am I supposed to Rest you?'

'I don't know. I suppose so.'

'But I don't want to die here. I want to go home and be burned on sacred copse wood. I want my ashes to be scattered at the World Tree. Is it wrong to want that, when I chose to leave? Can I have that? I want that. I don't want to die but I want to die on my island. What do you want?'

Callanish did not answer. She let the silence stretch, until Odell filled it by draining his bowl for the last time. She stood and walked over to his rowing boat. He followed unsteadily, leaving a line of wet footprints across the porch. She shouldn't have drunk so much; the sea pulled at her, stronger than ever.

'Can I come back?' Odell murmured. 'It's so quiet out here. Listening to records doesn't – I mean, it's not the same. Sometimes you need to say things and have someone respond.' His head was bowed. He seemed to be speaking to the flat water, the silvery fish, the uneven boards of the dock.

'I know,' said Callanish, doing her best expression of sympathy. Noble, restrained. She was a good gracekeeper.

Odell got into his boat and rowed off through the neat lines of grace-cages. Callanish watched until his shadow disappeared. She kept her back pressed to the wall of her house, away from the pull of the sea. Her breathing sounded as loud as waves. She went inside and lay down on her bed, face turned to the window, until light came back to the sky.

3
North

North and her bear poked their heads up out of their coracle to watch as they approached the first island. Though it was not a capital, it seemed wealthy. Guards were stationed to steer their convoy into harbour, and there were strings of spirit lamps between the tower blocks to light the way. Even the tower blocks themselves seemed healthy: instead of pitted metal sidings, the buildings had plants growing from them in neat rows. It looked as if the residents would be able to lean out of their windows and pick food for dinner. It was a shame that landlockers were so snobby about dampling food; they could probably hook fish and seaweed from their windows too. Then they could stay in their houses, and would never have to put their feet on that grubby land at all.

At these signs of wealth and order, North flicked her eyes to the lead boat, where Red Gold stood at the wheel. In preparation for going ashore he'd put on his most expensive shirt - the one with rows and rows of paper ruffles across the breadth of his chest. It was ludicrous to use something as expensive as paper to make clothes, but the landlockers were always impressed by it. It made the *Excalibur*'s warped wooden hull and the rash of rust on the coracles seem glamorously faded, rather than decrepit. After all, if a man were too poor to look after his boats, he wouldn't spend money on a paper shirt.

North could only see the back of Red Gold's head, but knew from the set of his shoulders that he was thinking dangerous thoughts. Sometimes traditional islands liked a traditional show. Sometimes they wanted more subversion than even this circus could provide. Often their preference only became clear when they got the opposite of what they wanted; many circus folk had spent nights on the prison boat for going too far, and many more were scarred from being pelted with shells and stones by bored crowds who felt they had not gone far enough. North had a jagged dash of scar tissue on her arm from the edge of a mussel shell, and there was a notch in her bear's ear that would never close.

Ainsel emerged, unhooking his coracle from the *Excalibur* and attaching it to the mess boat. The coracles formed an anchored circle, with the *Excalibur* floating separately, attached only by a rope. When it was time to perform, the crew would pull themselves ashore on a raft using that rope. It was awkward, but it was the only way. The land-lockers didn't want the damplings to be on land any more than they had to be – and North was quite happy with that.

Red Gold bowed to a landlocker, and a contraption of hooks and chains eased the *Excalibur* up on to land. The ringmaster swaggered down to greet the port crew with barely a wobble in his legs. North frowned: maybe he really was a landlocker. It made sense to her that someone would give up a pile of bricks on a patch of dirty soil, even if it were only to live on a run-down circus boat. The *Excalibur* might be a little dented, but it was still a boat. It could get you from one end of the world to the other. Land was useless; it couldn't take you anywhere at all. She knew there must be a reason that Red Gold had left his home island, but she was afraid to ask.

As North watched, the crew piled on to the raft and pulled them-selves to the *Excalibur*, ready to begin the work of turning the boat into a circus. They'd get no help from the people on the island; landlockers didn't like to go closer to the water than the blackshore – the line of seaweed brought up by the high tide – and sometimes you'd think they believed the seaweed itself was cursed. North didn't know where the superstition had come from, but she was glad of it. It meant that if the damplings ever had to escape, there was the safety of distance. Weapons could be thrown across the blackshore, but landlockers would be reluctant to cross, and so they couldn't follow the boats. North tried to relax. There was no reason yet to think that escape would be necessary this evening, but she knew from experience that a crowd could turn in an instant. Still, no point worrying: they were ashore now, so they had no choice but to perform. She turned away, back to her bear.

Together they ate their meagre dinner and began their preparations for that night's show. The glamours from the beauty boat had made North a collection of coloured powders and liquids, all of which were safe on her bear's fur. Even if he ate them, he'd be fine – though North would rather not have to scrub green goop off his tongue. She knew from the dread weighing heavy in her stomach that Red Gold was going to ask her to do the funeral waltz. She twisted open the tub of black powder and got to work.

Behindcurtains smelled of seaweed and soil. North's bear was in their coracle, resting before their act, but North could not stay still. Red Gold had listened to none of her worries about the funeral waltz; the crowd would bay for it, and that's all that mattered. Instead of getting more and more frantic, she was calming herself by watching the show.

The evening began with the maypole, feral and fleshly as ever. Then the horse show: Ainsel turning backflips and cartwheels on the narrow space of his horse's trotting back; Avalon riding around him in circles, simpering side-saddle like a queen, draped in flowers, her belly round as a full moon. Her pregnancy fitted the fertile springtime theme of the show, but the bump had to be visible from the highest seats, so most of it was still padding. Her horse was pure white, though North knew that its bridle had to be carefully positioned to hide the red birthmark on its cheek. In the circus, nothing was as simple as it seemed. Avalon used to leap through fire, but since the pregnancy she did nothing but posture, her horse merely a prop.

Ainsel was painted in shades of gold and purple, and his horse's bridle was studded with silver bells, each movement making its own music. Even North had to admit that he was beautiful when he performed.

The circus acts continued. Bero the fire-breather toyed with hot coals, the glamours flirted in suspenders and waistcoats, the clowns stalked them laddishly while dressed in corsets, and the applause increased with each passing moment.

Between acts, North peeped out from behind the curtain to get a look at the crowd. As ever on the islands, the men and women were separate, with all the children on the women's side. She looked for the subtle signs that they'd identify with the Circus Excalibur's gender-play: women with shorn hair, men sitting close enough to touch. Nothing. Still, the more conservative the island was, the more the landlockers might be desperate for subversion. The small, fenced-off section reserved for visiting damplings was full to overflowing; North could only hope that they weren't from a revival boat.

The last act before the interval was North's favourite: Melia and Whitby. Tonight they were aerialists, their ropes strung up high between the *Excalibur*'s two masts. They began on the ground, their turquoise hair and silver body suits rendering them mirror images. In the centre of the stage hung a pair of long ropes.

As the music began, the acrobats wrapped a rope around their wrists and began to roll up it in a series of planches, their bodies rolling, their delicate legs pointed like compass needles. Higher and higher they climbed, tilting the crowd's heads further and further.

At the highest point of the big top, they spiralled off and landed neatly on a tiny platform strung with ropes. The spotlight was trained only on them, leaving the rest in darkness. For a moment they were lost in an explosion of white as they smacked chalk between their palms, letting the excess drift down into darkness. Wrapping his wrists and ankles in ropes, Whitby bent his body into a crescent moon. Melia dropped from the platform and hung from the curve of his body for two breaths before letting go, falling to the ground like a comet. At the last moment she hooked her arm into a loop of rope, muscles pulsing. The crowd let out a smudge of noise; a mix of screams, gasps, moans.

She began to sway her body, building up momentum, letting her weight widen the circle, until she was swinging a circuit around the entire big top, far above the tilted heads of the crowd. Even from behindcurtains, North could see the incredible strain on Melia's arms; she shifted position to get a better hold, and North let out an *oh!* as Melia seemed to lose her grip. She fell two body-lengths on the rope, unable to hold it, and there was no net, and there was no safety line, and there was not enough time for anyone to run out and catch her. North screwed her eyes shut.

But there was no scream, no thud of a fallen body. North looked up to see Whitby, knees wrapped in the rope, arms spread, holding Melia's wrists. Their smiles stretched wide.

They were not siblings or spouses, as they pretended; they were two halves of the same whole. Not everyone found the key to their lock, the answer to their question. But they had. They took their bows high above the crowd, letting the applause float up like birds.

North was still catching her breath, trying to calm herself, when Red Gold dropped the curtain for the interval. It was time for the bear-girl to die.

Hidden from the audience behind a curtain, North was centre-stage, all in white. She was luminous, motionless, her spread arms bound to a huge whalebone cross that was wrapped in the blood-red ribbons of the maypole. Her bear was still behindcurtains, at the edge of her vision; he was wrapped in golden chains with his fur powdered black as night. At the other side of the stage crouched Bero, readying the needle of the wind-up gramophone. They each wore a tiny brass bell tied around one wrist. Even when performing, they could not forget what they really were.

Usually Red Gold introduced each act in lascivious detail, his voice booming halfway across the island to entice latecomers. But not this act. Although she couldn't see him from behind the curtain, North knew what he was doing: walking out onstage, standing serious-faced in front of the curtain. Now he was removing his hat. Now he was dropping his head in a play of grief. Now he was walking offstage, feet dragging. She threw her head back and closed her eyes.

The curtain lifted in silence on North, white as ice, crucified, lost in the throes of ecstasy or agony. The audience did not make a sound. They didn't seem to dare. The spotlight stayed on North for far longer than was comfortable; she could hear the audience shift in their seats, not sure what to think, not sure if this was all part of the act. North kept her face tilted upwards and tried not to let her chest rise. She felt her tiptoed feet begin to slip on the support at the base of the cross, and tensed her thigh muscles as hard as she could. She would not fall. Whatever happened, she would not fall. There was nothing more important than putting on the perfect show.

A moment more, then: a crackle from the gramophone, a shift in the spotlight. Violins juddered as her bear thudded four-pawed on to the stage. The crowd flinched back as one at the sight of the bear, then, after a heartbeat, leaned forward in a wave of curiosity. No one was looking at North now. At that cue, she extended the first two fingers of both hands, freeing the razor blades tucked against her palms.

Her bear approached. His black fur merged with the black curtain so that all that was clear were the fine lines of his chains. He raised himself up on his back legs, the violins reached a shriek, and, unnoticed, North used the razor blades to slice through the ropes. The music stopped, the spotlight burned bright, and North tumbled off the cross and into her bear's arms.

She knew that all the audience could see was the hulking shadow of the bear – and herself, draped pale and silent in his grasp.

The violins increased, denser, louder, swooping and diving as the bear staggered around the stage with North's lifeless body in his arms. He lifted her, presenting her to the crowd in his grief. His heart beat thud-a-thud, thud-a-thud, in contrast to the uneven wails of the violins. On the outside, grief was expressed in judders, faltering and unsure, but inside it felt as constant as breathing.

As the violins reached a crescendo, the bear raised his snout and released a roar loud enough to shake the entire island. From the crowd came scattered screams, children's sobs, a collective shift of feet as they got ready to run.

The bear collapsed in the middle of the stage, cradling North as they landed, wrapping his paws around her. The spotlight shifted to centre on them. So great was her bear, so thick his fur, that only the tiniest gleam of her skin was exposed to the air.

The violins died.

The crowd held their breath.

And then North was resurrected.

One arm swayed up, slender and pale as an anemone. It reached to cradle the bear's shadowed face. He lumbered to his feet as if he'd been hit, backing away from North, into the shadows. She was left alone in the spotlight. Her body was curved into a comma, her white dress spread. In silence she twisted on the ground, arching her back and looking over her shoulder at the bear, as if taking strength from him. The violins slid back: a single note, wavering.

Slowly, slowly, she got to her knees, as if in a trance. Slowly, slowly, she used her hidden razor blade to slit the front of her dress. The white fabric fell to the ground, and the crowd shifted in their seats: on the female side, the women tilted their heads away and the children peeped from between their fingers; on the male side, the men leaned forward with their elbows on their knees. North stood, and she was not a she.

Her body fitted the silhouette of a boy's. Her small breasts, her growing belly: all wrapped tight, all padded and bound in white. Her body gleamed like a marble statue. The styled tumble of her dark hair, now that the crowd looked more closely, seemed more like the mane of an unkempt boy. Blink and she's a girl. Blink again and he's a boy. Once more he turns to she, right in front of your eyes.

The violins fattened into a rhythm: from a dirge for loss, to a tango for love. North reached into the shadows and pulled the bear into the spotlight. He seemed confused, standing hunched at the edge of the light. She took his paw in her hand and turned, pirouetting into his arms. They swayed together, boy and bear, now girl and bear, but always lovers. North's bear had brought her back. She had returned to him, as she would always return to him.

They circled the edge of the spotlight together, North twisting in and out of the bear's grasp as they turned. In the centre of the stage they stopped, North's back to her bear's front. She brought her ankles together and stretched out her arms, lifting the bear's paws with them. They stood, white on black, aping a cross.

Then the bear folded his front paws around her, enclosing her in fur, his darkness covering every bit of her. Gripping his paws, she rolled her body up into his grasp, and they exited the stage to a chaos of violins. But no matter how loud the music, how bright the lights, none of the crowd could have failed to see the bear's peeled-back lips or hear his steady growling.

Red Gold swept past them to the stage, patting North and the bear on their shoulders. North's heart was beating so hard that she felt sick, but she forced her mouth into smile for the ringmaster. She glanced past the curtains to Bero, hoping for a wink of reassurance, but he was hunched over the gramophone, fiddling with the needle. His thick beard hid his expression. From the stage came the boom of Red Gold's voice announcing the next act.

North pulled her bear into the salty embrace of the curtains. In the narrow confines of behindcurtains, circus folk were all around her, preparing for their acts. Everything was the flash of colours and movement and frantic whispers. The growl still vibrated in the bear's chest. His jaw was clenched, his teeth bared. North still held the razor blades in her shaking hands. The bear's canines were as long as North's fingers. The scent of his meat-rot breath grew as he growled louder. She raised her hand. She hesitated.

Then she tucked away the blades, unclipped the bear's chains and stroked her hands along his broad neck, murmuring platitudes, soothing him with familiarity. His growl died down and he dropped to all fours. He seemed ready to lie down and sleep, right there among the curtains. North wished he could; she wished they both could.

A hand on her shoulder. She spun round, fists raised, teeth bared, ready to shout. Melia and Whitby backed away, eyes wide.

Sorry, mouthed North, lowering her hands. *Sorry. Tense. The show.* She nodded towards the stage. *Funeral waltz.*

The acrobats smiled and squeezed North's hands consolingly. She hoped they couldn't feel how badly she was shaking. *Our second act. Clown military*, they mouthed to her. *The clams will love it.* They nodded towards the crowd.

North knew how Melia and Whitby felt about the military acts. It was one thing to parody the resurrection; although the revival boats were getting popular, most people weren't religious, and those that were often didn't speak out for fear of being thought strange.

But to mock the military? It was suicidal. The *Excalibur*'s crew had spent time on a prison boat for it before, and there was no way to know how these landlockers would react. North hoped that Red Gold knew what he was doing.

North nodded to the acrobats to show her support, then turned back to her bear. Her hands still shook and her head throbbed with panic. No matter what went wrong in the acts, a happy crowd mollified · Red Gold. But North was not worried about the ringmaster. She was not worried about the military or even the prison boat. She was worried about her bear. They'd done the funeral waltz before, but not like this.

He was not supposed to lift her.

He was not supposed to roar.

Did he understand that it was just a show? When she was lying in his arms - when she would not speak or move or open her eyes - did he know that she was only pretending?

Not for the first time, North wondered what would happen to her bear when, inevitably, she could no longer do her act - whether she married Ainsel and moved to land, or was forced off the *Excalibur* by Red Gold. Either way, the ringmaster owned her bear. She doubted anyone else could learn to perform with him. He could not be used for farming or kept as a pet. He was meat for dinner, a fur coat, claws and teeth perfect for weapons.

North led her bear back to their boat. She would wash the colours off their skins, and they would be themselves again. Alone in their coracle, they were not performers, not burdens, not dangers, not weapons, not food. They were family.

After the music had stopped, after the performers had taken their final bows, after the crowd had applauded until the big top's canvas started to droop, and – most importantly – after her bear was lost in sleep, North climbed across the coracles to the mess boat. It was late, but the crew would congregate there to eat and drink away the night. The canvas was bright with lamps and she could hear the laughter from three boats away. She pulled back the edge of the canvas and climbed inside.

The *Excalibur* had been allowed to dock overnight on the island, which meant that the landlockers had enjoyed the show. No one would be reporting anything to the military. Red Gold had been right. When it came to judging the wants of crowds, he was right more often than he was wrong – although the consequences of wrongness were much more serious. North did not like to gamble.

'North child!' boomed Red Gold as North refastened the canvas over her head. He was still in his stage make-up and paper shirt, holding court at the head of the long metal table with his wife perched on his lap. Her smile was brittle.

'Good evening, Jarrow,' said North.

The mess boat was five times the size of North's coracle, but it was packed with the entire circus crew. A warm glow filled the boat; though the seal-fat lamps stank in the small space, they lit up as bright as sunshine. That old superstition about fire on a boat only had to be observed on the wood-hulled *Excalibur*. There were no windows in the metal-shelled coracles, and the need to see was more important than superstition. As long as the flames didn't reach as high as the canvas, they were safe, because almost everything in the coracles was made of metal or bone.

Spotting Melia and Whitby in the corner, North made her way over to them, but was stopped by Red Gold's hand on her wrist.

'Sit by us, my little Stirling-to-be.' He pulled her on to the pitted bench beside him, where a tin cup and plate were screwed on to the table. If she didn't drink, Red Gold would want to know why – and she was going to tell him, she really was, but not in front of the entire crew. And definitely not in front of Avalon.

North unscrewed the cup and lifted it to be filled. Bero the fire-breather, who also manned the gramophone, and was also the cook, also the barman, filled her cup with a clear liquid. Its smell burned the inside of North's nose.

'Thank you, Bero.' She tipped the cup so that the liquid touched her closed lips. No one would notice whether the level went down or not.

'I saw your act this evening, North.' Avalon's tone was prim, clipped, but she managed to fake a kindly expression in case Red Gold was looking.

North bought some time by standing up from the bench and blowing Avalon an elaborate air-kiss, then curtseying like she did after a maypole performance. She took her seat again with a wink to Red Gold. It was cheeky, but he was drunk enough to love it; he cheered and applauded, his meaty arms squashing his wife each time he clapped.

North hoped that this would count as a response, but Avalon wasn't letting go that easily.

'Your act seemed a little different to last time,' she said. 'I don't recall your bear roaring before. It all seemed less controlled. Louder. Wilder.'

'That's how we like it, eh? Got to give the islanders a good show if we don't want empty bellies!' Red Gold raised his cup to the canvas ceiling. 'Cheers, cheers, cheers! That's three cheerses so we all must drink.' He drained his cup, and then, with a tenderness only seen in the very drunk, he rested his free hand on Avalon's belly. 'Except for you, my flower bride. You cannot drink, so we drink to you. To Avalon! To my darling baby!'

There was a wordless roar as the rest of the circus crew raised their cups to toast the baby. North knew that most of them had gossiped and sniped that the baby was not Red Gold's, that Avalon lay with her horses, that she wasn't even really pregnant, that she wasn't even really a woman, that she was just a parcel of devils wrapped in skin. But Red Gold told them to drink, so they drank.

'To the baby,' whispered North. She wrapped her hands around her cup so that she wouldn't press them to her belly.

When people are cruel it's often said that they have no heart, only a cold space or lump of ice in their chest. This was never true of Avalon. She had no heart, everyone knew, but there was nothing cold about her. In her chest burned an enormous coal, white-hot, brighter than the North Star. North knew the truth about Avalon: she was made of fire, and she would burn them all.

Red Gold tipped Avalon back over his knee, smothering her with kisses. She struggled out of his grasp and slid on to the bench beside him, her chin raised, proud as a cat. She was probably trying to look noble, but the effect was spoiled by the gold glitter smeared across her cheek.

North took her chance to slip away and creep over to Melia and Whitby. When they weren't slick-haired and wrapped in ribbons for the maypole, it was easy to tell which was which. They had matching turquoise hair, but Melia's sat in neat pin curls while Whitby's was a mass of braids and dreadlocks. North took two steps towards them, and stopped.

Ainsel had unfolded himself from the bench and was standing in front of her, blocking her way. He was dressed all in black and his lips were stained red.

'Hello, Ainsel,' she said.

He took hold of North's shoulders – surprised, she jerked her hands up, ready to hit him – and he pecked a kiss on her lips.

'I look forward to our wedding, North,' he recited. All in one motion, he let go of North, sat back down, and drained his cup. The whole thing took less than a breath. After a few half-hearted whoops and table-slaps, the crew returned to their conversations.

North was glad that she hadn't hit Ainsel. They'd kissed plenty as children, lips too wet, eyes and mouths shut tight. Since Red Gold had decided that they were to be married, they'd been alone together just a handful of times – and most of them were spent discussing how to get out of the marriage. As children they'd pretended to be pirates and octopuses and priests; stolen the skin-diving helmets to explore the night-dark sea; crept to the blackshore to share a stolen plum, its flesh softened to the colour of meat. She didn't know what had gone wrong between them. Perhaps nothing had; perhaps she'd never liked him. The close quarters of the *Excalibur* could make it seem that two people were close, when really they didn't have a choice.

As he'd kissed North, Ainsel had been looking over her shoulder to the head of the table, where Red Gold and Avalon sat. Was this some test that he had to pass – a challenge, an agreement, proof of his intentions for North? She felt as cold and functional as the metal bench.

She took a seat beside Melia. 'That damn family,' she muttered.

'*Your* damn family, you mean,' replied Whitby, his eyes only slightly unfocused. 'You'll be one of them soon enough. Not long now until the wedding. North-East 19 isn't so far.'

'How did you know we were getting married there?'

Melia rolled her eyes. 'Gossip is the blood of the *Excalibur*.'

Whitby groped around for an unclaimed cup, and handed it to North. She tapped the rim of her cup against his, then screwed it to the table without even pretending to drink.

'So everyone knows everything about everyone,' she said.

Melia and Whitby shrugged in unison. In every group of people there is a hierarchy, and the circus was no exception. The acrobats were right in the centre; half the time they were allowed to tell others what to do, and the other half they had to do as others told them. Red Gold was at the top of the pile: lord of their tiny kingdom. Avalon was his lady, and then came Ainsel – at least, officially, though everyone disobeyed Avalon behind her back and Ainsel right to his face. He never complained to his father. Melia said it was because he didn't want to look bad in front of Red Gold, but North thought he was too self-absorbed to care what anyone else did.

Next came North – she wished this was because of her bear, but knew it was due to her betrothal to Ainsel – and then the fire-breather and the acrobats. Bero was above Melia and Whitby, because as the cook he also caught fish for their meals. The three glamours were at the bottom of the pile, but they had the sort of haughty beauty that meant they had to care for little else. And then the three clowns, who were their own separate fiefdom. They didn't follow anyone else's rules, but didn't expect others to follow theirs either. They were given some leeway for being the skin-divers, tasked with collecting seaweed to supplement their meals. If the water was shallow and unpopulated enough, sometimes they could also find tiny caches of coral or mother-of-pearl to trade for better food. North was a little scared of the clowns, though she'd never admit it. The clowns loved the military acts and would have done them on every island, given the choice. In choosing their performances each night, in denying them what they most wanted, Red Gold had saved them a hundred times.

Melia and Whitby were the best company on the *Excalibur*, and North wanted to talk with them, drink with them, pretend that things were normal.

'North!' Whitby leaned forward and tapped her on the nose, as he'd seen her do with her bear. 'Drink up. No time to mess about. There's a storm coming soon, you know.'

'And we should all get as pissed as stoats in preparation?' said Melia.

'Well, it's as sure as tides that we don't want to be sober.'

North lifted her cup and let a drop of the liquid on to her tongue, enjoying the burn as it went down her throat. Such a tiny amount wouldn't matter, and if she didn't drink it then she'd have to explain herself to the acrobats. Instead of a dizzy joy, the alcohol only made her feel sick. She had to tell someone. She couldn't deal with this alone. That night on the shore, and the secret growing inside her. She'd tell them everything.

She practised the words in her head: *Melia. Whitby. I have to tell you something. It might not make sense, but – listen.*

But she could see that they were in no mood to hear confessions. Whitby had reached over the table and was trying to tickle Melia, so she'd shoved handfuls of her hair into his face as a distraction. He backed away from the onslaught, raising his hands in surrender.

'Mercy, mercy! I'd rather choke on my drink than on your hair.'

'Well, I'd rather you choked on my hair than said another word about that storm.' Melia, seeing that her cup was empty, took a gulp from North's. 'It's not like we've never got through a storm before.'

'It's been ahead of us for days, Melia. See how it taunts us? We may need the good grace of the sea, but she couldn't care less what we do, or whether we're alive when we do it.'

Melia shrugged. 'Serves us right for being daft enough to sail into it. We could stay here.'

'Stay!' Whitby snorted. 'I'm sure the clams would love that. Staying still is not for us, my love. We're sharks. We move forward or we die.'

North climbed into her coracle long before dawn. The party was still going, but all she wanted was the comfort of her bear's heart beating against her back. She crawled in beside him, still in her day clothes.

How silly to think that she could have confessed to the acrobats. They were her friends, but they weren't her family. The clowns on the *Excalibur* were the children of clowns on the *Excalibur*, and their children would be clowns on the *Excalibur* in turn, assuming they lived long enough to make children - but not Melia and Whitby. They'd bought their way on to the *Excalibur*, adopted it as their newest home. Who knew how many families they'd had before this one? North was born on the *Excalibur*'s deck, and she'd never known another life. The acrobats wouldn't understand. There was only one creature alive that loved North unconditionally. She lived in a family of two - soon to be three. It would be fine. Her bear was safe. He loved her, and he would learn to love her baby too. She let the coracle rock her to sleep, with her bear's heartbeat at her back and the laughter from the mess boat sounding an echo.

4
Cash

The clowns were hungry. Every day the feeling grew. All damp-lings hungered – but Cash, Dosh and Dough wanted more than food.

Stuck under the swollen thumb of Red Gold – which was really the icy thumb of his horse-bitch wife – the clowns could not fulfil their true purpose. Clowns are mind-readers, megaphones, shouting out the things that the clams think but don't dare say. There's power in saying what no one else will. They wanted to scream and rage and have the whole world listen. They wanted sex and death and power. They were silenced, and it was starving them.

Cash broke away from working on Dosh's face and snorted.

'What?' mumbled Dosh, keeping still to avoid smudging the white paint.

'Red Gold lets us do the military act one night, and not the next,' said Cash. 'Where's the logic in that? Why does he get to choose when we're free and when we're chained? He should let us decide. We know better than anyone that the clams love it.'

'They love to hate it,' chimed in Dough, succinct as ever.

'Even better! Who wants to be loved? Hate is a much stronger emotion.'

'Finish. My. Face,' mumbled Dosh, lips pursed so the make-up wouldn't crease. Cash was getting frustrated. It was always hard to get more than a sentence out of Dough, but Dosh could usually be counted on to join in. Not tonight, it seemed.

'There are more important things here than our painted faces! There's no point if we can't use them to speak. Is this really enough for you?' Cash motioned around their coracle. It was sparse and scrubbed, the walls painted matte black, everything packed neatly in chests made of lashed-together seal bone. 'Is this all you want our lives to be? Parading our muted voices, flashing our fly-by-night skin, nothing but flesh for clams? We have things to say. We need to say them.'

Dosh shrugged. 'This is how it is. And now you made me move my face, so you can fix it.'

'But it doesn't have to be like this. It could be different.'

Cash knew that this night would be like every other. The clowns would draw on masks, wrap their limbs in costumes, tuck and pad their torsos strategically so that the audience got their gleeful little genderfuck. Then they'd pretty-up their coracle for the after-show, make it all mysterious for the clam girls: layers of coloured fabric, strange bones, abandoned objects they'd found while skin-diving. When landlockers bunked up with a circus performer, they expected something special. They had all the slow-witted farm-boys they wanted on their grubby home islands – now they wanted exotic animals in unlocked cages. They wanted to blink glitter for at least a week after. They wanted a secret to keep from their future husbands.

'You don't want a clam girl to warm your bunk tonight?' mumbled Dosh.

'Yes, I do. No, I – I don't *not* want that. I want...' For years, another body in the bunk had been enough to distract Cash. But not now.

'While you're deciding what you want, let me tell you what I want: for you to shut up and finish my damn face.'

Cash smudged two black eyes into the white. 'Dough, help me out.

Our fellow clown has no ambition beyond what's between our legs. But you – I know you see the bigger picture here.'

Dough, sprawled across two bunks, glanced up. 'Well –'

'Clowns!'

They looked up. The coracle's canvas top was peeled back at one corner – and who should be peering in but Avalon, the horse-bitch. They all turned their backs to her and returned to their business.

'Clowns, I am speaking to you.'

'Mmm,' mumbled Cash, resuming work on Dosh's make-up.

Cash knew that Avalon wouldn't dare climb down into their coracle. Her pregnancy dictated everything she did – everything the whole damn circus did, it sometimes seemed – and she wouldn't risk a tumble down the rope ladder. Instead she'd be squatting on the canvas, trying to look regal in case any clams lifted their eyes from the shore to peer at the circus freaks.

From above Cash, there was a rustle as Avalon pulled the canvas back further. 'Did you not hear me, clowns? I am ordering you to listen.'

Dough and Dosh managed to stifle their snorts of laughter, but Cash was not so quick.

'Are you mocking me, clowns?'

'No, mistress,' chanted Dosh, painted lips barely moving. 'Never, mistress.'

Avalon took a deep breath, as if gathering her strength to deal with the simply *awful* clowns and their simply *awful* manners.

'I am here to ensure that you are *not* getting ready for the military show,' she said. 'You should be preparing for the banker show, as you agreed.'

'Don't you trust us, mistress?' simpered Cash. 'Don't you think we mean what we say?'

'Not for a moment.'

'Well, mistress, that's rather rude.' Cash paused to let the other clowns chime in, but they stayed silent. If he was the only one brave enough to openly defy the horse-bitch, then so be it. But Avalon was not finished.

'This is my circus, just as much as it is my husband's,' she said, 'and the crew must obey me as they obey him.'

If that were true, thought Cash, you wouldn't need to say it. Instead of responding, the clowns got back to work.

Avalon wouldn't climb into the coracle, but she did drop her head in to stare at each of the clowns in turn. Her voice became a hiss. 'Just do as you're told. Soon you won't be my problem any more. North and Ainsel can have you, and good riddance.'

'Is that so?' murmured Cash, cheeks stretching with a grin. Dosh and Dough pursed their lips at one another.

'It is so. My husband is buying a house for us. And then I will be free of this stinking, tarnished circus for ever – which, I can tell you, will be the finest day of my life. I'll be a landlocker, and the rest of you can burn. I'll even watch from my house.'

'I heard that house was meant for –' burst out Dosh. But Cash's hand on Dosh's wrist stopped the words.

'Meant for what?' said Avalon, eyes narrowed.

'Meant for nothing, mistress. Meant for you, mistress.' Cash made an elaborate bow, forehead to feet.

For three long breaths, Avalon hung above the coracle. The clowns kept their faces straight as knife blades. Avalon opened her mouth as if to speak, then seemed to think better of it. She threw the canvas over with an angry flourish. The coracle swayed as she stepped off it, back to the *Excalibur*.

In the dim light the clowns huddled together, foreheads pressed, faces split with glee.

'She thinks that house is for –'

'But it's not for her, it's for North. But Red Gold –'

'Red Gold hasn't told Avalon, and when she finds out she'll hate North even more than she already –'

'She hates the rest of us as much as she does North –'

'But when she finds out –'

'Yes, when she finds out there'll be –'

The clowns grinned at one another.

'Chaos,' said Cash.

The clowns were hungry. They did not want to wait to be fed. But when they sated their hunger, they wanted it to be in the right way, for the right reasons. They could wait.

After that night's performance, the crew of the *Excalibur* felt the storm finally stirring to life. They furled their big top, soothed their animals, weighed anchor; all under a sky bruised dark with clouds. As the sun set it lit the clouds from below, making them round and bright as fruit.

They drank up, slept it off, and moved forwards on to the next island. What choice did they have? Landlockers are not sympathetic to the problems of the sea – and circus folk would rather take their chances with the petulant waves. With glitter in their blood, coals in their chests, choking on their secrets, they sailed into the night. Soon they lost sight of land. The first drops of rain fell.

5
Callanish

For days, the sea had been fractious. Waves chuttered and shwacked against the moorings of Callanish's house, making it difficult for her to think straight. She ate her meals, performed the Restings, tipped dead birds into the water. Every night she drank her cup of milk on the porch, watching the distant silhouettes of passing boats.

At mealtimes she wound up the gramophone and listened to records as she ate, the music rolling and wavering. It felt almost like a conversation. But Odell was right: sometimes you did need to say things and have someone respond.

Silence was not her only concern: the supply boat was late and her cupboards were almost empty. No graces meant no Restings, and no Restings meant no food. If it didn't come before the storm . . . well, no point thinking about it. Wishing for a boat did not make it arrive.

Several times, as the day slipped towards night with no sign of the supply boat, Callanish took her rowing boat out among the grace-cages. She pulled off her gloves and let her fingertips hover over the surface of the water. The webbing stretched. She knew there was seaweed down there, and fish – but there were also bodies, and both the seaweed and the fish grew from the bodies. She pulled her gloves back on and rowed back to her house. Still, each time she rowed out, she let her fingers dip closer to the sea. There would be no harm in touching it. There would be no harm in slipping off her boat and into the water. And what would be the harm, really, if she stayed down there? When Callanish was a child, her mother told her that the trees were to be worshipped because they had been there before everyone who'd ever lived on earth had been born, and they would still be there after everyone who ever lived on earth was dead. But Callanish knew that the sea had been there even longer.

One evening, as her fingers dipped towards the surface, she saw the supply boat approaching. She pulled on her gloves and rowed back to her house. Now she would not need seaweed or fish or the swallow of the sea over her head. She tried to be glad. She felt scooped-out, hollow as a shell.

She accepted the delivery without speaking. Her silence did not seem to matter, as the deliveryman kept up a steady stream of words without leaving any gaps for a response as he hauled cages of graces from the boat to the dock to the porch to the kitchen table. He spoke of trading routes and wheat shortages; of an abandoned ship found floating, perhaps empty for years, crewed only by cats; of a baby born with gills and webbed hands, a half-fish monster buried alive at the World Tree by its landlocker mother, and good riddance to the beast; of a new trend for tattooing the bases of one's fingernails purple; of a boy who had his hand cut off for chopping down a tree; of whispered scandals among military officers. Over the years Callanish had heard all these stories, with small variations. Everything changed and nothing changed. His chatter felt like having a record playing quietly: a soothing background hum. She sat at her table, her gloved hands pressed tight between her knees, so he couldn't possibly see. She had received thousands of graces, delivered by dozens of different supply boats, and none had yet seen her hands. The government decreed that she should receive just as many graces as she needed to stay alive – but the exchange of Restings for food was not the only thing keeping her alive. Wearing her gloves and slippers was just as important as eating. Given the choice, she would rather not be buried still-breathing under World Tree.

Finally the supply boat was empty and Callanish's table was full.

'Farewell,' said Callanish, just as she always did. The deliveryman may have wished her farewell back, but it was getting hard to pick out individual words from his avalanche of sound. She was sure that he was still talking even as he sailed away.

The days passed. Callanish Rested bodies, took her payment, filled her aching belly. One morning, she rose to a storm approaching from the north: the sky dark, the water choppy and licking up over the edges of the porch. The anxious trilling from the grace-cages made her want to cover her ears.

She took her rowing boat out between the lines of graces, pulling open the cages as she passed. Most of them were too weak to fly. Those that could get out of their cages might make it some way before falling into the sea to drown. Those that could not fly would stay in their cages and drown. If she took them into the house, they would die because she had no food for them. Whatever she did, she could not save them. She wasn't supposed to free the birds, but who would know? Who would care? A small crime; another secret that could only hurt the one who kept it.

When all the cages were open, she lashed her boat flat to the dock. Of the newly delivered graces, not yet used for Restings, only two remained, caged in the corner of her house. She didn't have enough to feed them, and no one would approach with food for days after the storm. She opened the cages and flung open her front door, thinking that the graces would spread their wings and fill her house with a flurry on their swift path outside. Instead the pair took their time, pecking around the floor, shivering their feathers, regarding Callanish with their tiny black dots of eyes. Finally they made it to the door and opened their wings to the wind. They were stronger than the Resting graces, and soon disappeared.

When all the graces had flown she closed the metal shutters over the windows, then stood for a moment on the porch. It was almost beautiful: the water chopping up in white waves like petticoat lace, the delicate arches of the empty grace-cages, the clouds piled up in layers from charcoal to bruise-blue to black.

She wished that she could dive down into the water, that she could live down there under the water; that she could drink water and breathe water, let water support her limbs and lay a comforting weight on her shoulders. Down there she'd be safe from the storm. On the surface the waves and the wind could tear the world to tatters, but she'd be safe down in her watery cocoon. She went into the house and bolted the door. She waited.

6
Melia

Melia had not feared a storm since the day she'd met Whitby. All damplings have their own relationship with the sea, and Whitby's attitude was one of respect and acceptance, tempered with a generous helping of lust.

'The sea does not need us,' he would announce to Melia in the warmth of their bunk, bodies tucked together like spoons. 'That fickle mistress, it's all the same to her whether we live to be a hundred or drown before we even take a breath. We're parasites. Eating her offspring, drinking her salty blood, cutting through the waves of her belly. We're living off her spoils. No wonder she wants to devour us all.'

'So we should give up and jump overboard?' Melia would tease back, clasping her hands with his, stretching their arms together until the joints cracked. 'Let the sea have us?'

'You're assuming it's our decision to make, my love. She'll only take us when she wants us. I for one look forward to the embrace of the sea, when she decides that it's time.' At this he would wrap his arms around Melia, biting kisses along her shoulder. 'Just think of her rhythm! Her passion! Her relentless, depthless wetness! Oh, sweet relief for this unworthy man!'

At this, Melia would clamp her hand over Whitby's mouth, but could never resist turning her body in his grasp, replacing her hand with her mouth. Then they would make love, pressed close in the narrow space of their coracle, moving together with the rhythm of the waves. Their bodies wound up speckled like eggs, white on tan, from the touches of one another's chalky palms. Melia took care to kiss every one of Whitby's scars, built up over their years of performances at dozens of different circuses. Other damplings were born and worked and died as part of the same crew, treading the same deck, hoisting the same sails their whole lives. But Melia did not need such ties; Whitby was the only home she needed. With their skills, it was not so hard to buy their way on to a new ship.

Melia could not remember whose idea it was to sow misinformation about their relationship when they joined the Circus Excalibur. They were not siblings and they were not married, and Whitby found it endlessly amusing that anyone could believe either. They were simply lovers, though there was nothing simple about that. They were aerialists, the two of them: many ways to fly, but only one way to fall.

Afterwards, sweat-damp and tingling, Whitby would bury his face in her shoulder and whisper, *we are the sea.*

They had not had such an exchange last night after their drinking session in the mess boat. By the time they made it back to their coracle, they were so booze-slurred and woozy that they could barely manage to tie their canvas shut and strap themselves into their bunk before their eyes closed.

In the abyss between waking and sleeping, Melia thought of her own relationship with the sea. She did not lust for the sea the way that Whitby did. But when he said to her, *we are the sea* - that made the most perfect kind of sense. She was the sea, and so was everyone else. We all come from the sea.

Melia had heard that in the olden days, when the world had lots of land spreading out over miles and miles in every direction, seas and lakes were called 'bodies of water'. That made sense too. Her body was water, and Whitby's body was water, and Red Gold's and Ainsel's and North's and even the bear's – they were the sea, and so they could trust the sea. She wanted to tell Whitby this. But her tongue was too heavy to make the words. Sleep took over her thoughts, and she slipped away.

Melia woke in blackness to the boom of Red Gold's voice projecting across the coracles. Over his voice there was an odd whistling, a screeching, and Melia's half-sleeping mind could not understand it.

TIGHTEN THE CHAINS came Red Gold's shout, and there was a clanking of the chains that tied together the line of coracles, HAUL IN THE SAIL and there was a whoosh and thwack of canvas, LASH YOUR OVERHEAD and this call was almost lost in the wind, but still the phrase worked on Melia like an alarm, jolting her awake, her fingers scrabbling at the buckle of her bunk strap. It was the wind, the screech and whistle of the wind and the rain, and as she swung upright she felt how the boat was rocking and dipping in the rough waves.

In the dim light she could make out the shape of Whitby reaching for the canvas overhead, his knees bending and ankles rolling as he moved with the deep sway of the coracle. She staggered over to him. Her narrow legs felt as flimsy as seaweed, but she knew her arms were strong enough to fight even the roughest swell. Rain blew through the gap: the canvas had come unfastened and was flapping in the wind like a panicked bird. Melia was instantly soaked, and fought to keep her feet steady on the slick inside of the coracle.

Working together in the darkness, they yanked the canvas tight and knotted it shut. There would be no point in lighting a seal-fat lamp; the sea was wild enough to knock it from its hook, and if the canvas caught fire then there would be nothing to protect them from the rain.

When the canvas was secure, Melia went port and Whitby went starboard, running their hands over the shelves lining the coracle's curved sides. Straps and buckles and strips of canvas kept everything flat. It was impossible to see in the darkness, but they knew the shapes of their belongings well enough, and could feel that nothing was missing. Melia tightened the buckles so that things could not knock together and break. Rainwater sloshed around on the deck of the coracle, but there was nothing to be done about that now. They could drain it all in the morning when the sun came out. She kept sidestepping round until she bumped into Whitby at the end of his half-circuit. Done.

Overhead tight, belongings secured, they were safe. They lay back down on their bunk, frozen and sodden from the rain.

'Thanks,' whispered Melia to Whitby.

'For what?'

'For keeping us safe.'

'You're always safe with me, my lass. Besides, I knew I had to patch that gap up quick-smart. Wouldn't want that saltwater to get in here and cause damage, now would I? Just *think* about your hair!'

'You mean your hair,' said Melia.

'Of course I do,' said Whitby. 'I have to stay beautiful for my women.'

Melia sat up, pulling away from him in mock offence. 'Women plural, is it?' But she could not keep the laughter out of her voice; could not even pretend to be annoyed at Whitby.

'You and the sea.' He pulled her back down into his arms. 'You're better company than she is – but me and that briny temptress, we're like this.' Whitby crossed his index finger over Melia's so they were intertwined.

As if in answer, the sea sighed and boomed against the hull. Melia felt the gentle scrape of coracles on either side and knew that they were all safe now. The coracles seemed to be tiny, fragile things but they had been through many storms, bobbing up among the roughest waves, weathering the wind and salt-spray like miniature fortresses. The sea had never tried to claim one of them. Perhaps she did not bother with such small prey.

Melia turned to face Whitby, pressing herself into his body to lessen her shivers, and listened to the waves and the wind shriek and boom against the hull. In the centre of a storm, it was easy to believe the old superstitions. The gods of the deep, hungry for revenge; the earth as a flat plane, with the seas tipping over the edge into nothing. Here Be Dragons.

Melia smiled and rested her damp face against Whitby's shoulder, letting his heat dry the rain from her forehead. Colours and shapes began to flicker behind her eyelids as she drifted into sleep. She'd weathered worse storms, and lying awake all night would only make her tired, less able to carry out any repairs in the morning. She let herself drift.

A wave boomed against the next coracle – North's coracle, and wouldn't her poor bear be frightened by all this noise? – and Melia pictured its motion behind her closed eyelids. Cresting the wave, tugging on the taut chain, righting itself on the swell. Safe, like always. Even as it thudded into the side of their coracle hard enough to knock her teeth together, she knew it was safe.

Under the sea's tantrum, she heard another sound. Slosh-suck, slosh-suck: the rhythm of the waves, but closer and clearer. She opened her eyes to check that the canvas was still tight.

The boat tipped on the waves, and Melia saw a small circle of stars; it tipped back and the stars were gone, replaced by blackness and the slosh of water. Melia understood what had happened before the words could form in her mind. A crack. There was a crack in the hull. Their coracle was sinking.

'Whitby!' Melia's fingers scrabbled at the buckles of the bunk strap. 'The hull!'

Melia crossed the coracle on her knees so she wouldn't fall, the thin layer of water numbing her legs. She lit a lamp and held it high. Whitby was out of bed, reaching for scraps of oilcloth, reaching for the tin of tar, his movements calm and precise. She held the lamp closer to the hull. The crack was the size of an egg, and she breathed a sigh of relief. Whitby could patch that.

But, but. The oilcloth was too small. The lid was stuck on the tin of tar. And with each swell and push of the waves, the crack widened.

Whitby held the scrap of oilcloth to the weeping hull, but now it was not big enough to reach the edges. Melia grabbed another.

Lid, tar, fingers, oilcloth.

It was not enough.

It would not stick.

They were still on their knees, the water now halfway up their thighs, salt-stinking and dark. Melia felt sure that the coracle was sitting lower in the water. Panic blurred her thoughts. Her legs were numb. The light from the seal-fat lamp jerked against the sides of the coracle: her hands were shaking, and knowing that they shook was not enough to make them stop.

'Hush now,' murmured Whitby over the shriek of the wind and rain, and she realised that she'd been making a sound of distress, a low moan in the back of her throat, the same pitch and beat as the waves.

Whitby turned away from the hull, eyes casting around the coracle, looking for something that was big enough to patch the gap. Melia wanted to help him, but she could not tear her gaze away. As she watched, the crack spread wide as a yawning mouth, revealing a tumble of stars and the sea's white teeth. The coracle tipped into the swell of a wave. Water poured through the gap, knocking Melia and Whitby on to their backs in the freezing water.

'We can't,' said Melia. 'It's too big. We need to get out.'

Whitby did not reply; Melia was not sure he could bring himself to say the words. He tugged down two loops of the long rope they used for their show and knotted them around their waists. Melia reached for the floats strapped to the wall, then realised it was a waste of time. They wouldn't make a difference in a sea this raw.

Their coracle was only the third away from the main boat, and their ropes were long enough to reach across North's and Ainsel's coracles – assuming that North's had not also been damaged in the collision. Red Gold would be on the deck of the *Excalibur*, but the stars might not be bright enough to let him see the coracle's damage beneath the dark water and white froth.

Melia threaded the lamp on to its hook - a burning canvas was now the least of their worries - and began untying the overhead. The knots were tight and her fingers were numb.

'Whitby!' she shouted. 'I can't - it's too -'

And he was beside her, nimble fingers dissolving the knots, strong arms pulling back the canvas, calloused hands throwing the end of her rope out of the coracle and into the night. It thudded and splashed into the sea. Melia pulled herself up on to the edge of the coracle, wrapping the overhead ropes around one arm so that she wouldn't tip into the water. The coracle's edge was slippery with seawater and she overbalanced, jerking the coracle as she landed on her knees. The thud juddered through her bones – she didn't think that she had landed that hard, but still the impact seemed to vibrate through the coracle.

In the bleaching starlight she saw the outline of Red Gold, lashed to the *Excalibur*'s mainmast. She waved her free arm at him, but he did not notice. Now that Melia was out, she could see how low their coracle sat in the water; how it was already beginning to drag down its neighbours.

A split of lightning arced across the sky, echoed by a deep grumble of thunder. It lit up the world, painting Red Gold's wide red face as white as bone. Melia's head spun. It was all unreal. Pale shapes. Etchings on burnt wood. The ends of stories.

Red Gold raised an arm to hail her and she threw him the rope. He could not know what had happened to the coracle, but he knew that they were in trouble. She made sure that Red Gold had a tight hold of her rope, then reached down for Whitby's to throw that too. She could not find it.

'Whitby!' she shouted, but the wind stole his name. She kicked her feet in the empty space of the coracle, trying to find him. 'Whitby, stop trying to fix it! It's too late!' She ducked her head inside but couldn't see anything. She pulled some slack on her rope and dropped down into the coracle. All her breath was knocked out as she landed hip-deep in the icy water.

'Whitby, damn you to earth!' She groped around in the dark but could only find the sides of the coracle, her numb fingers bumping and scraping against the straps and buckles. Nothing, nothing. Then: a tug around her belly, pulling her backwards through the water. She pressed her hands against the walls and screamed out Whitby's name. But Red Gold had the end of her rope, and was pulling her out.

As she came free of the water she kicked her legs out as hard and wide as she could. They caught things, dozens of things, soft things and shattering things, but she did not know if any of those things were Whitby. Around her waist the rope tugged, tugged, and it was so tight that she could not breathe, could not call again for Whitby. Stars wheeled above her. The sea raged in long, deep heaves. She tried to turn, to untie the rope, to signal to Red Gold. As she slid over the edge of the coracle it scraped a long graze of skin from her forearm. A wave spat saltwater on to the wound, but she felt nothing.

She half scrambled, half dragged over the two coracles and on to the sodden deck of the *Excalibur*. Red Gold pushed her towards the cabin. Through the burn of saltwater in her eyes she saw that he was climbing across the coracles to save Whitby. Despite his tight and mismatched oilskins, his cracked and bloody cheeks, Red Gold at that moment was the most glorious thing that Melia had ever seen. She held tight to the mast, watching him.

Red Gold ducked his head into the coracle, emerging with the end of the rope in his hand. He steadied himself on the half-tied canvas and hauled on the rope. Then he hesitated. Melia squinted through the salt-spray. It seemed that he had seen what was on the end of the rope, and dropped it back into the sinking coracle. But that could not be.

Now the clowns and the glamours were emerging from their boats, ropes around their waists, faces sheened with rain. Together with Red Gold they grasped the chain attaching her coracle to the glamours' boat. Now they were unhooking the glamours' boat and hooking it into North's. Now they were standing on North's coracle, ready to unhook Melia's entirely. No. No. Why did Red Gold not pull Whitby out? She remembered the thud as she'd fallen, the judder through the coracle. The crack of bone she'd thought had been her own.

'No!' she shouted, though she knew Red Gold could not hear her. She launched herself off the *Excalibur* and on to Ainsel's coracle, not caring about its unsteady lollop, about the rain throbbing at her shoulders, about the thunder vibrating her insides. She grabbed Red Gold's arm.

'No!' she shouted into his ear. He did not reply, did not shake his head, but his intentions were clear. If they did not let the coracle go, it would drag them all down. But why would Melia care? If Whitby was in the sea, then they might as well all be in the sea.

She reached into the coracle. The water level was high, almost to the top. The end of the rope floated. She grabbed it, closed her eyes against the salt-spray, and pulled. She could lose the coracle, but she couldn't lose Whitby. Hand over hand, eyes shut tight, she pulled. She reached the end of the rope, the start of something heavy. She kept her eyes closed.

She felt Red Gold unfasten the chain and let the coracle sink. Still she held the rope.

7
Callanish

The storm seemed to last for days, though Callanish did not know how many. She slept heavily, the days and nights blurred into an argument of rain and wind. She wondered whether she was supposed to feel scared; if someone else had been with her, and they had been scared, she would have understood why. The wind screamed through the shutters and saltwater seeped in around the edges of the door. She couldn't see outside, but it seemed that her house was still in the same place. If it had come loose from its moorings and been tossed into the sea, she'd only know when she opened the door. It was soothing to think about things happening without her having to make them happen. She imagined opening the door to snow-tipped mountains, jewel-coloured lakes, rainforests dripping with heat and noisy with life. Daydreams became dreams. Her bed felt like the only steady point in the storm.

One morning, she opened the door to her mother. Veryan looked awkward, apologetic, and very pregnant. The sun was low, shining through the doorway and into Callanish's eyes, so that every time she tried to focus on her mother, she could not. Veryan wavered and pulsed, like the distant sea on a hot day. Standing there on the porch in the middle of the graceyard, she asked for help. Callanish was going to help her mother. She would get it right this time. She would be brave and wise and her hands would be steady no matter what. But she did not know how. She could not afford to make a mistake again. She closed the door, to buy some time to think, and when she opened it again her mother was gone.

This dream, unfamiliar as it was, ended up the same as all her other dreams: the ache in her hands and feet, the lullaby calling her, the soothing embrace of the sea. Even in the dream, Callanish kept enough of her conscious self to be glad that the door was closed and windows blocked. This dream would be different: she couldn't wander out of bed. She couldn't walk out on to the porch. She couldn't wake to the chill of water closing around her ankles.

Callanish came awake to silence, her dreams clinging. She got out of bed, unbolted the door, stepped out on to the porch. The sky and the sea were as flat and blue as china plates, so perfect that she couldn't see where they met. All of the grace-cages were empty. It was so quiet that she could hear herself breathing, a tick each time she blinked. The storm was over.

She went back inside and began sorting through her food, separating out the things ruined by seawater. Most of it was fine; only some bread was spoilt, and that was stale anyway. She had a few eggs, some dried meat, dehydrated peas, a bag of lentils and beans, a pot of jam. Enough food for a week; or two, if she rationed it. The storm might keep people away for a while, but there would be plenty of new dead to mourn – not that she could be of help yet, as she had no newborn graces. She couldn't perform any Restings until the supply boat came by. Gracekeepers weren't allowed to breed the graces themselves; it was a delicate process, as each bird's stated lifespan had to be accurate. It would be no good to tell a Resting party that they should grieve for two weeks, only for them to check back a fortnight later with their white mourning clothes packed away, and find the grace still alive.

She unfastened both the windows, then pulled the sheets off her bed and hung them on the rafters to air. The house was bright and dry and silent. It was as if the storm had never happened.

A fish was splashing outside her window. Callanish leaned out to see it. The sea stretched to the horizon, flat as polished metal. She leaned out of the other window and she could not see a fish, but still she heard it splash. The sound grew louder, and she realised it was the waves against a hull.

Out on the porch, she squinted her eyes, but she couldn't see a boat. She even tipped the rowing boat back on to the sea and floated out so she could check that nothing was coming towards the back of the house. No shadow, no smudge: nothing but blue in every direction. Still, the unsteady splash. She went back to the porch and waited. It was eerie to be able to hear something approach, but not yet see it. Everything acted differently in the doldrums: sound, taste, temperature. She didn't think she would ever really get used to it.

Finally, after what seemed like half a day, a shadow slid into view. Callanish ran inside and put on her gloves and slippers. She began to put on her white dress, then ran out on to the porch again when she realised she didn't need to. Or did she? She wasn't sure. She ran back inside and pulled on the dress. She wasn't performing a Resting, but she was still a gracekeeper. She should be properly dressed to play her role. She braided her hair loose and low to hide her scars.

The approaching boat was large and made of wind-scoured wood, its two masts carrying just one small sail. The boat was not moving properly through the water. As it turned to pass between the poles at the edge of the graceyard, Callanish saw that it was not only one boat: it trailed five coracles behind it, each of a different size, brightly painted and patched with rectangles of rusting metal. Usually larger boats anchored at the graceyard's edge and took a rowing boat to the house; this one sailed its sluggish way straight through, forcing empty grace-cages to either side of the hull with a series of thuds and scrapes.

She raised her hand to hail the figure at the wheel. He took slightly too long to respond, and in those moments the ground seemed to drop from under Callanish's feet. They were pirates, they were thieves, they were going to kill her and throw her body in the sea.

Then the figure hailed, and she remembered to breathe, and she saw several things at once: the captain had bright red cheeks, as if they'd been rouged; beside him stood a beautiful pregnant woman with long black hair and a pale blue dress; the canvas top of one of the coracles was peeled back; and poking up from it was what appeared to be a bear.

Callanish had seen a bear before. The memory was scratched and worn: a striped silk ceiling, a family dancing to a gramophone – and then the sound of screams, skin sheened red. That was her first and last bear, though she'd always loved them because of an illustration in a fairytale book her mother used to read to her. The picture wasn't clear, as the pages were made of silk and they had become damp and stretched. It was strange to see, right there in front of her, something that she didn't think existed any more. For a moment, she felt reality unfocus, as if she was seeing the land from the map hung on her wall.

Then the boat bumped up against the dock, and Callanish snapped back to reality.

'Welcome,' she said. 'I am Callanish Sand. I am the gracekeeper here. Please come ashore.'

The huge man with the red face bowed low, which was awkward as he was partway through dropping the anchor. He managed to drop anchor, finish his bow, and step on to the dock all in one movement.

'Thank you kindly, Ms Sand. I am Jarrow Stirling, the captain of the *Excalibur*.' He moved his arm as if to give the boat a pat, then seemed to think better of it. Callanish found that sensible; a good knock and the whole thing would probably fall apart. Instead he lifted his hand palm-up to help the pregnant woman step off the boat. She stumbled as her foot touched the dock. She was clearly a dampling – they could never quite get the hang of steady ground – but the captain seemed oddly at ease on the metal slats.

'I present my wife, Avalon,' said Jarrow, 'and my son, Ainsel, who is – ah, he's below deck, in the coracle with the horses. They did not like the storm.'

'Neither did any of us,' said the pregnant woman, presenting her hand to Callanish. 'Avalon Stirling. Charmed.'

She wasn't sure what she was meant to do with the hand, so she bowed her head and tried to look distant.

'I present also my crew.' Jarrow swept his arms wide with obvious pride, as if the tatty boats were made of fresh flowers. At the summons, the rest of the crew emerged from their boats, climbing on to the deck and then wobbling down on to the dock. The space was not large, and the damplings were unsteady on the planks; Callanish was sure that one of them would end up falling into the water. She hoped they were good swimmers. She felt a jolt of panic thinking of her tiny house crammed with bears and horses, and was relieved when she saw that the animals were staying in the coracles.

'Behold, the brave and wondrous performers of the Circus Excalibur, marvels of acrobatics and the taming of the most dangerous beasts.'

Behind Jarrow, the circus crew began to assemble on the dock. First came an elegant man around Callanish's age, with feathers in his long hair and coloured streaks across his cheeks. Although he bowed to her, he seemed distracted.

'My son, Ainsel, lord of the horses. Even the most jaded of audiences are struck dumb by the poise and bravery of his horseback skills.'

Next came three uniformly beautiful men, with hair dyed various shades of pink - though how they had made such vivid colours, Callanish couldn't imagine. It was years since she'd seen anything so bright.

'And here are Teal, Cyan and Mauve, our glamours. They can seduce a crowd of hundreds with their dances around the maypole.'

The three beauties were languid, unimpressed, knowing. They would be terrible gracekeepers.

'They also show their skill as artists of our attire and decoration, which I'm sure you will agree is like nothing you've ever seen. And – ah, steady now, watch your step on to the dock – I present our clowns, Cash, Dosh and Dough, who promise to shock and offend you. Not that you, ah ...' The captain coughed, seeming to remember the purpose of a gracekeeper. 'Not that you might wish to be offended. In which case they shall not. Keep moving, crew!'

Jostling up against the pink-haired men came three gangling, shifting women. They had their sleeves rolled up, displaying tattooed designs on their forearms: one grey-shaded bones, as if her insides were outside; one a constellation of pale stars on a blue background; one a mass of colour that looked like layers of birds' wings in flight. The starred one caught Callanish staring, and bared her teeth. A moment later she seemed to think better of it, and glanced away awkwardly. Something in that movement struck Callanish as strange, and then she realised that the tattooed women were the tallest she'd ever seen - and then, with a shock, she realised that they weren't women at all. She looked more closely at the pink-haired men, and felt suddenly foolish for not seeing that they were women. Or was it the other way around? She dared another glance, but still couldn't be sure.

As the crew shuffled along to make room for the others, she heard the faint *tink* of bells from their clothing. She wanted to tell them that they didn't need to wear them here – that her visitors were almost all damplings, and she didn't care anyway – but she did not want to embarrass them.

Next came a short, broad man with long-healed burns covering his right arm, a thick beard, and a braid of dark hair down his back. He nodded to her as he stepped on to the dock. Callanish couldn't understand why he was holding his left hand behind his back – but then she looked closer and realised that his left arm was missing, the empty sleeve pinned neatly to his shoulder.

'Bero, king of fire. It bested him once, as you can see, but now he is its master. Though his fire-show may make you gasp, I assure you he is in complete control. Now!' Jarrow clapped his hands and turned to see who was next on to the dock, but faltered in his speech. 'This is Melia, our acrobat.'

The woman – if she was a woman; Callanish could not be sure – waiting to climb off the boat had curly blue hair and huge muscles layered along her upper arms and shoulders, tapering to slender hips and legs, then impossibly small feet. Callanish wondered how she managed not to tip over. A younger woman with long dark hair, scattered with braids as bright as gold, came up behind the acrobat.

'And finally, our very own north child, performer of death-defying...'

The acrobat went to step off the boat, and stumbled. Her tiny feet didn't seem to be the problem, though; her entire body shook, and Callanish was sure she could hear her teeth knocking together. The dark-haired woman – Callanish thought that the man had said her name was North, but it was hard to keep so many new names in her head – had to help the acrobat on to the dock. Although North was not beautiful, there was a set to her jaw and a purpose to her movements that Callanish found striking. She wondered what this woman did in the circus; she did not seem fragile enough to fly through the air, nor sturdy enough to lift heavy things. She did not soothe the eye like the pink-haired women, or confront the gaze like the tattooed men. Perhaps she could have made a gracekeeper.

The acrobat's stumble seemed to have thrown Jarrow off his stride, but he tried to continue. 'All thirteen of these fine performers will ...' He cleared his throat and continued in a quieter voice. 'All twelve of ...'

He trailed off. For a moment Callanish was confused, and then she remembered who she was, why people visited her. Her gaze strayed to the deck of the boat, searching for the familiar shape. There: a bundle wrapped in striped silks.

Jarrow turned his back to the crew and addressed Callanish in an undertone. 'Please forgive my boisterousness, Ms Sand. It is merely a habit, born from years of addressing restless crowds. I meant no disrespect.'

'Mr Stirling. Please do not worry. I understand. But I must tell you, I fear I cannot help with what you need.'

'We require only one thing of you, and then we will be on our way. We can pay.'

Callanish glanced along the line of people. The *Excalibur*'s crew filled the entire dock, spilling over on to the porch so that she had to stand right in the doorway of her house. After the solitude of the storm, it felt strange to be in the presence of so many people. But it did not matter how many of them there were, or how much they mourned. She had no graces, and so there could be no Resting. She was about to turn to them, to explain, to apologise, when from the line of boats came a low rumble. Her mind cycled through memories of the sound: wind in the chimney, rough sea battering the underside of a dock.

'North,' said the pregnant woman, and she made the word sound like a curse. 'See to your beast.'

The rest of the circus crew turned away, embarrassed, and looked to Jarrow as if for instruction. Avalon did not check that North did as she was told, but tucked her arm into Jarrow's, smiling up at him. It seemed that she was used to being obeyed. Only Callanish, half scared and half curious, watched North's progress. She wanted another look at the bear.

North stepped across the coracles to the one that was growling. As she lifted the canvas she stumbled, and instead of putting out her arm to stop her knee hitting the edge, both her hands flew to protect her belly. She glanced up, guilty, and saw that Callanish was watching. The moment stretched as they stared at one another, both determined not to react. Then North lifted the canvas and disappeared into the coracle.

She might not be as visibly pregnant as the dark-haired woman, but Callanish knew what she'd seen, and she'd had enough. The mass of people was fine, the strangeness of their costume was fine, even the lack of grace was fine. But not this. She would do whatever was needed to get these pregnant women off her porch, and hope that they never came back.

'I am sorry,' said Callanish. 'I regret that I do not have the necessary equipment, and without a grace to mark the mourning I cannot –'

'Is that all?' said Jarrow. 'In that case, you must not worry on our account. We shall simply mark our own mourning.'

'I am sorry,' said Callanish again. 'The grace is a traditional part of the Resting. It would be wrong to perform the service without it.'

The woman with the muscled arms lifted her head and looked at Callanish. 'Please,' she said.

She spoke quietly, but her voice had the power of a shout. It wasn't clear whether she was addressing Callanish or Jarrow. The word was enough to make up Callanish's mind. If this were the quickest way to get the pregnant women to leave, then she would do it. Besides, if she didn't, then they would have to drop the body into the sea themselves. The end result would be the same, but without the dignity of the

Resting. There was no grace, but who would know? Who would care? She was not sure whether the growing list of her crimes made each one larger, or smaller still.

'Bring me the body,' she said, 'and I will prepare for the Resting.'

The acrobat climbed back into the boat and began lifting out the bundle wrapped in silk. The man with the burnt arm stepped forward to help her, but she turned her back and would not let him board. As she lifted the body and turned, the bundle fitted her exact shape.

Callanish did not mean to watch the woman struggle, but she could not take her eyes away. The woman stumbled on to the dock, landing with a thud on her knees. She managed to stand without letting the bundle touch the dock. Her arm muscles tensed as she lifted. She shook, but she did not drop the body. She made her slow, stumbling, graceful way to the house.

Jarrow broke the tension by placing an arm around Callanish's shoulders and leading her into the house, away from the rest of the crew.

'This is – ah – delicate,' he said. Callanish waited. 'We need the fabric back. It's our mainsail and our big top. Without it, we can't move on and we can't perform. Can he be put in the – that is, can you sink him, or ...' He seemed to struggle to find the right words.

'I understand,' she said. 'I will provide fabric for the Resting and return your silks. What is the man's name?'

The acrobat appeared in the doorway. 'Whitby,' she said. She raised her arms, presenting the body to Callanish, and tipped her head to the ceiling as if she was about to roar. Instead, she spoke in a whisper as quiet as a ghost. 'He's the reason that the sea is calm. She wanted her sacrifice, and now she has it.' The acrobat blinked and swallowed hard. 'His name was Whitby Gaunt. Please Rest him well.'

'Of course.' Callanish gestured into the house, where the acrobat slid the body on to the table. Callanish went to the window and stood with her back to the room, to give her a moment to say farewell. Moments passed. Callanish knew without looking that the acrobat was still there; she could hear the ragged sounds of her breath. From outside the house came the shuffle of feet on the boards and the gentle thunk of the boats bumping together. Callanish wanted to say something – to comfort the acrobat, to assure her that the Resting would be noble, to explain to her that the grieving would soon be over. The practised words would not come.

'Do not feel ashamed that you are still alive,' said Callanish.

When she turned to face the room, she saw that the acrobat had walked out of the house. She had spoken only to herself.

Callanish closed the door, pulled off her white silk gloves, and began to prepare the needles and ointments for the body. *Whitby*, she repeated in her head. This time, she did not want to feel nothing as she tipped the body under the water. She would think of her mother, and the crew would think of Whitby, and the words of the Resting would not be meaningless. For that moment, they would all be connected.

8
North

Most of the people North loved were dead, but this would be the first time she attended a Resting. When she'd lost her parents, she had been too young to mourn, or even to truly understand what had happened. That loss brought new responsibilities, as losses tend to, and a small bear was enough to keep a small child very busy. She could not miss her mother and father, as we cannot miss what we do not remember having. Instead she could only miss the idea of a family – though she found that the *Excalibur* was not a bad substitute, considering the options.

Although North did not know what to expect for Whitby's Resting, she did not have time to wonder. Her only concern was to make sure that neither her bear nor Melia cracked under the weight. In the days and nights since the storm, Melia had been travelling in the Island of Maidens with the glamours, as her own coracle was at the bottom of the sea.

'I can't stand it any more,' she whispered, red-eyed, to North as they queued for their dinner in the mess boat. 'They barely sleep, always chattering about something or mixing up endless pots of colours. I know they're being quiet now, but I promise, as soon as they get back to their coracle they'll have to spatter out all the words they're saving up.'

'They can't be that bad, Melia. They fixed up that scrape on your arm, didn't they?' North used the mention of the wound as an excuse to pull Melia's hand away from it. She hadn't stopped picking at the graze, and so it would not scab over, and so it would not heal. North had asked Cyan to tape a dressing on, but Melia had peeled it off again.

'I don't care about that. You don't understand, North, it's – Everything in that boat is so bright that it hurts my eyes. I can't rest. I can't grieve. There's no peace anywhere.'

Melia could not know that there was a spare bunk in North's coracle. The only reason it was spare was that North shared with her bear, and she had not told the rest of the crew for fear that they would find it strange. But there were more important things than appearing strange.

'Stay with me,' whispered back North. 'Me and the bear. We'll make room for you.'

Instead of replying, Melia tucked her hand into North's and gave it a squeeze. North was still finding her way with grief, but helping Melia lessened the ache.

The dinner rations were small, and consisted only of dampling food; they hadn't been able to perform without their big top, and with only one sail their progress had been slow. Then again, progress through the doldrums was always slow. The food was strange, too: it looked like cockle and sea-kelp stew, but it had a salty-sour aftertaste that North could not identify.

She chewed her stew, saving half for her bear. It would not last long, this time spent motionless. Soon they'd feel the wind in their hair, and eat eggs and bread, and come alive in the spotlight in front of hundreds of adoring eyes. Soon this would all be over, and things could go back to normal.

The next morning, the circus crew assembled on the dock, dressed in their plainest, palest clothes. North wasn't sure if it was disrespectful to wear the white dress from her funeral waltz, but it was the lightest-coloured fabric she owned, so it would have to do. The grace-keeper wouldn't know it was part of her act, and the rest of the crew would understand. They were dressed in a mishmash of clothing: Mauve in creamy scraps of silk, Dosh in panels of faded blue canvas, Bero in a white shirt that strained over his chest. It was the best they could do, and North was sure that their ragtag appearance would have amused Whitby. The gracekeeper, at least, had a decent outfit on: white dress, white gloves, white slippers, all made of silk. She'd fit in beautifully at the circus in that get-up. North couldn't help imagining her doing somersaults on the back of a horse, its jewelled reins held between her teeth.

She took her place on the dock beside Melia, trying to control the shake in her legs. It felt wrong to be surrounded by sea yet be standing on something that did not move with the steady flow of the water. Even though it wasn't really land, it still juddered her knees, messing up the sway and flow of her movements.

There were too many people to fit in the gracekeeper's tin boat. She seemed to have anticipated this; the lines of empty birdcages stretched for half a mile in every direction, but she had put Whitby into the sea as close to the dock as possible. Maybe that wasn't for their benefit, thought North. Maybe she couldn't be bothered to sail out to the faraway cages.

Red Gold and Avalon took the rowing boat with the gracekeeper. Ainsel headed the line of crew on the dock, though he didn't seem pleased about it.

'Let us think now of Whitby Gaunt,' said the gracekeeper, 'and of the ones who mourn him.'

Her voice was the exact opposite of Red Gold's crowd-pleasing gusto. She spoke calmly, quietly, but with enough power to silence an entire big top. As soon as she began the Resting she seemed to go into a trance; she tilted her head to the sky, almost glowing, like those paintings the revival boats unrolled over the sides when passing the 'heathen' ships. The Virgin Mother. The Holy Queen. Gracekeepers were holy, in their way, but were they virgins? North couldn't remember. She focused on the gracekeeper, trying to imagine her kisses on a stranger's mouth, her pale limbs wrapping around a stranger's body – and if she could imagine it, did that mean it was true? She could imagine that Whitby was still alive, waiting behind curtains for his cue, grinning to think of them all mourning for him as if he were gone. She could imagine it, so...

North pressed her feet hard against the metal of the dock. She must concentrate. It was easier to think about the gracekeeper's gloves, the gracekeeper's voice, the way everyone was went quiet when the gracekeeper spoke. If she thought about that, she would not have to think about Whitby. North shut her eyes, took Melia's hand, and allowed herself to miss Whitby as if he was really gone.

North could not sleep. The inner deck of the coracle was even less comfortable than the bunk, and at least on the bunk she had the softness and warmth of her bear's fur. But she still didn't want Melia to see them sharing, so Melia and the bear had a bunk each, and North slept on the deck between them. Or at least, she tried to.

It didn't help that Red Gold and Ainsel were still pattering around on the *Excalibur*, hissing at one another and trying to do repairs by the light of the seal-fat lamps. They'd attempted to set sail that afternoon, but the *Excalibur* was too damaged in the storm. Red Gold had to turn back before they'd made it to the posts that marked the edge of the graceyard. The gracekeeper seemed even less pleased than Red Gold at their return to her house. She'd allowed them to dock, though, and said they could stay until the boat was fixed. She had not offered to help, she had not joined them for dinner on the mess boat, and she had not spoken to anyone else in the crew. North assumed that she thought she'd done her job and that she didn't owe them anything else. Did she think they wanted to be there? That they enjoyed floating pointlessly above hundreds of corpses? North could not wait until they set sail again.

From the darkness outside came a thud, a scuffle, a shouted curse.

'Fine!' shouted Ainsel, his voice echoing in the quiet of the night. 'Sink the whole damn thing for all I care!'

North held her breath.

Silence.

Then footsteps. Her coracle swayed as Ainsel jumped down off the *Excalibur* and on to his own boat. She waited and heard the unclipping of his canvas, the whicker of the horses, the muffled soothing of his voice. She heard Red Gold bumbling about on the *Excalibur* for a few moments, then he seemed to give up and go to bed too.

Finally, the circus was asleep – but North was not. She tried not to count the passing time, but she didn't even have the steady rhythm of the water to lull her. Here in the doldrums, the sea was flat and the air felt too heavy to breathe. She tried to relax her limbs, to let sleep slide over her, but it was no use. She stood up and unclipped the edge of the canvas, heaving herself up on to the edge so she could look out.

She'd expected it to be dark, but the moon reflected off the metal bars of the cages, lighting the sea silver. It was too eerie to be beautiful. Even North – who had never been a victim of imagination – couldn't help picturing the corpses under the water. The fish would have eaten the bodies, but fish didn't eat bones. Perhaps it wasn't the water that was reflecting the moonlight, but piles and piles of gleaming bones.

North stuck her head back into the coracle, listening for the snuffle of her bear in sleep. If he was there, then nothing bad could happen to her, not even if the sea swallowed the bones of everyone in the world. Reassured, she straightened up and put her hands on the edge of the boat, leaning her weight back so that she could look up at the stars.

There was someone on the porch, silver-haired and silent. North jumped, her hand scraping off the side of the coracle. Heat throbbed across her palm and she bit down on a curse. There was no point slipping back into the boat; whoever was on the porch had already seen her.

The figure raised its hand in greeting. Moonlight caught her white silk gloves. Without thinking, North raised hers back. It was the gracekeeper – and what was her name? Had she told them? North couldn't recall. Her shoulders tensed as she remembered her thoughts during the Resting: the gracekeeper's kisses, the stretch of her limbs. It was inappropriate, and North was ashamed. But the gracekeeper couldn't know that. She might be a holy hermit, but she wasn't a mind-reader.

Cradling her raw palm against her belly, North got to her feet and made her way across the coracles. She stumbled when she stepped on to the dock, but managed not to fall. In the moonlight, the grace-keeper seemed unreal, beautiful, as if she was carved out of white stone. It was only when North sat down on the porch that she realised she'd forgotten to tie on her silver bell. She pulled her sleeves down over her arms, despite the humidity, so that the gracekeeper wouldn't see.

'It can be difficult to sleep here,' she said. 'The call of the sea. It's so loud.'

North shrugged a reply.

'Sometimes I feel I haven't slept a full night since I got here. It's hard to let go. It's not safe.'

She wasn't looking at North as she spoke; instead, she kept her gaze on the horizon. A house surrounded by water and dead birds: what was unsafe about that? Nothing but the grey sky and the silver sea, and the cages lit up bright as seal-fat lamps. It was horrible, but it didn't seem dangerous.

'You're not an acrobat,' said the gracekeeper. 'Or a clown, or a fire-breather. And you don't have a horse.'

'No,' answered North, even though it wasn't really a question. 'I'm North. I'm the bear-girl.'

'The bear-girl. Now I see. I'm Callanish, the gracekeeper. And I'd very much like to see your bear. It reminds me of my –' She seemed to check herself. It was a moment before she spoke again. 'It reminds me of something that happened, a long time ago, when I was a child. It reminds me of being saved.'

North liked the fact that Callanish was interested in the bear. Not everyone recognised what he was: bears and pictures of them were both rarities. Maybe Callanish had seen the circus perform long ago, in another life. After all, she must have come from somewhere; no one was born into the graceyards. They weren't a home.

'You can see him,' said North. 'Tomorrow. It'll have to be early, though, because I'm sure we'll have the boat fixed soon.'

'And then you'll leave as soon as you can.'

'We have to. If we want to eat, we have to work. This far from the islands, we'll get through our supplies in no time.'

'That's not the only reason.' Callanish never seemed to ask any questions, and yet North felt that every sentence was a question.

'I'm restless. This place, it's…' North couldn't find a way to describe her discomfort. She suspected that Callanish, as someone who lived above hundreds of dead bodies, knew anyway. 'I prefer to be at sea.'

'You want to move on. I understand. I want you to go too.'

North glanced over at Callanish. It didn't seem as if she'd meant to be so abrupt. She probably didn't spend a lot of time around people who weren't mourning, and anything you say to someone in mourning is the wrong thing. Maybe she'd stopped worrying about what she said.

'I want to get back to normal. Everything since the storm feels wrong. If we can get back to how we were before, it will all be fine.' She laughed. 'Except that when Whitby finds out that his coracle sank, he'll be –'

She stopped. She knew that Whitby wasn't coming back, but also he must be coming back. It didn't make sense otherwise.

'I haven't been away from him for more than a day since we met,' said North. 'The boats, they're so small; not like those huge revival cruise ships, or the military tankers. We're so close – we live so close, anyway, and sometimes that feels the same.'

'I'm sorry. I can't imagine how it must feel to lose –' Callanish seemed to stumble on her words. 'I can imagine it a little. I had that once. Where I lived – before I lived here. Seeing the same faces every day. Knowing them better than your own.'

She put her gloved hand on the porch, then stretched out her pinkie until it was touching North's pinkie. North almost flinched – but why not have some contact? Why not tell Callanish things? She was a landlocker, but gracekeepers weren't like other landlockers. They were outcasts, just like circus folk. It was either talking to her, or the hard deck of the coracle and the loneliness until dawn.

'I want you to leave because of the baby,' said Callanish, her fingertip still touching North's. 'It won't be long now.'

North sighed. 'She'll be even worse when it's born. It's bad enough with her pregnant. She had this apple, and she quartered it, and I really thought – oh, never mind. She's the ringmaster's wife and so there's nothing we can do.'

'Not her baby.'

North turned to Callanish, ready to laugh, ready to deny, ready to draw back her fist and land a punch that would draw blood. Callanish wasn't looking at North; her gaze was still out on the inky horizon. There was a tension in her body, as if she was holding herself back against the wall of the house. North couldn't tell whether her expression was one of calm or sorrow.

'There's nothing there,' said North.

'There will be,' replied Callanish.

North's breath caught in her throat. She could keep telling herself that the baby couldn't be a baby because it was hidden, unreal, just a growing part of herself. But soon it would be there. It would be real.

If the gracekeeper could tell just by looking at her, then other people would be able to tell. So far the crew had been blinded by familiarity, but that couldn't last much longer. For a moment, North was stuck between stomach-clenching panic and a quiet, distant acceptance. Then she leaned back, lying flat on the porch. The sky stretched above her, pinpricked with stars, and the boards seemed to sway with the rhythm of her breath. After a moment, Callanish lay down beside her.

It felt like a long time since North had lain like this; she'd spent the past months hunched over, in constant motion, trying to distract, desperate to hide her swelling belly. But that didn't matter now. She could let Callanish see. She *wanted* Callanish to see. She pressed her hands to her bump and looked out across the water.

'I want to tell you something,' said North. 'I don't think you'll believe me. But it's true.'

She'd tried to tell the people she'd known for almost her whole life, and hadn't managed to get the words out. She might as well practise on a person she'd only just met.

'I'm listening,' said Callanish, and with a shock North realised that she really was.

'Well, this – it's hard to explain.' North shifted, leaning her head on the front wall of the house so that she was closer to Callanish. The closer they were, the more quietly she could talk, and the less likely they were to be overheard. 'I've never actually got this far before. I've tried to tell people, but I couldn't manage it. You already know so I thought it would be easier.'

'The child's father is not part of your crew.'

'No. The father isn't really the father. He's - she's - oh, I don't know.' North breathed out, emptying her lungs until her stomach ached, then pulled in a breath as deep as she could. 'I'll tell you, and it doesn't make any sense. But I'll say it.'

North closed her eyes, comforted by the warmth of Callanish's skin and the sway of water underneath them. She remembered.

One night, months ago. Drunk and aimless at the edge of an island. All day she'd been distracted, catching a silvery gleam at the corner of her vision, squinting her eyes, sure she could see the angles and features of something beautiful swimming far out to sea.

Evening fell and she was drained from a night of forced conversation with Ainsel, tired of feigning interest in his spoilt-child dreams. He'd been woozy-drunk, telling her how he was born with a caul and so he was eternally blessed, meant to rule from an ancient castle beneath the sea. In shallow water those structures were visible – they'd all seen them – but they were just rock formations that people imagined into palaces. North had told Ainsel that he was a ringmaster's brat, that there was nothing for him to rule, and he'd sulked, and she'd turned away from him to stumble on to land, clumsy and disgusted but desperate to get closer to the person out at sea, purposefully not tying on her bell, glad to be courting danger. It turned out that there was no danger because there was no one there; no guards, no alarms, nothing on the island precious enough to be protected from the wicked, lawless damplings. Every time North blinked, she caught a glimpse of the sea-swimmer just before her eyes closed – but when they opened again a split second later, there was nothing. The world spun and spun and spun, but still she could not get any closer.

She had lain along the blackshore, seaweed tangling in her hair, the water stroking her legs, and let the stars pulse above her. Perhaps if she stayed there long enough the tide would claim her, pull her out to the sea-swimmer. She let sleep drag her down, right to the bottom of the sea, and in the dreams there really were castles, and Ainsel really was a king, and she still didn't like him.

Then: a slow pull out of sleep, reality seeping into her dreams. A mouth pressing against hers, cold as the ocean. The weight of a body on her own. The limbs, the angles, the planes of the body matched her own – but not a man, not a woman. In the dim light of the stars, she saw the silvery gleam of scales. The sea-swimmer had finally come to her. *Yes*, she'd said, *yes*. She'd tilted back her head and opened up her body, letting words repeat inside her head, names she'd heard only in stories: selkie, nereid, mermaid.

Then the gracekeeper moved her hand away, and the wall of the house was too hard against North's head. She had put it in words as best she could, but it was like trying to describe the logic of dreams.

'So I woke at dawn,' she said, 'and I went back to my coracle. I thought I must have imagined it. I thought I'd wanted it so much that I'd dreamed it happening. Until –' she motioned to her bump. 'And I know you won't believe me, but I had to tell someone. So there it is. I've told you.'

'I believe you,' said Callanish. Her voice was so quiet that it could have been the sound of a bird shifting in its cage.

North got to her feet. Cradling her belly with one hand, she reached the other down to Callanish. 'I want you to see him,' she said. 'With strangers, he can be a bit – but it will be safe if you're with me.'

Callanish hesitated, then pressed her palms to the boards and stood. She looked away from North's proffered hand, as if she knew she was being rude but didn't want to acknowledge it. Could it be a gracekeeper thing? North had noticed that she never took off her silk gloves, so maybe she wasn't allowed to touch anyone's hands because she had to keep her gloves white. It was odd, but then most things about being a gracekeeper seemed odd.

They walked together across the porch, neither seeming sure which should lead. The porch belonged to Callanish and the boats belonged to North - and also, these things belonged to neither of them. For them, everything was borrowed.

North wondered if she should tell Callanish to step cautiously, to stay quiet; she even considered raising a straightened finger to her lips like a strict mother. There was no need. Callanish seemed lighter than a bird when she stepped on to the deck of the *Excalibur*. They made their way across the coracles, silent as shadows in the still night.

North got cocky. She did a little leap, a flirty pirouette, as she stepped off Ainsel's coracle and on to her own. A cloud had darkened the moon, and it was impossible to see whether Callanish smiled at the theatrics. But North liked to think that she did.

The canvas of North's coracle sagged in the middle - she'd forgotten to pull its edges tight, too shocked to see the figure on the porch - and she felt Callanish stumble as she stepped on to it. North imagined the thud of her knees against the edge of the coracle, the undignified tumble as she toppled over. Before she knew what she was doing, she'd reached out and caught Callanish's hand, stopping her from falling. They crouched together in the darkness, hands pressed, breathing in rhythm.

The moon blinked bright again. North looked down at their linked hands and saw how close they were standing, saw that her thumb had smudged dirt on to the white silk glove; saw too that they were standing so close that her bump was pressed rudely against the gracekeeper's middle. She dropped the grip and hunched her body, pulling back the edge of her canvas without looking at Callanish.

They dropped silently into the coracle. Quick as blinking, North slipped a razor blade from its holder and into the pocket of her dress. Her bear would be fine. He would stay asleep. But if he growled, if the gleam of moon lit up his curved teeth – then what? Could she really use the blade on him? But it did not matter. He was safe. He was.

The grumble of the bear's breath filled the tiny space. North had wanted Callanish to see the bear, to meet her family, but it was too dark. Instead she took the gracekeeper's hand and pressed it to the bear's broad back. At first she flinched, but then she let North's hand hold her own.

The bear's snuffles caught from one breath to the next, but he did not wake. They kept their hands pressed to the bear's fur, feeling his heart beat strong and steady. Callanish smelled of warm breezes and saltwater. North breathed in deep, holding the scent inside her.

Suddenly Callanish pulled her hand away. North heard the shush of silk, and Callanish's ungloved hand was in hers. Her skin was cool and smooth. Their hands were linked, but their palms did not align – North could feel a high ridge of skin linking Callanish's knuckles, soft and solid. Webbing, like a fish. Like a mermaid.

North knew now why the gracekeeper had believed where her baby had come from – why the gracekeeper was the only person she'd ever met who would truly understand. She was suddenly sure that if there were light, she'd see the gracekeeper's skin gleam silver. She pressed their hands tighter, holding them close to the bear.

It was then, with their hands linked, that North first felt her baby: three taps, low down in her belly, like knocking at a door. She'd heard a word for this during Avalon's endless wittering about her own baby, and she repeated the word in her head. *Quickening*. It was the quickening. She kept her hands tangled in her bear's fur. The four of them there felt good, and safe, and real.

'Thank you,' Callanish said, her voice as soft as breathing as she pulled away and put her gloves on. North did not know what to say in reply, so she said nothing at all.

She tugged back the canvas, led Callanish over the coracles, and left her on the porch. She made her way to her boat without looking at the gracekeeper. She did not dare. If she looked at the gracekeeper in the moonlight, if she saw the silver gleam of her skin, how could she leave? How could she sail away and leave Callanish there alone, knowing how they were connected?

Back in her bunk, tucked in beside the musty warmth of her bear, North fell asleep with her hands linked tight over her belly. In her dream, she was her child: tiny as a bulb of seaweed, tight as a balled fist. Above her, the beat of an enormous heart shushed and roared like waves. Through her closed eyelids, the world showed in reds and purples: the branching lines of anemones, the nodules of coral, the hard lumps of rock and mussel. Inside North was the sea. Her child had come from the sea.

For so long, the bear had been her only family. But soon that family would have to expand to fit her child - and perhaps there could be room for someone else too.

9
Red Gold

J arrow dreamed of the storm. All night he had the same dream, slightly different each time but always with the same end, always losing a life to the sea. Layer upon layer of drownings. Whatever he did in the dreams, he could never save Whitby.

His final dream before dawn was of a sea monster with eyes as huge as a galleon's wheel, bloodshot and staring. The creature reached into the coracles one by one and retrieved its prize. In the dream, Jarrow's hands were stretched wide with daggers and machetes, harpoons and flensing knives. But all his weapons were useless - or rather, Jarrow himself was useless. However hard he tried, he could not move. He stood there, armed but impotent, as the coracles emptied. The monster had twelve tentacles, enough to grab every member of the Circus Excalibur. It saved Jarrow's wife and son for last. When its tentacles were full it turned its leering eye on Jarrow and sank down into the shadows, leaving him untouched and broken among the bones of his fleet.

He choked awake. His heart was hammering in his throat, and his chest was chilly with sweat. Breathe out. Breathe in. Don't panic. Don't wake Avalon. Don't die. Don't die. You're not ready yet.

Captain's wisdom said that those who encounter monsters at sea are those who bring monsters on board. In all his years as captain of the *Excalibur*, Jarrow had been soothed by that thought. There was no monster on board his fleet. His beautiful wife, his noble son, his loyal and talented crew – there was no room for monsters to hide.

When he was sure that he wasn't dead, Jarrow opened his eyes. On the bunk beside him, his wife's face was lit by a ray of morning sun, her expression rapturous in sleep. Her black hair spread in a curve across the pillow, smooth as a fish hook. She was still the most beautiful woman he had ever seen. After the death of Blanche – his life's love, mother of his firstborn, the reason he'd left the land for the sea – he'd thought his heart would stay broken. But Avalon and their baby, Ainsel and North – he had a second chance. He'd get it right this time.

Gently, so as not to wake her, he slipped his hand beneath the blanket to rest it on her swelling belly. His baby, his son. He had never known such bliss. He'd lived almost forty years – not bad, considering he now lived the life of a dampling. Life at sea was hard and hungry and full of dangers. Most damplings were lucky to make it to thirty. He was lucky. And soon he would have a baby to coddle, to delight in; a glorious plaything to light up his twilight years.

He hadn't understood what it meant to love Blanche. Many landlockers saw the circus that night, and many fell in love with the beautiful horse-dancer – but only Jarrow loved her enough to marry her and buy a whole new circus boat, just for her. Only Jarrow loved her enough to become the ringmaster. He'd built the Excalibur up from nothing, and he couldn't let it go now.

He and Avalon had waited so long, had lost so much – child after child, gone before their first heartbeats. He'd come close to giving up, but she'd convinced him to give it one more try, hope for one final miracle. He should have known that when Avalon wanted something enough, she could make it happen. He knew it from the moment he met her. With Avalon, he had found the land of bliss.

But there was no use in dreaming away the day. The crew needed to be fed, and for that the circus needed to perform, and for that they needed to get away from this damned graceyard. He wanted to kiss his wife, but knew that the scrape of his rough skin on her face would wake her. Instead he kissed the tips of his blunt fingers and touched them to Avalon's lips.

From the deck, Jarrow surveyed their situation. The *Excalibur* was tucked against the dock, sitting high and noble in the water. Behind it, the line of coracles curled around in a neat semicircle. How fine they looked. How proud, how respectable. Not the same sort of respectable as land, but not bad for a dampling. He felt the weight in his heart lift a little. Soon they would be at the island of his birth – and, true, there would be someone else's home on the old land that should be his. But this time the ache would not be as bad. This time, his son would be leaving the circus and living on the land. Ainsel would reclaim what Jarrow had lost.

All around him the sea was mirror-flat, the sky lightening to blue without a scrap of cloud. Even when they got the mainsail back from the gracekeeper girl, it wouldn't be much use in the still air. They would have to drift until they picked up a decent wind – and that's assuming they could fix the rudder. He'd have a hard time steering their way out if he couldn't damn well steer.

As Jarrow moved towards the stern, he noticed that the *Excalibur* did not seem to be listing in the water any more. That meant one less thing to be fixed, and he sent up a silent thanks to the gods of the sea and of the earth.

His gaze settled on the wheel. Something was different. He grabbed the wheel and turned it gently, left to right. He leaned over the stern of the boat: in the clear water he saw the rudder swing from right to left. It was not bent, it was not cracked, it was not trailing fistfuls of seaweed. It had been repaired.

Jarrow's mind swerved. Ainsel must have come back – crept across the deck in the darkness of the night and fixed the boat while his father slept. Anger burned through Jarrow, settling as a hot pain in his belly. His son was trying to show him up. He had no idea how hard it was - what it had taken to establish the circus, what it still took to keep it going. Ainsel could never make it as a captain. There was no room for weakness. No chance for beauty. The sooner the boy was safely on land, the better.

Movement caught at the corner of Jarrow's eye. He glanced up. The sound of his feet on the deck had roused the clowns: they sat in a row on the rim of their coracle, watching him. The steadiness of their gazes, the anticipation held taut in their limbs. They were waiting for Jarrow to notice.

'You,' he called across the sleeping line of coracles. 'You repaired the rudder, hmm? The three of you. You dived down and fixed it.'

Cash shrugged. Dough and Dosh picked at their fingernails and stared out across the water. Others might see the clowns as a threat, a gang of three existing only to mock and scorn and attack anything that mattered. Jarrow knew them as they really were: their delicacies, their sensitivities, their quiet afternoons spent in thought. He saw that their tattooed skin and aggressive sneers served as masks.

'Good work, gents,' he added. He felt the pain in his belly cool, gratitude washing through him like cold milk. He wished, for one fleeting moment, that he were their father. But their fathers were long dead, the same as the fathers of everyone else in the *Excalibur*'s crew. How fortunate Jarrow was to have another chance to be a parent so late in life - and he could be a father to this baby, and to the clowns, and to his whole crew. He strode across the taut canvases of the coracles and slapped the clowns briskly on the shoulder. 'The Circus Excalibur would be nothing without you.'

He strode back and stepped down on to the gracekeeper girl's porch. Then he called to the clowns, loud enough for the rest of the crew – and Ainsel in particular – to hear. 'Let's get this beast back out on the sea where she belongs.'

He walked across the porch and knocked on the gracekeeper's door, ready to collect his sail.

Jarrow felt, for a moment, at ease. His hands were on the wheel and his feet were spread wide on the deck of his boat. His beautiful wife was belowdecks, his noble son tended to his horses, and his crewmembers were all tucked away safely in their coracles. The wind was lazy and progress was slow, but at least they were moving. All was well now that they had left the bones and silence of the graceyard. If they could get a few days of good strong wind, they would be able to make port at North-West 1 archipelago – and from then it was only a few months to the North-East archipelago. On maps the islands look crowded together, but distance lies. Between almost all pieces of land there is nothing but miles of sea.

Despite his flash of good cheer, Jarrow felt ashamed at the payment he'd given to the gracekeeper girl. Four strips of oilskin, a tub of seal fat and a half-dozen eggs was surely not enough. But it was all they had to spare. The circus's usual payment was a show, but it did not seem appropriate to perform in a graceyard – not to mention to an audience of one, which would have made the whole endeavour ridiculous.

No, it was not just that. Something else was nipping at Jarrow's sense of well-being. Something else was wrong in the Circus Excalibur.

'Avalon?' he called.

The hatch slid back and Avalon climbed up on to the deck, cradling her bump with one hand. She raised her eyebrows at Jarrow in a way that was half questioning, half teasing, and entirely seductive. He kept one hand on the wheel and stretched the other out for his wife, turning her under his arm in a pirouette. Avalon laughed. She was the same height as the cabin, so no matter how fast the boat went the slipstream never affected her. Jarrow bent his knees so he was closer to his wife's height, feeling the strain in his thighs. There was no wind to hide his words, and he didn't want to be overheard.

'What is your wish, my king?' she purred, tucking her body close against him so that he could feel the swell of her belly. His smile stretched wide. He felt the skin of his cheeks crack. No matter: such bliss was worth a little blood.

'Simply the pleasure of your company, my queen.'

'Oh, no. I know you much better than that. Have you called me on deck to show me the dubious glory of the doldrums? Or is something needling away at that big brain of yours?' Avalon reached up to tap one delicate finger against his temple.

'You do know me, sweet queen.' Jarrow sighed, unable to continue their game against the weight of his concerns. 'My worry is for Melia.'

Avalon tutted. 'Oh, Melia. She'll be fine. You worry too much about your performers. You let them question your orders, when they should silently obey. You will find Melia a new partner for her performance, and in a few months she will have forgotten all about what she lost.'

'I fear her relationship with Whitby was more complex than that. I think none of us really understood it.'

'Weren't they just sleeping together?'

'I assumed so. That's why I chose them – I only had a coracle with a double bunk. I hoped that would be enough of an answer for everyone. But they were more than that, Avalon, don't you see? They were connected in a way that was more than their act. I can't name it, but I could see it. I fear that she will never forgive me for letting go of that coracle.'

Out of nowhere, Jarrow felt the hot prickle of tears in the corners of his eyes. He stayed still, his eyes unblinking and his hand on the wheel, until the feeling faded.

'Hearts stop every day,' said Avalon, pressing her hand to Jarrow's broad chest. 'Tomorrow it may be yours, or mine. But this time it was Whitby's. You did what you could to save him, but it was too late – and that coracle could have sunk the entire circus.' She dropped her voice to a croon, tiptoeing her fingers along his chest. 'We have mourned him, have we not? His body rests in its proper place. You have done all that you needed to do, even more than he deserved. What more could that little acrobat possibly ask?'

Still their bodies touched, still her hands caressed him, but Jarrow felt himself pull away from Avalon. After a moment she seemed to realise that her words might be interpreted as unkind – though Jarrow knew that although she was petulant and passionate, she could never be truly cruel.

'Life at sea is hard, Jarrow,' she said, her tone becoming distant. 'And Melia will not be our concern for much longer. The bear-girl will take good care of her.'

Jarrow sighed. 'North is looking after her now, but that can't last. Eventually Melia will need her own coracle – though perhaps she could inherit North's, and the bear with it. In time, Melia could learn to train him. Although the state she's in, I can't see her learning anything at all.'

'Let Ainsel and North worry about that after the wedding.'

Jarrow frowned. 'After the wedding they will have their own worries. There's the house, and the promise of children, and North learning to fit in among the landlockers. She will have to fit in, and quickly, if the Stirling name is to be restored.'

Avalon pulled away. 'What do you mean?'

'I mean that North will have to learn how to play her role. The landlocker life might not come naturally to her, but given time she'll get used to –'

'No. No, you said a house. Why would North have to worry about the house?'

'Avalon!' Jarrow was caught between a frown and a laugh. 'I told you that I was buying a house. All the things I've been saving – what else would it be for?'

'But that house...'

'It can only be on reclaimed land, I know, not real land. And certainly not the true Stirling land.'

'The house.' Avalon's tongue seemed to stumble over the words, as if she was speaking a language she didn't fully understand. 'We won't live in the house. It's not for us.'

The wheel turned, bumping into Jarrow's arm. He realised he'd dropped his hands.

'Avalon. My love.' He kept his voice soft, trying not to let it waver. 'You knew that, didn't you? You knew that the house was for Ainsel and North?'

The sea, the sky, the dozens of scattered archipelagos: the whole world shrank to the expression on Avalon's face. Jarrow forgot to breathe. His head throbbed to the beat of his heart.

Breathe out. Breathe in. Don't panic. Don't let Avalon leave. Don't let anyone die. Breathe.

'Of course,' Avalon finally said. Her face stretched into a smile, so tight it looked sore. 'Of course, my king. We are in total agreement, and your mind is my mind. We have no secrets from one another. I simply meant –' Her smile faltered; she looked as though she was going to be sick. 'I meant... Excuse me for a moment, my king. Our child is restless.'

Avalon closed her eyes and leaned over the bow. She took several deep breaths, her head hanging out over the water. Jarrow's head throbbed harder.

'Avalon?' he said. It came out in a whisper, lost beneath the lazy slap of the sails in the breeze. She knew about the house. She must. He'd told her, he was sure – he'd told her when they ... but when he tried to hear himself saying the words, he could not remember. Had they discussed it? Had they truly understood one another? He and Avalon exchanged many words, but it felt as if those words were in different languages.

When Jarrow's wife turned back to him, her smile was as open and bright as the sun. 'My king. I apologise. You took me by surprise but now I've gathered myself. Lately I have been concerned about North, and I fear it's making me ill.'

'Concerned?' Jarrow had to tread carefully. He could not risk the health of Avalon or the baby – but he could not risk the house either.

Avalon sighed prettily. 'Oh, it's probably me being silly. I don't know if our north child will be able to pick up landlocker ways. She is a sweet child, but she *is* a child.' She took Jarrow's free hand and held it to the swell of her belly. 'But let's not think about her. You have your own child. Your wife and your baby need you.'

Jarrow kept his breathing steady, ignoring the throb in his head. 'You have me, my queen. Both of you have me. Everything I have is yours.'

'Everything but what we need.' Avalon's voice was so quiet that Jarrow might have misheard her. But he knew he had not. He swithered between adoration and irritation. He could not possibly love his wife more – and yet no matter how many apples he bartered for, no matter how many fresh flowers he placed in her hair, she was never satisfied.

Seeming to sense his swaying emotions, Avalon turned to Jarrow and peppered kisses along his ragged jawline. She spoke in a purr. 'But listen, my king. I'm being a silly thing. I just wish ...' She sighed and waited for Jarrow to prompt her, which he did not.

'I just wish,' she continued, 'that I could help give you a fresh start.

I give you a new baby, you give me a new home – together, we have a new chance to restore the Stirling name. Ainsel is not a baby, and can look after himself. Is the father not more worthy than the son?'

'Do you want the house? Is that what you're saying?'

Avalon pealed out a laugh. 'Oh, my king! I want for nothing. I never think of my own desires. I'm merely thinking of what's best for our child.'

'I cannot leave, Avalon. Who will look after the Excalibur? Who will be the ringmaster? This is my home. Our home.'

'It doesn't have to be. Ainsel can look after the circus. Ainsel and his new dampling wife. They're more suited to it, my king. We're not meant for a life at sea. You are a true landlocker.'

Jarrow gripped the wheel until his knuckles throbbed. 'It's too late to go back, Avalon. I've made my decision. There is one house, and that is for my son.'

'If you say so.' Avalon had switched her smoulder to a sulk, bottom lip pouted out, body turned away from Jarrow. 'But we still need a house. Your wife and child can't be expected to live at sea for ever.'

'Hmm,' replied Jarrow, hoping that would be answer enough. He had been saving for most of Ainsel's life; this baby would be grown and Jarrow long dead before the same again could be saved. Surely Avalon knew that. Surely she saw that this was the only way.

Jarrow bent to drop a kiss on his wife's forehead. She tilted away from him, swaying belowdecks without looking at him. He couldn't bear to watch her go. He kept his gaze ahead, on the merge of sky and sea.

Over the following days, Jarrow watched North. She performed her circus duties perfectly – couldn't she just as perfectly slip into the role of a good landlocker wife? It was true that she did not spend much time with the rest of the crew, preferring to stay in her coracle with her bear. But that proved her diligence, surely – it was not easy to keep a bear so well trained and docile, and North did the best she could. Jarrow had seen what a beast like that could do.

The one good thing about their lack of progress was that the animals could be exercised. North's bear paddled in the sea for hours, and judging by his silence it tired him out so much that he slept the rest of the time. The horses, of course, were far too precious for the water, and instead were exercised by circling the *Excalibur*'s deck. Jarrow's thoughts were punctuated by the steady clop of hooves.

He'd slipped so deep into his thoughts that he barely noticed the first breath of wind that signalled their emergence from the doldrums. It was Cash, in fact, who alerted him. The clowns had taken to peeling back the canvas of their coracle and perching on the edge, allowing the sun to brown the skin that was not covered with tattoos. Jarrow found their presence comforting. In the still air of the doldrums, alone on the wide sea, with no sign of life from the covered coracles, it would be easy to feel alone in the world. But Jarrow needed only to glance over his shoulder and see the edge of a brightly coloured limb to know that his circus continued.

'Easterly!' came the shout on their second afternoon. The sky was flat and blue as an upturned bowl, and the sun glinted silver off the kicked-up waves. Those waves should have been Jarrow's clue to the breeze, but his worries seemed to clump inside his brain and obscure his vision.

'I feel an easterly, Captain!'

He turned towards the call. Cash was on the port side of the coracle, ideally placed to feel the first breath of wind from the east. Jarrow lifted his face to the sky. Sure enough, he could feel the push of a breeze against his skin. Relief flooded through him.

Cash's call roused the rest of the crew. Jarrow waited for the head count before announcing: 'We are free of the doldrums! Hoist the sails, crew, hoist the sails. Hoist! Hoist! Hoist!'

Usually the crew would join the chant, but the only response was a smattering of watery smiles. Well, that was all that could be expected. Perhaps they thought Jarrow callous for continuing on in the face of such loss. But what was his choice? There were still eleven other members of this crew, and it was his responsibility to ensure that they were fed and clothed and kept safe. Better to be a callous captain than a negligent one. He kept the smile pinned to his face and turned to retrieve the mainsail from its cubby under the port bow. He knew he should have hung it before now, but he was as superstitious as the next captain: the mainsail had touched the dead, and it would take a strong wind to blow that away. No point in letting a mild breeze whisper ghosts around the ship.

Understanding that there would be a wait while the sails were hoisted, the rest of the crew busied themselves with individual tasks. The clowns tugged out their skin-diver gear and the thick glass sphere of the lung, ready to collect food for dinner; Mauve and Teal sat on the edge of their coracle and dipped their feet into the water, shouting over to Cash the names of the undersea items they needed for their beauty supplies; Ainsel led the horses back to his coracle.

The distance up the mast to attach the mainsail was not far, perhaps twice Jarrow's height. From there, it could be hoisted by ropes on the deck. It was easiest for the acrobats, so used to monkeying up ropes and platforms. But he had already asked so much of Melia. The world was still turning and bellies were still hungry and the circus still needed to perform, and soon enough she would have to do her duty. But not yet. The rest of the crew could manage, and North was small and skinny enough to shin a little way up the mast.

'North!' called out Jarrow. She had ducked back down into her coracle to dry and settle her bear after his daily exercise, and took a moment to reappear. He made a note to ask her how Melia was faring. 'North, please help me to hang the sail.'

'Oh, I - yes, Jarrow.' She ducked down into her coracle once more, then climbed out and began to step across the line of boats to the *Excalibur*.

Ainsel, who had already stepped on board to help with the sail, gaped at his father. Jarrow regarded him with a slight smile.

'Thank you, Ainsel, but I can manage this ship quite well. I should practise for after your wedding, no? You may tend to your horses. I imagine that they are still restless from the storm, and we must have them ready to perform when we reach land tomorrow. We all wish to eat.'

Ainsel muttered something that Jarrow could not discern. As North passed, he swept his arm wide and dropped to a deep bow in a parody of manners. Jarrow watched, the sail in his hands.

North did not react to Ainsel. Instead she stepped past him and on to the *Excalibur's* deck, then waited for Jarrow to pass her the sail. He held it out, but hesitated. He could feel the heat from North's skin, so close to his own. When the boat was not moving, the air was oppressively hot. Sweat itched along Jarrow's top lip, and the rough skin of his cheeks began to ache in the humidity. He knew that he should stay out of the sea-spray as he sailed; the saltwater only made his skin crack more, but it felt so soothing on the reddened flesh. He was anxious to get the circus moving again.

'North,' he began. 'I knew your parents for many years before you were born. I know you didn't get much time with them, before - that is, perhaps they never spoke of their hopes for you. But all of this - the house, and your marriage to Ainsel - I am sure that it's what they wanted for you. I am sure it's even more than they hoped for. Ainsel is my firstborn son, and I loved his mother very much. I do not give him away lightly.'

She kept her eyes down on the deck. Jarrow waited, wondering if perhaps he should repeat the words in case she hadn't heard. The silence thickened. The sail was heavy in his arms.

'What I am saying, North, is that I am proud of you. I am giving you my son because I think you are worthy of him. And you know that if there was anything – that is, any reason that you might not be able to start your life on land – live properly with Ainsel as his wife...' He faltered.

From the coracles came the ting of glass against metal. Jarrow glanced up. Dosh was in the water, lung balanced on the surface, ready to start diving, pulling faces at Cash and Dough through the scratched glass sphere. Damn: Jarrow had forgotten to ask him to bring up some of those pinkish seaweed shoots, the ones that Avalon liked. And he needed Cash to scrape any barnacles from the undersides of the coracles while the clowns were diving. And he needed to discuss a tweak to Bero's fire-breathing act. And he should check that Cyan had properly mended the costumes for the maypole. And Melia needed a new coracle, and the *Excalibur's* seams needed caulking, and Avalon needed things for the baby, and he still did not have quite enough saved up for the house, and the days were slipping away towards their arrival at the island. And, damn it, North still had not answered him. He cleared his throat.

'Well,' he croaked. He coughed again and passed the corner of the sail to her, keeping the mass of it in his arms. 'Thank you, North. I am glad that there is nothing to stand in the way. You will be an excellent landlocker, and you will make us all proud. Now we had better get the sail up.'

As North began to climb the mast, the sail's edge tucked into the back of her trousers, Avalon popped up from belowdecks. Her anger seemed to have blown over. It never took long – and at least Jarrow hadn't had to sweeten her with gifts this time. She tiptoed to peck a forgiving kiss on his cheek, murmuring that she wished to sun herself on the deck. She waited for a kiss in return then stretched out, one hand behind her head, elbow cocked.

Jarrow had intended to watch North, but instead he watched Avalon watching North. Her eyes were squinted shut against the sun – but no, not quite shut; just enough to mask the direction of her gaze. He pretended to busy himself with the wheel, checking again that its movement was smoothly oiled. From above came the click of bone hoops, the shift of limbs, the shush of fabric dropping. North had hung the sail. But still he kept his eyes on his wife.

Her pose was one of absolute relaxation: head tipped back, one arm stretched along the gunwale. He held his breath, all the better to observe her.

He saw Avalon's head tilt up, following North's movement as she slid down the mast. He saw her eyes widen; saw an unpleasant little smile sneak across her lips. He glanced up at North, but she had already shinned back down to the deck and was fussing with her clothes, rearranging them where they'd rucked up during her descent. She stood with her back to him, and he could not see what had so intrigued Avalon.

He flicked his gaze between them. As North turned to go back to her coracle, Avalon stood to meet her. If North was surprised, she did not show it; she simply stood with her hands at her sides and her gaze on her feet, waiting.

'Oh, North', sighed Avalon. She took both of North's hands in her own, turning them so that the palms faced up. She opened her own hands so the two pairs were in a line, as if she was showing North something held in her hand. But Jarrow could see that her hands were empty.

'Our little north child,' continued Avalon, her voice as soft as a breeze. 'Our child,' she repeated, to let North know that she and Jarrow really did think of North as their own dear daughter. The throb in Jarrow's head lessened. Avalon was happy once more, and that meant he could be happy too.

Avalon took hold of North's hands and pulled her close, so close that the swell of her belly pressed against North's own middle. Despite her moods, Avalon really was the sweetest of women: reminding North of the baby, showing her that North should see the child as a new part of her family. Jarrow would never have known how to show North this, and he was grateful to Avalon for her kindness.

'Ready to hoist!' he called out. There was a rush of activity: Dosh tugged on the cable attaching Cash to the boat; Teal and Mauve pulled their feet from the water and fussed over their canvas; Avalon slid belowdecks; and among it all, North slipped away from the *Excalibur* and back to her coracle.

Jarrow tugged on the rope that would hoist the sail and get the fleet on their way.

Don't let Whitby's blood be on the sail, he thought. *Please, please, all you gods of the earth and the sea, let that gracekeeper girl have rinsed the sail. Don't let there be blood.*

He hoisted the sail.

The striped fabric was bright and clean, as spotless as the day it was made. It bellied in the wind, already tugging the *Excalibur* and its line of coracles on to their next port. Jarrow double-checked his compass and his sextant. Then he took hold of the wheel and steered them in the right direction, letting the wind soothe his throbbing skin.

10
Callanish

After the circus left, Callanish passed the time in looking at the map pinned to her wall, and stitching up the worn patches in her white dress, and polishing the grace-cages until they gleamed as bright as the sun. This last exercise was the most effective, as by the time Callanish had polished the final grace-cage, the first had become tarnished by the seawater and she could begin all over again.

The supply boat returned, so her grace-cages were no longer empty, and her belly did not need to be empty either. Boats passed on the horizon. Some of them approached, offering up their dead to Callanish. She stitched their faces, folded up their fists, and caged a bird above them. Every night she dreamed of the bear-girl.

One morning, she tore a finger-thick strip off the hank of fabric and sat down to write a letter to her mother. She imagined how the words would look, printed on the fabric. They all seemed wrong. She wanted to say ... she wanted to say ... she closed her eyes and imagined the bear-girl. Her lips opened and she could speak. The bear-girl, and the bear-girl's baby – she knew them, deep down in her guts, her heart, the base of her spine. They felt real, like family. But how could they be when she already had a family?

Callanish wanted to say so many things, but the most important thing was something she could not say. She wanted to tell her mother that she remembered. And that she was sorry.

She stood up again, and got into her rowing boat, and went all the way out to the furthest-away grace, one she'd caged last week. It didn't have long left; she checked whether it was breathing, but its time had not yet come. Tomorrow, probably. She'd have to row back then to unclip the cage door and tip its tiny body into the water. She was almost at the edge of her graceyard, the outer circle of thirteen spindly stones with the look of weathered wood. Real wood was far too precious for such a thing, but the salvaged metal had been etched and shaped so that, if you weren't looking too closely, it could almost be wood. From this distance, the house looked like wood too; at first Callanish had worried about rust, but now she encouraged it. The metal had lasted this long. It would last after she was gone.

She poked her fingers through the dulling bars of the cage, ruffling the grace's feathers until she found the largest, brightest one. When she tugged it free, the grace did not flinch. It did not look at her, or at anything at all. It did not seem to know that she was there. She tilted the feather in the light, watching the colours shift from green to blue.

Callanish had never meant to be cruel. She remembered her mistake, and she would continue to remember it even if she could be forgiven. She wanted her mother to know that, although she could not say it. She sat for a long time in her boat on the flat sea, surrounded by dying birds, with a single feather in her hand. Then she went back to her house, wrapped the grace-feather in the strip of fabric and wrote her mother's name and island on the outside. She waited.

When the messenger finally came, it was night. This was not unusual; good messengers spoke the language of the constellations, which communicated more than an empty blue sky. Callanish was in bed, face turned to the window and the busy stars, waiting for morning. The first she knew of him was the steady splash of the waves against his boat as he approached.

The graceyard had been visited by many messengers, so without looking she knew what was out there: a single-masted boat the size of her house, sails fluttering, deck overwhelmed by a huge waterproof chest; and at the helm, hands on the wheel, a man in blue with his head shaved to the skin: the standard uniform of a messenger.

The beat of the waves grew louder, louder, and then it stopped. Callanish heard the thud of the messenger's boat bumping up against the dock. He would not be rude enough to climb out of his boat until she came to greet him. She pulled on her gloves and slippers and stepped on to the porch.

A little boat with its sails now furled and its rope fastened to the dock. A man in blue. He climbed out of the boat and stepped towards Callanish.

'I need you to take something for me,' she said. 'A message.' From the pocket of her dress she pulled a canvas-wrapped feather. 'The address is on it.'

'Hello to you too,' he replied. Callanish said nothing. He lifted the parcel, tapping it with his fingertips. 'I don't hear any paper inside. Is the message written on the other side of the fabric?'

It seemed rude to say that it was none of his business, so Callanish kept saying nothing.

'Or is it a verbal message? Seems odd to take the cheap option when you've already got the fabric, but I don't mind. I'm good at verbals. One of the best, if you want to know. I don't just remember the words, I remember the *intent* of the words. That's what really matters.' He grinned at her, teeth bright as bones in the moonlight.

Callanish knew that the messenger had travelled far and probably wanted to rest, but he could not rest here. She had nothing. There was nothing.

'I have payment,' said Callanish. She went into her house and scooped up chips of quartz and copper and gold: a month's worth of Resting payments, the parts she couldn't eat or wear or wash with. She went back out to the porch and dropped the chips in the messenger's waiting hand. He poked through the offering.

'This isn't enough,' he said. 'Not even for a verbal.'

Callanish swayed, dizzy with panic. 'But it has to be enough.'

He shrugged. 'Sorry. I'll be back around in six months or so. You can save up and I'll take it then.'

Six months. What did it matter if she waited six more months? But it did matter. It did.

'You have to take it,' she said. 'Please.'

'Look, I'm sorry, I really am. But I have to eat. Messages mean money, and money means food.'

No one was more shocked than Callanish when her tears began to fall. She hiccuped out a sob.

'Hey! Hey, now. No need for that.' The messenger slid his arm around Callanish's shoulders, and she let him. Her knees gave up and she collapsed on to him, both of them dropping to a clumsy embrace on the porch. 'Hush now. Hush now, little fish. It's okay. It's okay, I'll take the message. You can pay me when I come back. Or we can trade for something. We'll figure it out. Don't cry, now.'

Callanish leaned forward and kissed the messenger, their lips slick and salty with tears. After a heartbeat of hesitation, he kissed her back.

She pulled away, took his hand, and led him into her house, wiping her cheeks dry on her shoulder. They lay down on the bed.

Around them, the graces shuddered in their cages and the sea sucked at the moorings. It was not difficult to pretend that they were the only people left in the world. It was so easy, in fact, that perhaps it wasn't pretending. No one would ever know what happened out here. Such small crimes.

Afterwards, they sat together on the porch, feet tucked up, two hand-spans of empty space between them. Callanish could not offer the messenger anything. She had no spare food, nothing to drink.

'What's your name?' asked the messenger.

Callanish picked a flake of rust from the boards and cast it into the water. It left a reddish smudge on the finger of her glove.

'What's with that map you've got pinned up on the wall?' asked the messenger.

That was a question that Callanish did not mind answering. 'My great-great-great-great-grandfather,' she said. 'He made lots of maps, but that's the only one left now. He was a cartographer. From back when there was still land to map.'

'There are still plenty of maps, little fish.' The messenger stretched his arms up over his head, letting the bones crack. 'Sea roads, trading routes, the locations of the archipelagos. Even if people can read the constellations, they need maps. There are still cartographers around. Lots of them.'

'I didn't say that there weren't,' said Callanish. 'But it's different now. Before, the land was a proper home, not like – it doesn't matter.'

The land that her ancestor had mapped no longer existed. The contours of mountains and valleys, the lines denoting when one country became another, the shaded colours to show kingship: all of it was gone under the endless ocean. Back then it had shown the real world. Now it was only history, stories of a place that once was. Callanish knew all about mourning – she only had to think of the hundreds of bird skeletons, picked clean by fish, resting for ever beneath her house. But she did not know how to mourn the world that she had never seen.

The messenger seemed restless now that their bodies were separate. He was shifting on the boards, rubbing his hands over his scalp, prodding a toe into the water to scare off the fish.

'I should move on,' he said. 'You never know when the next storm is coming. If I don't go now, I could be stuck here for a while.' He left a long pause, watching Callanish from the corner of his eye. He went to take her gloved hand, then seemed to think better of it. 'You could put a pot of coffee on and I could stay for a while longer. We can talk about your great-great-whatever and the maps. Come on, little fish. It'll be good for you.'

Callanish stood and walked over to the messenger's boat. She waited until he lumbered to his feet with a sigh. When he got back into his boat, she tugged his rope off the dock and threw the coil into his boat without a word.

'Aren't you even going to say goodbye to me?' The messenger leaned his arm along the boat's edge and looked up at her, the coquettishness an awkward contrast with his shaved head and muscled shoulders.

'Farewell,' she said, and the messenger turned his boat and sailed back into the night.

She knew that she would sit on the porch every evening and watch for him until he returned. Not for the man that he was – he could end up under her house, picked clean by the fish, for all the difference it made – but for his message. If the feather meant anything to her mother, she would know by the response. If there were no response, then Callanish would know that she had not been forgiven. Without forgiveness, she would be forever haunted by her mistake; nothing more than the ghost of a ghost.

11
North

The scent of North-West 1's pine needles crept from the trees, across the fields, over the houses, past the harbour, and all the way into North's nostrils as she dozed in the swaying cocoon of her coracle. She was dreaming of Whitby: his long, strong limbs wrapped tight in net, dropping down into the water. His fingers and toes nibbled by fish, his body dropping piece by piece to the ocean floor to be buried in sand. The earth exhaling, pulling him in.

She coughed awake, her nose full of soil. An afternoon nap before the show had seemed like a good idea, but now she regretted it. She didn't want the image of Whitby fish-nibbled and land-buried.

Landlockers spoke of North-West 1 in favourable tones; they loved the woody, earthy scent of the pines, and believed that the needles brought luck. That was all nonsense, North knew. Pine trees smelled of dirt and mould, like all other trees. She breathed in deep so that her nose would become accustomed and blunt the sharpness of the smell.

On either side of her, shadowed figures snored. North listened for the rhythm of Melia's breath, and decided that she still slept. She hoped that Melia dreamed of shifting colours in far-north skies, or a bed stuffed with feathers, or pork-dumpling stew. Anything but Whitby.

She got to her knees and pressed her face to her bear's furred belly to steady herself. That was a good smell. Why couldn't everything smell of warm fur and saltwater and fresh seaweed popping in the fire? Then the world would be perfect. Well, not quite perfect: she remembered the soft web of the gracekeeper's fingers, the sun-clean scent of her skin, the flutter of North's baby inside her. That was a new world; a kind of perfect she had never thought to imagine.

She peeled back the edge of the canvas and peeped out, careful not to let too much light seep into the coracle and wake the sleepers. The *Excalibur* had already docked in the harbour.

Red Gold, in all his raw-cheeked and paper-shirted glory, stood amongst the chaos of the harbour, charming the landlockers. If they weren't moonstruck by the excitement of his stories, then they were certainly reassured by the steadiness of his feet on the ground. North knew that landlockers found Red Gold familiar in a way they could not quite explain. They would not accept him as a true landlocker, but although he wore his tiny brass bell like all the other damplings, they knew he was not a dampling either. She would never understand how Red Gold could talk to landlockers with such ease. They chose land over sea, stagnation over motion, the stench of rotting wood over the fresh ocean breeze. They were another species entirely.

She tried to tell from the set of his jaw whether Avalon had told him about the baby. It would be difficult when the child came, she knew: to make sure the bear was never alone with it, and carry on doing her act, and somehow get enough food for all three of them, but she would just have to ... she would ... she had no idea what she would do. All she could do now was carry on.

North glanced down to check that her bear was still sleeping, then pulled herself up to sit on the edge of her coracle. She raised a hand to greet Dosh and Dough, who were already sunning themselves on their coracle's taut canvas. Her dress was loose, so she did not worry that they would notice her bump. She hadn't minded the gracekeeper seeing, but that had become a trade, an exchange of secrets: the outline of a bump for the touch of webbed fingers. The opening of a box she hadn't known was locked.

Past the tight line of coracles and the docked *Excalibur*, the island rose. Northern islands were usually uneven, and this one dipped and stretched messily, the central copse of pines obscuring the other side of the island. North knew from an overnight stint on a prison boat a few years ago that it was a conservative island, and revivalism was popular. She hoped that Red Gold would remember, and save the subversion for another night. Judging by what was being loaded into the trade boats, the fields here were mostly wheat, peas and broad beans – unusual, as the southern islands were usually better for farming crops, the northern better for animals. Bread with honeyed peas for dinner, then, and North couldn't argue with that. She only hoped that the landlockers would love the show enough to include some of their hard-traded meat in with the payment.

She took a deep breath, grateful that her nose had got used to the smell of the trees, and leaned back against the taut canvas. The *Excalibur* had been lucky to find a berth; every other space was occupied by messenger cutters and medic galleons and fruit-trading clippers. Looming over them all, its sides draped with painted depictions of the blue-eyed, blue-robed Virgin, was an enormous revival cruise ship. North shivered; it was several spaces away, but so huge that its shadow would soon be cast over their coracles.

Above her, the sky was barnacled with clouds. The sun was starting to fall, spreading swathes of orange and pink as it went. Junk traders sculled in the shallows; when flotsam washed ashore it belonged to the landlockers, but if the damplings could drag it up when it was still in the water, it was fair game. North would hail one of them later, to see if she could trade some treats for her bear.

Behind North there was a rustle, a sigh, as one of the clowns shifted position.

'I hear the clams on this island make a decent pine-needle vodka,' said Dosh. Perhaps the trees were good for something after all – though North wasn't sure she'd ever drink something that tasted of pine.

'Can't be worse than the liquid fire that Bero usually serves up,' she stage-whispered back without taking her gaze down from the sky. 'I bet it's the same stuff he uses to breathe flames for his act.'

No response. North sat up, resting her weight on her elbows, and tipped her head right back to look at the clowns upside down.

Dosh was regarding her with a serious expression. 'Sweet North, I know you jest, but you speak a true fact. Bero has spent his whole life filling us with fire. Inside each one of us is a raging inferno waiting to take hold. Inside me, and you, and Red Gold, and even Red Gold's kind and generous wife.' Dosh rolled over and gave her an exaggerated wink, turning each tattooed limb to tan the underside. 'Now, when you go ashore to seduce those clam boys, you watch yourself among those trees. You've got a flame inside you. Don't set them alight.'

North laughed and tipped her head back to the sky. She would be going nowhere near the trees, but she didn't need to tell Dosh that; the clowns wouldn't venture any closer to the shore than they had to for tonight's performance.

North ducked back into her coracle, ready to wake her bear and Melia so that they could get ready. The islands might not be North's favourite places, but they needed to perform tonight. They needed to eat, of course – but more than that, they needed the distraction. The ghost of Whitby lurked in the corners of every coracle. If glinting lights and Red Gold's roar and the scratch of the gramophone weren't enough to distract Melia, then North was lost.

Behindcurtains, North and her bear waited. Most of the circus stayed in their coracles before a performance, but tonight North wanted to watch the show. It was good to see the grace and glory of her fellow performers. Sometimes she needed to be reminded of the point of all this. The glamours had re-dyed the blonde braids among her dark hair and draped her body in brown fabric. She'd do the simplest version of their act: a dance, a kiss, a bow to the crowd. Then back to the mess boat to feast and comfort Melia and try to avoid Avalon's spiked, knowing gaze.

Red Gold played it safe, beginning with a subdued version of the maypole. In the olden days they'd called maypole dancing a sin. It was pagan superstition, worshipping false gods. But things change. Now even the most devout revivalists didn't dare reject the gods of the land, for fear the crops would fail. North admired the way that Red Gold managed to braid the revivalist beliefs together with the old traditions – not forgetting a healthy dose of sensuality from the andro-gynous, ribbon-bound bodies. She couldn't help wondering what Callanish would make of the maypole if she were here.

BEHOLD THE BEAUTY OF THE DANCERS' RIBBONS, boomed the ring-master's voice around the big top, AS RED AS A TULIP, AS GREEN AS THE GRASS – at this he swept his arms wide as if glorying in the joys of spring – AND WITH THIS DANCE WE GIVE THANKS TO THE GODS OF THE LAND FOR BRINGING NEW LIFE TO THE WORLD, and out slid Avalon, demure and maternal as the revival boats' Virgin in her pale blue dress, AS I TOO THANK THE GODS FOR THE NEW LIFE, and Red Gold beamed from ear to ear, pointing his smile from one side of the big top to the other, OF MY BELOVED SON, and the audience broke into applause as Avalon curtsied, her padded belly swollen as a poppy about to burst.

Such nonsense, thought North. Red Gold was far too clever for the landlockers, and they didn't even realise. Damplings did not worship the gods of the land, and if Red Gold were thanking anyone for that child, it would be the real gods, the ones of the sea. But then again –

Red Gold was born a landlocker, and he had slapped her when she had gone to snap a twig from the tree. Maybe this was not just an act for him.

The clowns cartwheeled offstage, and North pulled her bear into the embrace of the curtains to keep out of their way. Her bear had been so good about having Melia in their coracle, and despite the fluster of tonight's show he stayed quiet and calm. As a reward, after tonight's performance she would find something to trade for the fish-belly and purple seaweed that he liked.

Ribbons off, costumes on, a trio of grins at North and her bear, and the clowns raced breathless back onstage. As the ringmaster's voice echoed across the island and North peeked out from behind the curtain, Cash, Dosh and Dough began the act for which they were named.

Dressed as old-fashioned bankers, in suits and garishly patterned ties, they plodded around the stage, dragging their briefcases along the ground as if they were full of rocks. Just as the crowd was getting riled up, throwing decades of pent-up rage at the clowns, they opened their suitcases. Inside sat stacks and stacks of paper money – it was genuine, too, scavenged and traded and stitched back together when it tore. And it certainly did tear when the clowns began to throw it into the crowd. The clowns' white-painted faces and blackened eyes blurred to skulls as they threw the money faster and faster.

Whatever the truth, over time the landlockers had learned to blame the banks, the relentless drive for more money, for the rising seas and the loss of their land. Once upon a time they'd had a whole planet of fields and plains and deserts and forests. Now they had to make do with the patched-up corners of gutted cities, to cluster their homes around half-dead copses, to scrape what they could from their tiny footholds in a swallowing sea. They needed a scapegoat, and the clowns provided it. North should have known that this island would like this act the best. Revivalists were always angry.

As the clowns' act continued and the clams in the crowd grew more aggressive, she shrank back into her bear's furred embrace.

Out the clowns tossed the money! Loudly they crowed about their wealth! Sneakily they rubbed together their greedy hands and discussed their nasty plots!

The clams were on their feet, stamping and braying, crumpling the notes and throwing them back onstage along with the curses. North tried to glance over at Red Gold, but her view between the curtains was narrow and she could not see him.

It seemed to North that the clams were shouting louder than ever, and her back vibrated with the beginnings of a growl from her bear. She turned in his grasp to tap his nose - but, if she was honest, she felt like growling too. Even though she couldn't see him, she knew that Red Gold would be watching carefully. They'd all suffered violent crowds and chilly nights on the prison boat, but the ringmaster knew better than to risk that now. Although he had not spoken to North about it, she knew that he had noticed Melia's emotional state. There was a time for risk - and there was a time for safe acts and full bellies. North would never make a ringmaster, but she knew that much.

She took her bear by the paw and led him deeper into the shadows, ready for their cue.

That night on the mess boat, Bero served the crew endless cups of fire. North found it easy to refuse without anyone questioning her. They seemed grateful that she was looking after Melia; although they all loved her, caring for the bereaved is a burden that few people want to carry.

So North delivered the meagre portions of sweetened peas and seeded bread to her coracle, ready to ensure that her bear and Melia both cleared their plates. She dropped into the coracle to find Melia perched bird-like on the edge of her bunk, smacking chalk between her palms. Her bear was hunched on his bunk, eyeing Melia as if he was not sure whether she was a threat. The coracle vibrated with the growls sounding low in his throat. The lamplight gleamed on his teeth as his lips peeled back.

'Look, North!' crowed Melia, smacking her palms and letting the dust fill the coracle. 'Ghosts!'

Chalk snowed down on the bunks, the boards, her bear. He blinked it out of his eyes but let the rest cake his fur. North would bring him all the fish-belly he could eat as a reward for not biting Melia's hands off.

It did not take long to calm Melia; just an acknowledgement that yes, there were ghosts, and no, they did not disappear because they could not be seen. The peas and bread were dusted with chalk, but they ate them anyway. A little chalk on the tongue was worth it for something for their bellies to grip.

As North washed and groomed the chalk from her bear she kept an eye on Melia, who was eating her dinner in silent slow motion. If she needed to wash and groom Melia too then she would, but she would rather not have to. Once crossed, certain boundaries could not be forgotten, and she hoped one day to look up to Melia once more.

Finally her charges slept, and North stepped across the coracles to the mess boat. Red Gold and Avalon held court at the head of the table with Ainsel looking on sulkily, the clowns seemed to take up more space than their lanky bodies suggested, the glamours whispered and crowed among themselves – and so North sat at the far end of the table, hoping that Bero would not be too busy with his bar-tending duties to talk to her. Most of the seal-fat lamps hung at the top end of the table, and she felt soothed by the shadows.

She'd just slid on to the bench when Bero, ever the eagle-eyed, thumped down beside her.

'Evening, bartender,' North said solemnly. She picked up the end of Bero's long braid and held it above her top lip like a moustache. 'I am honoured to frequent this gentleman's establishment.'

'Evening, young sir,' Bero replied. 'And may I say what fine facial decoration you have there. Why, it must soak up your alcohol like nobody's business. How does it ever reach your mouth?'

'I'll thank you not to think of my mouth, you impudent seahorse. Now apologise and kiss my salt-hardened feet.'

'I shan't, you old dogfish. And now we've got that out of the way, tell me –'

At this, Bero leaned in to North, so close that his beard tickled her cheek. He wiped a smear of chalk from her shoulder where she had missed it during her wash.

'Tell me,' he said, 'how are you?'

North let go of Bero's hair and reached for her tin cup, unscrewing it and then screwing it back to the table. 'I'm – it's – Melia won't talk about Whitby. She eats and sleeps, and she'll nod if I ask her a question, but she's like a doll. If I threw her into the sea I bet she wouldn't even swim. And when she does speak – Bero, it's nonsense. She says she hears bells. Under the water.'

'Like that old superstition?'

'Right. I can't even remember what it is, really. That the bells are a curse? That they herald storms? But we'd know if another storm was due. Red Gold would know, at least. And sometimes I . . .' She tailed off, her indecision lost in the chatter of the mess boat.

'Go on.'

'I worry about my bear, you know? Who will look after him?'

'Don't lose today in worries about tomorrow. No one knows what's coming with the dawn.'

'But I do know what's coming, Bero. Red Gold is going to make Ainsel and me live in a house on land. He's going to make me be a landlocker.'

'*Make* you? It sounds more like a gift to me. Life is short – look at where we've just been. That graceyard. It won't be the last time we're there, North. We have to grasp what little joy we can before it's our turn. There's no shame in living.'

'And you think I'll find joy in pretending to be a clam with Ainsel?'

'North. Listen. Are you hungry?'

She laughed. 'Of course. I'm always hungry. Aren't you?'

'Yes. I'm hungry, and you're hungry, and everyone on the *Excalibur* is hungry, and every damned dampling between here and the equator is hungry. You know who's not hungry, North? The landlockers. They might be beasts and bury children alive and –'

'What?'

'You didn't hear? The landlockers at the last island were gossiping. Some baby born with webbed fingers and great gaping gills on its throat. They buried it alive at their World Tree – said it was some wicked spell cast by damplings, the curse of the sea. The curse of *us*, North. It's only a matter of time before they tire of damplings and try to bury the whole cursed lot of us. Get yourself a foot on land before that happens.'

'I don't want to be one of them, Bero. There are more important things than full bellies.'

'Are there? I'm not so sure.' Bero tensed his left shoulder, moving the empty sleeve pinned up on his shirt. 'We fell into a hard life here. Imagine what we could do if we weren't hungry all the time.'

North should agree. She should take a drink and smile as wide as a crescent moon and say that she would be a landlocker and she would live with Ainsel and everything would be a joy for ever and ever. But she could not lie to Bero. He seemed to know it, too; he turned his broad body sideways on the bench, creating a Bero-shaped wall of privacy. Or at least, as much privacy as could be expected on a tiny boat crewed by people who had known each other for most of their lives.

'North, I didn't ask you about Melia, or about your bear. I asked about you. We're a crew here, and none of us has to be alone.'

North saw herself split into two. One North defied the ringmaster: said she wouldn't marry his self-absorbed son, and instead she'd carry on as she always had, caring for her bear and also, later, her mysterious baby which was clearly not born of anyone on the *Excalibur*, and she'd somehow ensure her bear didn't eat her child out of jealousy as soon as her back was turned, and somehow Red Gold wouldn't force her off the boat for rejecting his firstborn son, and somehow the grace-keeper would come to the *Excalibur* and they would be a family together, and – the vision crumpled.

The other North married Ainsel, and never let anyone see the baby so they'd believe it was her new husband's, and ate her fill at the dinner table every night, and lived for ever unsteadily on land, sharing the tiny space with her ragtag family and a bear living – where, in the back garden? – and never saw Callanish ever again.

Neither North would stay, not even in her imagination. Being alone was not the problem. Perhaps being alone would be better.

'Bero, will you promise me something?'

He rested his right arm on the table, scarred palm up, ready for North to put her hands in his. 'I will,' he said.

In the shadows she could see the dark dots of stubble on his cheeks and the lines etched between his eyebrows. Perhaps not everyone in the circus slept as soundly as North's bear.

'North child! What are you doing down there?' Red Gold's voice cut across their whispers. North jumped as if she'd been caught doing something she shouldn't. 'I didn't even see you there. Hiding away from me, eh? You must have crept in here like a little minnow.'

'Of course not, Jarrow. I'm just talking with Bero. We're discussing those changes to his act.'

But the ringmaster was already scoffing, chewing on North's

response and spitting it out. 'Bring yourself up here, my north child.' At this he lifted Avalon, ignoring her disgusted expression, and deposited her further down the bench. 'Look, I made a space for you. Up here is where you belong, not down there with the riff-raff!'

North flickered Bero a pained smile. She tugged on his braid as a farewell and made her way up the mess boat to the head of the table. The glamours hunched their shoulders as she passed, their backs forming walls. Tomorrow she'd go to their coracle and explain to them that she didn't think anyone was riff-raff, least of all her crewmates. But no, there was no point. The glamours had taken that old preacher's words to heart; they believed that glamour was grammar, that words were magic spells. Nothing was spoken in truth, only as a means to deceive.

She addressed Red Gold. 'Do you want me to –'

He swept a dramatic hand at the space beside him. 'Yes, I most certainly do. Sit sit sit, my future daughter.'

She slid on to the bench between Ainsel and Red Gold. For a moment it seemed as if the ringmaster was going to wrap his arm around her, or pull her on to his lap, or pepper her face with kisses as he did to Avalon. North would not flinch. Even if he smeared blood and glitter all across her face and into her mouth, she would not flinch. Red Gold deserved better than that.

'Hello Ainsel,' she said, because he was gazing down at the pitted metal table, toying with his cup and ignoring everyone. She felt a burn of annoyance. What a self-centred little prince he was.

'Hello North,' he replied. He looked up at her, and she regretted her annoyance. Ainsel was a brat, but she had never seen that expression on his face before. He must be thinking about Whitby. Or maybe his horses were sickening. Or – North felt a churn of relief at the thought – perhaps he was worrying about how to get out of this marriage as much as she was. He'd promised that he'd speak to his father. The time

was getting close now, and in North's opinion he'd better hurry up –
but she knew that Red Gold was not an easy man to disobey. She'd
rather Ainsel waited for the right moment than rush and get it wrong.

'Now then, my favourite lovers,' boomed Red Gold. He swooped
his arms wide as if to embrace North and Ainsel, one on each side,
then seemed to think better of it. Instead he took their hands in his,
squeezing them hard. His skin felt as hot as a seal-fat lamp. He linked
North's hand with Ainsel's, pressing them together until her bones
ached.

'Soon we'll be at North-East 19. I know you've been counting down
the days until we make it there, because your wedding, my loves, will
be the most glorious day of all our lives. Isn't that right, crew?'

He raised his cup in a toast, gleaming his grin round the mess boat
until everyone else followed. North tried not to shrink down under
the table.

'I have the islanders ready to set everything up by their World Tree
– and I don't need to tell you what an honour that is. We have ribbons
of all colours, and I know you're thinking that they can't possibly be
as bright and beautiful as the ones made by our glamours. But they
will be almost perfect, I can tell you that. There will be songs, and
offerings of paper, and the finest leaf-crowns. It will be glorious.'

'It will be glorious,' echoed Ainsel.

'*You* will be glorious, my son. And now I may as well make it official.' Red Gold raised his voice to fill the mess boat. 'Crew, you have
long suspected that I wish to buy a house on land. And if I understand
the way gossip spreads on this ship, you'll all have known my intent
for that house since minutes after I decided it myself. But I will say it,
so you know it's true. My firstborn son, my glorious Ainsel, will be
leaving us to live as a landlocker with his beautiful new wife.'

The sound of claps skittered through the coracle, but the crew did
not number enough for true applause. North looked up to lock eyes

with Bero, but was distracted when she saw that the clowns were staring at Avalon. She did not know what they saw; she did not dare look at Avalon herself.

'It is no easy decision to select a wife for my son,' continued Red Gold. 'But I have chosen well. I know that North will make us all proud. The landlocker life is very different to the *Excalibur*, and North will have to build strong foundations if she is to –'

But then he stopped, because Avalon was standing, her spine straight, her arms spread, her hands palm up.

North cringed at the thought of what was about to happen. Would it be a repeat of Avalon's power struggle from the deck of the *Excalibur*? A comparison between Avalon's white, cold hands and North's red, chapped ones; a reminder of North's inferiority, her place in the hierarchy of the crew. And then, once again, Avalon would press her brazen bump against North's own secret one; she would call North 'child' over and over until everyone had guessed, until everyone knew that she was not a child any longer.

Avalon leaned towards her. North's heart stuttered. She took North's hand from Ainsel's and pulled North towards her, forcing her body to stretch. She had to tense every muscle in her back to stop her bump from pressing against the metal table.

'Oh, little urchin,' Avalon crooned, her voice echoing in the silence of the mess boat. 'It warms my heart to see how much you love our sweet Ainsel. You do truly love him, don't you?'

Eleven pairs of eyes stared at North; eleven pairs of ears waited for her to speak. She stretched out the best smile she could. She didn't trust her throat with words.

'I am glad, north child. For you know, only true love – real, honest, lifelong love – is worthy of such a noble home. The sort of love that my husband and I have for one another.' Avalon did not look at Red Gold. She kept her eyes on North, her smile tight as if she was swallowing something bitter. 'That is the only sort of love that can restore the Stirling name to the island.'

North managed to nod. Avalon was holding her hands so tightly that they were turning white.

'You love him,' soothed Avalon. 'You love him, don't you? Enough to build a home with him, and live with him for ever. You love him enough to have his children some day. Tell us, North.'

North tried to pull her hands away, but Avalon would not let go.

'Tell us all how much you love Ainsel. Tell us that you will carry his children. Tell us now, North.'

A wave licked the boat, rolling it in the swell. From outside came the scrape of metal on metal and the distant ringing of a bell. North felt her heart beating hard in her throat.

'Avalon,' said Red Gold in the voice he used to soothe the horses.

The spell broke. Everyone turned their gaze away from Avalon, bowing their heads to the pitted metal table. North waited until her hands had stopped shaking, then slipped them from Avalon's loosening grasp and dropped back into her seat.

12
Callanish

The days passed and routine swept Callanish in its wake. Resting parties arrived, so she prepared the bodies they brought and performed their Restings. Her house grew dirty, so she cleaned it. The graces died, so she tipped their bodies into the water. The supply boat came with new graces, so she refilled the empty cages.

She found herself amazed at the quantity of actions required simply to ensure that she woke up every morning. How had she ever found time for idle thoughts among all these necessary actions? Even this thought took up too much time, for now she had to scrub the grace-cages again. She stepped on to her rowing boat, and polished the cages until night crept in and it was too dark to see.

One day, weeks later, sails blinked on the horizon. Callanish could not see whether it was the messenger boat or the battered, bright-sailed *Excalibur*, but whichever it was, she knew that it was the boat she had been waiting for. She went into her house and sat at the table with her spine straight against the chair-back and her gloved hands cupping her knees. Eventually she heard the steady plash of waves against a hull and the bump of a boat against the dock.

This, then, was her fate. One home, one world, awaited her – either on land, or at sea.

She considered barring the door in an effort to delay the moment, but knew it would not make any difference. These things had already happened, and her ignorance could not undo them. She went out on to the porch and looked at the answer to her question.

A little boat with its sails furled and its rope fastened to the dock. A man in blue, head shaved, hands empty.

He climbed out of the boat and stepped towards Callanish.

'Hello, little fish,' he said.

She looked again at his hands. Still empty. She turned away from him and went back into her house. There were a dozen graces in cages, stacked in the corner of the room, and she paused to drop a handful of seeds in each cage.

'Aren't you going to say hello?' asked the messenger from the doorway. 'I thought you'd be pleased to see me.'

'You didn't bring a response.'

He shrugged. 'There wasn't one. Look, why don't you make us a pot of coffee and I'll tell you the whole story.'

'Is there a story to tell?'

'Not really. But I'd like some coffee.'

Callanish got up, drained water from the filter, ground a few precious beans, and put the coffee on to boil. When she turned around, she saw that the messenger had sat down in her chair. There were no other chairs, so she stayed standing. The messenger leaned back and thunked his feet up on to the table. The new graces ruffled their feathers and turned circles in their cages, unsure how to react to this stranger in their midst.

The messenger. Had she ever asked his name? Of all the things that mattered, this was not one.

'Why didn't you tell me your name?' he asked, as if reading her thoughts.

'It doesn't matter.'

'It matters to me. My name is Flitch. And your name is Callanish, isn't it? Callanish Sand.'

'How did you know that? You must have spoken to her. To my mother.'

'Oh, a mother, is it? Well, aren't you the lucky one? I wouldn't mind a mother myself.'

'You've seen her.'

'Got yourself a father too, little fish? Got a lovely little family on that lovely little island?'

'My father is dead. He died when I was young.'

The messenger snorted. 'So did mine. So did everyone's.'

'Please, tell me what my mother said. I have to know.'

'Bring me some coffee and I'll tell you.'

Callanish pressed her palms against the sharp edge of the kitchen counter until the urge to throw the coffee in Flitch's face had passed. She waited for the pot to boil, poured the coffee into her bone cup, and put it on the table in front of him. He took his time in blowing the steam before taking a sip. He let out a lip-smack sigh.

Callanish thought about the coffee-pot: it was metal, and still hot from the flame; she could smack him around the head with it and it would give him a satisfying shock. It might even leave a scar. She would count down from ten, and if he had not spoken by zero then she would give in to the urge. Five, four, three –

'I didn't see your mother,' he said.

'You're lying. You know my name.'

'I know a lot of things, little fish. And I'm telling the truth. I got to North-West 22, and I found the address you'd written on the parcel. I knocked on the door, and I waited.' He sipped his coffee again, eyeing Callanish over the rim of the cup. In the corner the graces pweeted; having received an unexpected treat of seeds, they would soon become bold and ask for more.

Callanish kept her face blank. Flitch could play all he liked, but she would not react. Her teeth were gritted so tightly that her jaw ached.

'So I waited, and she didn't answer – but then the neighbour came out, and she took the parcel. Said she'd give it to Mrs Sand. I asked – any response? No, she said, Veryan has nothing to say. So I left. And here I am.'

'That's it? You went all the way there and you didn't even see her?'

'Sure. What's she to me? I delivered the parcel, like you asked.'

'You didn't. You didn't deliver it. Give me back my payment. Go back there. Go back right now and bang on the door and tell me whether she's really there. Tell me whether she wants to respond. That's what I wanted. That's what I paid you for.'

'I bloody well did deliver it. That's how I know your name, little fish. *Is it from her daughter?* the neighbour says. *Is it from Callanish?* So I said, I don't know, because you never told me your name and you never told me if this Veryan Sand was your mother. You're a grown-up, why should I think you still had a mother? So I couldn't say yes or no to the neighbour. And she takes the parcel and says she'll pass it on, and she goes back into her house and shuts the door. That's it. That's how it happened.'

'That's not what you said before.'

Flitch shrugged and sipped his coffee. 'Close enough.'

'Did the neighbour really ask that?'

'Of course she did. How else would I know your name?'

'You could have asked around. The names of gracekeepers aren't secret. You could have gone by the next graceyard – Odell could have told you.'

He rubbed at the shaved skin of his head. 'I could have asked him. But that's assuming I cared to.'

Callanish went and stood by the window so that she would not have to look at Flitch's face.

'So you didn't see her,' she said.

'I told you, no. Why should I fuss about seeing her? Your mother is nothing to do with me.'

'Then you have to go back.'

'Oh no, little fish. That wasn't the deal. You didn't say anything about seeing her. You just wanted me to deliver it, that's what I thought. I'm allowed to leave parcels with a neighbour, unless it's a verbal or unless you pay extra – that's the rule. You check if you don't believe me. I didn't do anything wrong.'

Callanish pressed her hands against the windowpane, feeling the cool glass through the silk of her gloves.

'Take me with you,' she said.

'Take you where?'

'Back to that archipelago. Back to my mother.'

'Not going back to the north-east, not for a while yet. I have messages for the south-east now. I only came back this way to deliver something to your man there.' He nodded towards Odell's graceyard. 'Otherwise I wouldn't have bothered. You never said anything about me coming back after I delivered the parcel, but I thought I'd come by anyway. Trying to do a good thing, you know?'

'I'll pay you. Take me as far as you can. I'll find my way from there.'

He shrugged. 'I'm not going anywhere near it. It's a fair trip, and I don't see you sailing that far. I only made it so fast because I hitched a ride on a military tanker for most of it.'

'Then I'll do the same.'

He laughed. 'You? They'd shoot you down before you even managed to climb on board. You need to have governmental business to get on a military vessel, little fish.'

'I'll manage. What do you care?'

'Get your supply boat to take you. They come by a lot, don't they? Someone's got to bring you those birds. Ask him.'

'I can't. He won't. I'm not supposed to leave.'

'You're not allowed to leave the graceyard? Well then, won't they kill you if they catch you?'

'No. I don't know. I'm not supposed to go, but I don't know – they never said what would happen. I don't think a gracekeeper has ever left before. But I have to know if –'

Callanish did not want to beg. But if she did beg, who would know? Who could ever know what happened to her out here, trussed to the equator, alone with her dying birds and the rotting bodies of strangers? She did not want to beg, but she could. She could do whatever it took to get back to her mother. She turned to face Flitch.

'Please,' she said.

Even from a distance, Callanish could see that Odell's grace-cages had not been polished in a long time. The bars were reddened with rust, dark as meat. Only two or three seemed to be occupied. Flitch's boat weaved an unsteady path through the cages, bumping against the rusty bars.

'He hasn't been taking care of these,' murmured Callanish.

'I can see that. Not like your shiny ones, eh? Bloody awkward trying to sail through here when I delivered his parcel.'

'You didn't tell me about the state of his cages before.'

'Why should I tell you? You didn't ask.'

Callanish bit down on her frustration. 'But I told you I was going to bring my graces here.'

'Little fish, you didn't ask.'

She let Flitch have the last word on that. She didn't think that he would change his mind and take her back to her graceyard, but they were still close enough for it to be a danger. She would mind her words until there was nothing around them but sea. Although Flitch was annoying, she didn't think he'd drown her.

It had not taken long for Callanish to pack her things. She didn't have any things, really; she filled a box with the small amount of food she had left, then tucked her white dress in the extra space. It seemed silly to take it, as she wouldn't be able to perform any Restings, but it was in good condition and she would have to look respectable if she wanted to be taken on as a passenger on a military tanker or revival boat. The sea-stiff dress she wore was fine enough for the eyes of Flitch and Odell, as long as she kept her gloves and slippers on; she would change into her decent things later.

She spent a long time looking at the map on the wall. It would have to be left behind. She shut the door on Flitch and pulled off her gloves. She finger-walked along the lines separating countries, spreading her fingers wide to feel the pull of the webbing; pressed her eye to the places where the cities met the sea, so close that she couldn't see the distinction. She knew that no two maps were exactly the same. Every map was the world seen through a different lens; every mapmaker proof that there was not just one way of looking at things.

But there was no room for the map. It would be ruined. She might lose it for ever. It would be a mistake to take it. It was idiotic to even think of taking it. But still she ached at leaving it behind. She put her gloves back on before opening the door.

Most of the packing had involved transferring her few still-living graces to Flitch's boat, ready to be given to Odell. And now that they had almost arrived at his dock, she was questioning that decision. She should have let the graces go, to fall into the sea or fly to another grace-yard as they chose. She would no longer decide their fate for them. But the boat was bumping up against the dock, and Odell was opening his door, and it was too late.

'Well, well, well,' he purred, leaning the length of his body against the doorjamb, pointing his foot daintily out on to the porch. 'If it isn't Miss Callanish. And she's brought herself a playmate.'

'Odell.' Callanish tried to continue but did not know what to say. Odell looked ridiculous. His white suit was crumpled, the fabric dulled to a dirty ivory. He was barefoot and had coloured ribbons wrapped around his thumbs. He bowed unsteadily, waving his arm in an elaborate gesture that seemed to be welcoming them into his house.

'Come in, come in, my finest friends. Any friend of Flitch's is a friend of Callanish's. Or Callanish is Flitch. And I am a friend.'

Odell disappeared into his house. He was drunk. How could he be drunk? The supply boat would not have brought him alcohol, or the equipment to make his own. Callanish was suddenly aware of Flitch, pointedly not looking at Odell as he furled his sails and knotted his rope to the dock. It was not just supply boats that passed through the graceyards. If you had something to trade, you could get whatever you wanted.

'Odell,' called Callanish from the dock, not wanting to see the state of his house. 'I need you to take these graces. And if anyone comes by looking for me, I need you to do their Resting.'

Odell shouted something back, his meaning lost on the journey between house and dock. Callanish began taking the grace-cages off the messenger's boat and stacking them on the dock.

There were as many ways to die at sea as there were feathers on a grace, from storms and whales and infighting to attacks by strangers on unlicensed boats. Before long, her Resting parties would lose another of their loved ones. They would return to Callanish's graceyard, and she would not be in her house, so they would come here instead. And Odell, drunk and crumpled Odell, who she knew even from a distance would smell of hangovers and boredom, would tarnish whatever scraps of a reputation she had. But still, she was grateful to him. She did not have a choice. She kept stacking.

Then: the thud-thud-thud of Odell's steps as he stamped back out on to his porch.

'Come *in*, I said!' His shout was so loud that his voice cracked. 'In!' He spun on his doorstep and disappeared back inside.

Callanish had finished stacking the cages, so she scattered another handful of seeds for the birds and followed Flitch into Odell's house.

It was not as bad as it could have been. There is not much to make a mess with in a gracekeeper's house. There was his bed and his table and his cooking equipment, and it all seemed normal enough. There was a stack of empty bottles in one corner, and in another was a pile of grace-cages that reached almost to the ceiling. Some of the graces raised their heads as Callanish approached them, but most just lay on the floors of their cages.

'Odell, have you been feeding these graces? Some of them are already dead.'

'Not meant. To feed. The graces,' he pronounced.

'That's after you've used them for a Resting.'

'No! Not meant to feed them. At all.'

Callanish did not correct him, because she was not sure that she was correct. She'd been feeding her graces for so long that she could not remember the exact rules. Perhaps he was right, and these point-less deaths were as it should be.

'I want you to feed mine, Odell. If anyone asks, say that I forced you to.'

'Forced me?' Odell let out a mushy laugh. 'How could you force me to do anything? You're a little scrap of nothing and I didn't miss you at all. I never thought about you, and I never watched the horizon for you, and I didn't care a whit whether – whit whether ...' He pursed his lips again around the words. 'A little bit whether you visited me or not.'

Callanish retreated to the doorway, anxious to leave.

'That's good, Odell. I won't be bothering you again.'

'You won't?' Odell swayed upright and swaggered over to Callanish. 'You won't. You will. Will you? You will.'

Callanish shut the door. She did not want to be in this tiny space with two men whom she needed almost as much as she disliked. But she did not want Odell to veer out of the door and tumble into the sea.

'That's what I meant. I will come back, Odell, and very soon. Then I can visit you every evening, and we can listen to records, and drink together, and cool our feet in the sea. You can say things and I will respond.' She waited until she was sure that Odell was listening. 'All I need is for you to look after things until then, okay?'

'You're going with him.' Odell glared at Flitch. 'I bet you'll love that, won't you, Callanish? I bet that's why you never came to see me. You had him instead. Well, what's so special about him?'

Callanish bit down a spasm of irritation. Of all the things she'd expected from Odell, jealousy was not on the list.

'It's not like that, Odell. He's helping me to do something, and I am very grateful to him because I know that he is a good man and wants to help me. And soon I'll come back and see you.'

Lies upon lies upon lies. But Odell seemed content enough with them, and that was the best she could ask.

She turned to leave and saw the bird skull hung on the back of the door. She didn't want to touch it, but couldn't help reaching out a hand. The bone was warm and smooth. The bird's beak stuck out like the prow of the rowing boat, and above the thoughtful eye sockets was a dent, an impression, as if someone had pressed a thumb there.

'Why do you have this?' Callanish said.

Odell sighed loudly, as if he was trying to blow a fly off his lips. 'Found it.'

'Where?'

'In the water.'

Callanish failed to suppress a shudder. 'You went in the water? It's not safe down there, and – look, never mind. Odell, I'm going. We're going.'

She opened the door, ignoring the gentle thud as the bird skull fell back to rest against the metal. The temptation to leap into the boat and sail away from the dock without Flitch rose, rose, and disappeared. She stepped on to the deck and waited.

The trip might be easier if she could hate Flitch, but that emotion was far too strong. All she could feel was a mix of irritation and regret. She regretted having to ask for his help. She regretted the way he swaggered across the dock, the way he rubbed his hand across his shaved head, the way he threw a glance back at Odell as if he'd won a fight. Most of all she regretted her own nature, and that she had not thought to invite him into her bed and steal his boat as he slept.

But now was not the time for regret. If this was what it took to speak to her mother, then this was what she would do. And if she needed to do more, then she would do that too.

Callanish had had everything, and then she had lost it. Now all she had was this caged bird fluttering inside her: the need for her mother's forgiveness. Soon she would have her answer.

13
Ainsel

Fourteen islands, fourteen nights, fourteen performances. It did not take long for the Circus Excalibur to slip back into the comfort of routine. Behindcurtains they were individuals, each full of doubts and concerns; on stage they were the circus, with glitter for blood and glass for eyes.

Each night the curtain rose. Ainsel turned cartwheels on horseback, Avalon pranced gloriously around him, Jarrow boomed their introductions and exits. They were the picture of a perfect family, and the revivalist landlockers lapped it up. Every night the circus ate scrapings of baked cabbage and honey and raisins, black pudding and chicken hearts and pig snouts. There was never quite enough, but at least they were not sitting down to empty plates.

With every passing night, Ainsel became more convinced that Jarrow really believed their performance. The old man had always had a knack for storytelling, and he made best use of this in telling tales to himself that conflicted utterly with the cold facts of his life. Otherwise, Ainsel knew, he'd never have made it through all these years on a leaky, rusting boat when his rightful place was on land. Unfortunately for Ainsel, he had not inherited his father's skill for self-deception. He knew that the *Excalibur* was rotten to its core. He needed to get ashore before the whole thing crumbled. The only good thing in the *Excalibur* was Avalon. But she didn't want him – she wanted a house. And there was only one way for Ainsel to get a house.

At first he'd wanted to call off the wedding too. He'd just been waiting for the right moment. But then his father had taken them ashore and told them about the house, and Ainsel had seen the pieces of his life click perfectly into place.

He had to make sure that North went ahead with the wedding. He waylaid her one evening as she carried three dinner bowls back to her coracle. 'Good show tonight, North,' he said, though of course he had not seen her act; what with the horses and Avalon and his father, he had no time to watch a bear dance. 'Your bear looks well. Perhaps you could come and see the horses some time. Give me some tips.'

North smiled and nodded, so the words were worth it – but it had hurt him to speak them. His stallions were glossy-coated, bright-eyed, sure-footed: more elegant than that violent beast could ever be. But Ainsel had known North a long time. She scowled at praise for herself, yet glowed if you complimented the bear. If Ainsel didn't know better, he'd say that North and the bear loved each other.

A week passed, and North did not visit his coracle to see the horses, but there was time enough for that – because now, finally, they had reached the North-West archipelago. Soon they'd be through it and at the North-East archipelago – and that meant North-East 19, and his father's home island meant the wedding, and the wedding meant the house, and the house meant Avalon. She'd refused him so many times, but that would change when he had the house. She would love him then. She would.

That night – after the performance, after the dinner, after the drinking, after the slow slide of the circus into sleep – Ainsel tapped on the side of North's coracle. It was tricky as he was wearing heavy diving boots and held a skin-diver lung under each arm. The thick glass was scratched, and he did not know how much would be visible through the domes underwater, but they would have to do. He'd stopped by the glamours' boat before dinner, allowing them to coo over him as they tied his hair in an elaborate knot and dabbed lilac powder under his eyebrows. It wasn't strictly necessary to look beautiful for North, but it couldn't hurt.

He'd resisted the urge to stop by the *Excalibur* before going to North's coracle. His father would be there, and he wouldn't be able to speak properly to Avalon, but it was enough just to look at her, to hear her voice, to see the growing press of his baby inside her. His need for her was a physical ache, heavy as stones in his belly. But it was fine. They would be together soon.

He tapped on North's coracle a little louder. When Red Gold had first decided on their engagement, Ainsel had not minded the thought of marrying North. He didn't love her, but he liked her, and perhaps that could have been enough. But then Avalon had come to him, and he found what love really tasted like. Everything since then had been an act: shadows and lies, the worst sort of circus fakery. But if he wanted Avalon he needed that house, and so he needed the marriage – and for North to go back to the sea afterwards.

He knocked again on the coracle. Still no answer. Through the canvas, he heard the snuffles and snores of North's bear. He unfastened one of the canvas-knots.

'North!' he hissed through the gap. No reply. The bright eye of the moon peered over his shoulder, lighting a blurred circle in North's coracle. Ainsel waited for his eyes to adjust. He leaned further in, tensing his back so that he wouldn't lose his grip on the lungs.

In the silvery moonlight he surveyed the innards of the coracle. There was Melia, her body curled tight as a knot, her turquoise hair ratty and faded. There was North's bear, blacker than a storm cloud and just as unfriendly. There was North's tin chest of clothing, and her dimmed lamp, and her rack of whale-tooth combs, and her neat shelves of thread and oilcloth and tar. But where was North? Ainsel leaned in further.

'North!' he hissed again. The bear shifted, turned, and a finger of moonlight landed on something pale among his dark fur. For a heart-stopping moment Ainsel thought that the bear was dead – that he had been gutted, carved out, and that long white patch was the cage of his ribs. Then he saw how silly that was. The bear was just holding something. A stretched, pale object, one of North's dresses perhaps, though why he would be holding a dress Ainsel could not...

He frowned. He placed the lungs down on the canvas so that he could grip the edge of the coracle and lean further in. Yes, he had been right: that pale thing was North, cradled in the arms of the bear, sleeping as soundly as if the bear was a fur coat. And where were his chains? Why was he not strapped to the bunk?

'North!' said Ainsel, his voice loud in surprise. Quickly, before she could react, he pulled the canvas shut and picked up the lungs. He waited.

A whisper of feet, a crumple of canvas. Up she popped out of the coracle.

'Ainsel? Is that you? What's wrong?' Her voice was thick with sleep.

'Hello, North.' He kept his words honey smooth to hide his shock. 'Nothing's wrong. I'm sorry to have woken you.'

'It's fine, I was just – I mean, I wasn't – did you ...' She didn't seem to know how to finish the sentence. Ainsel blinked away the image of North curled in the bear's arms, tucking it into his memory. He couldn't worry about it now. Later, maybe, it would come in useful.

'Yes, I saw,' he said. 'Melia's hair looks like old seaweed and you need to wash your combs.' North still seemed unsure, so Ainsel followed his words with his finest grin. It took a moment, but her face cracked into the beginnings of a smile.

'Now,' he continued, hefting the lungs. 'We're going for a dive. I want to show you something.'

'Ainsel, no. It's late, and it'll be dark down there, and...'

'Go on. For old times' sake.'

From the coracle, the bear gave a wet-sounding snort. Ainsel let his eyes stray towards the sound, his eyebrows raised in a challenge. North hesitated.

'Look.' Ainsel took North's hand and pulled her out of the coracle, then took hold of her hips. He pushed her down so that they were both sitting cross-legged on the taut canvas. 'Look up there.'

He examined North's profile as she tilted her head to the sky. In the moonlight she was almost pretty.

She turned back to him and shrugged. 'I don't know what I'm supposed to be looking at.'

'What do you see?'

'I see the sky. I see stars and the moon.'

'Which star?'

'All of them.'

Ainsel leaned in to North so that their temples touched. Her heart was beating so hard that he could feel the pulse throb. He took hold of her chin, tilting it so that they were both looking in the same direction. 'There. That star.'

'The Pole Star?' she said.

'The North Star.' Ainsel paused to let that sink in. 'The North Star is the most beautiful because it's always there. It can always show us the way. North –' He took her hands in his, gazing down at them as if he was too shy to meet her eyes. 'Do you see what I'm saying?'

North seemed to hold her breath. He could feel the nervous tremor in her hands and the quickening of her heart, thudding in her temples. 'I don't – there's something I should tell you, Ainsel. Everyone will know soon enough.'

'Later, North. We have time. That's what I'm trying to tell you. We've seen each other almost every day of our lives. We've always been there for one another. I really think we can make this marriage work. You're my North Star, and I can be yours.'

Before North had time to reply, Ainsel leaned over the side of the coracle and dropped the lungs into the water. They landed with a plimp, cupping air between the water and the glass sphere. He slid into the sea, shivering at the chill.

'North,' he called, but she had already put on her heavy sea-boots and was slipping into the water after him.

He tipped the lungs to refresh the air. He placed one over North's head, making sure that it rested flat on the water's surface, then settled his own lung. When it felt steady, he tied a long red string between his left wrist and North's right wrist.

'Now we can't lose one another,' he said, the words echoing inside the glass sphere of his lung. North smiled uncertainly through the clouded glass. The moon reflected in the water's surface, turning the world monochrome. Ainsel got a grip on his lung. When North was ready, they twisted their bodies in the water and kicked their feet off the outside of the coracle to force the lung underwater.

Black, black, black in every direction. Ainsel's insides shrank, rebelling against this dive down into blindness. It turned his stomach to feel the water close over him. The sea was an endless battlefield, and the deeper you went the worse it got, because everything that died had nowhere to go but down. In its darkest depths, the sea was nothing but an endless rain of bone, teeth, scales and flesh. Ainsel was not surprised that the revival boats preached about hell being at the bottom of the sea.

But still he held on to his lung. Still he kept kicking. He hated the sea, but he knew that North loved it. She'd never settle to a life on land. But that didn't matter – all that mattered was that she married him, and that Red Gold gave them what he'd promised. Then Avalon would come to him. It would be too late for his father to take back the house then, and he could live happily with his love for ever. A proper landlocker family, with their proper landlocker baby. Once he had Avalon, everything would fall into place.

He blinked hard, trying to force his eyes to adjust. There was nothing to focus on, no sense of scale; they might as well be in outer space. Vertigo overwhelmed him. His breathing seemed loud and wet in the confines of the lung.

He turned to check on North; the light caught in the scratches on her lung, reflecting it back so that he could not see her expression. But she was still kicking, so he kept going. He knew that above them ranged the undersides of a dozen boats; that below them, the sea floor spread. He could see none of it, and it seemed that the entire world had fallen away. They were alone.

Ainsel held his breath, trying to hear over the tidal beat of his heart. The sea brought back muted booms and the distant keen of whalesong. He held tight to the red string linking him to North. Finally, from the gloom, came the sound of bells.

He opened his eyes wide, and he could see. Below his feet, moonlight slid off a rooftop. He took hold of his lung and pulled on the string, forcing North deeper. He wanted to tell her not to panic, to soothe her like he did for his horses, but he knew that the words would come out tinny and muffled.

One moment they were floating aimless in the black of the sea; the next, a spotlight of moon appeared, and there was the city.

Dim light bleached the world silver. Ainsel and North swam past mosaics of leering peacocks, enamelled carriages shaped like swans, fish flickering through the eye sockets of giant carved skulls. Below them, the sea floor sparkled with shattered glass.

Floating along the flooded streets, they opened their eyes as wide as they could. Together they tiptoed along the top of a tower and caressed the stone faces of gargoyles. Together they slid down the seawater-smoothed gutters of a church roof. Ainsel ducked into the bell tower to show North the enormous bell, whose sound had led them to the city. The clapper inside was too heavy for a person to move; only a strong current could cause it to chime. He led North further on.

A horse's head, huge as a tower block, loomed towards them with its nostrils flaring – but its stone ears had broken off and algae rimmed its eyes. Ainsel led North past the horse and onwards through a menagerie of stone animals. He trod water while she ran her hand along the back of a deer, its antlers tangled with seaweed.

Ainsel closed his eyes and the ruins became his palace. He passed through his burnished gates, the gold curlicues gleaming bright as the sun. He walked through rooms furnished with blue marble fireplaces and green satin carpets. He reached out his hand to his carved birds: at his touch, their enamelled beaks opened to let out their clockwork song. Finally, he took his place on his wooden throne. He raised his head to receive his leafy crown.

What more could be said? What could the sea provide that was more glorious, more noble than this drowned kingdom? No matter how wide the sea opened its maw, there would be some land it couldn't swallow, and that land would always be superior. He knew North would not see it that way. She was a child of the sea, and she would never leave it. She would never understand his true place as lord of the land.

But the city was large and the lungs were small. They had to leave now, or stay for ever. Ainsel turned away from the sunken city and straightened his body in the water, kicking his feet to bring them back to the surface.

He pushed aside his lung and gasped at the air. After the stale heat of his own breath, the harbour smells were overwhelming: soil, saltwater, the skin of strangers.

Without a word, North removed her lung and used the canvasropes to pull herself back on to her coracle. Water sluiced off her body as she climbed. Ainsel threw the lungs up to her, one by one, then followed. He watched North as he climbed: she was leaning over the edge, wringing the water from her dark hair; she was peeping into the belly of her coracle; she was rearranging the ropes so that they didn't dangle in the sea.

North waited until he'd climbed the ropes. 'It's from before, isn't it? It's where people used to live when there was still land. That's where you want to be, isn't it?' she said.

'My great-great-great-great grandfather lived there.'

'And you want something real. Something ancient. Like your ancestors had.'

Ainsel nodded. Perhaps North understood after all.

'But it's gone,' she murmured, more to herself than to him. 'The sea took it.'

'We will take it back,' he whispered. 'We will make the new land our home. There will be Stirlings on the island again.'

'Home …' said North. Or was it just the suck of the sea against ships? Her eyes drifted away from Ainsel and she dropped down into her coracle.

He shook water from his limbs and closed North's canvas. He tied the knots tight.

After the usual routine of performing and eating, Ainsel slipped away with a vague mumble about grooming his horses. The other circus folk bored and frustrated him: their small words, their small dreams. They would never be the lords of anything. They would never know real love.

His coracle was the second largest, after the mess boat; it was easily three times the size of North's, but that was as it should be. His horses could not be bundled into a tiny bunk like North's beast. Ainsel needed space to prepare for his performance, to allow himself enough sleep, to sit quietly and contemplate his future. He slid into his coracle, leaving the canvas open to freshen the air.

'Hello, beauties,' he crooned to Lady and Lord as he ran his hands along their necks. They snorted in reply, their breath hot and damp on his palms. Lady was a pure white mare, with a birthmark on her cheek the shape and colour of a ripe plum; Lord was a beautiful silver-grey, his muzzle velvety black as if he'd been sniffing at charcoal.

Both their manes were braided with green and silver ribbons from that evening's show. Ainsel noticed that some of Lady's were coming unfastened. Rather than try to tidy the braiding, it would be better to do it all over again. Lady's mane could do with a rinse anyway. He pulled down his horse-brushes, filled a tin basin from the filter, and got to work.

On the boats there was never quite enough space, just as there was never enough food or water or privacy. A dampling's life was one of lack. Ainsel deserved better. And he would have better – he and Avalon, together.

His heart was Avalon's, from now until eternity. How strange that to be with her he had to marry someone else. What would it be like to have North for his wife, however briefly? His memory strolled through moments with North: the pair of them, six years old, prising abalone off salt-crusted rocks; sharing a pomegranate on a lazy, dozing morning; helter-skeltering across an eastern island, screaming half in terror and half in glee with a landlocker's dog snapping at their heels; aged ten, playing doctor; fourteen, practising kisses. In another life, perhaps he could have loved her. But not in this one.

'Ainsel,' whispered Avalon into his ear.

He jumped and tipped over the bucket. Water crept across the deck of the coracle, making Lady and Lord skitter their hooves and flick their ears.

Ainsel soothed the horses, turning his back to Avalon so that she wouldn't see his elation. His heart throbbed in his ears. He'd been alone with her only a handful of times, and it made his head spin. 'My love. How I have wished for you to visit me again.'

Avalon dug through the box of sea sponges, spreading a fistful across the deck to soak up the water he'd spilled. 'I won't be long. I don't want Jarrow to notice I've gone.'

'I knew you would come back to me.' Ainsel's hands had stopped shaking. He turned to Avalon. Her night-black eyes, her throat as smooth as pearls: she was so beautiful he could barely look at her.

'I haven't come back,' she said. 'I will never come back to you. Not in that way. I just need to speak to you.'

Ainsel traced her lips with his finger but she could not summon a smile.

'Enough, Ainsel. I told you, that won't happen again. Jarrow mustn't know.'

'Are you worrying, my love? There is no need, I promise! Trust to me, and I will give you all you want.'

In the light of the seal-fat lamp, Avalon's skin gleamed as white as a shell. Her black hair was still braided in ribbons from the perform-ance; with a slow smile, Ainsel reached over to unfasten it. It came free, teasing Ainsel with the scent of jasmine. Avalon snatched her ribbons back, her nails scratching Ainsel's fingers. 'Stop it! I only came to speak to you – to tell you – Ainsel, you have to refuse the house. It's mine. It should be for me and for Jarrow.'

'Forget him. The house is rightfully yours, my queen. Yours and mine.'

'Ainsel, don't be ridiculous. Give up the house. You can have the circus, all of it. You can be the ringmaster.'

'I don't want to be the ringmaster. I want to be with you. Listen to me, my love. All I have to do is marry North, and my father will sign the house over to me. Then you can leave him and we can be together. It's so simple.'

'What about North?' asked Avalon.

'What about her?'

'You'll be married, Ainsel. Do you imagine that she'll quietly consent to live in the house with you and your father's wife? Do you think she'll go without a fight? Listen to what you're saying. This plan is nonsense.'

'When it all comes out, when everyone knows that you and I are in love, North is bound to leave. She can run the circus with my father. Or she can buy her way into another circus. Or she can take that mangy bear and jump in the sea. It really doesn't matter. Since when did you care about North?'

'I don't care about her. There's no point arguing about this because you can't marry North anyway. She's pregnant.'

Ainsel couldn't hold in his laugh. 'The little north child! What secrets we all hold. It's a wonder we don't burst open with them all. Whose child is it?'

'I don't know. Whitby's? Bero's? Some dampling she picked up? She probably doesn't even know.' Avalon pressed her hands to her belly, breathing deep. 'Look, Ainsel. This is what matters. I can't leave with you. I don't *want* to leave with you. And you can't have that house. You have to tell your father that you don't want it. That you want to stay here and be the ringmaster.'

Her words stung, but Ainsel knew she didn't mean them. She loved him. She must, or why would she have crept into his coracle all those nights? Why would she have slid on top of him in the dark of his bunk, whispering sweet words in his ear, the length of her hair forming a curtain between them and the world? If she didn't love him, why would she carry his child?

'But I do want it,' he said. 'And that's not all I want.'

He pulled his shirt off over his head, one-handed. Avalon looked away.

'Please, Ainsel. Tell your father you don't want to live on land.'

'Oh, my love. There are lots of things I could tell my father.'

He stepped closer to Avalon, so close that her bump pressed against him. Lady and Lord tapped their hooves on the deck of the coracle, and he took Avalon's hands, holding them tight so she couldn't pull away. Lady and Lord tapped again, and he pulled Avalon closer, slipping his arms around her – and no, that couldn't be right, horses did not tap that way, and they could not reach to scratch at the canvas, and he had not fastened the canvas so how could they –

'Ainsel?' called North into the coracle.

'Wait, North! I'm – just wait!'

His breath felt too heavy. Avalon stood in the centre of the coracle, her hair wild, her eyes wide. 'She mustn't see me here,' she whispered in a panic. 'She'll tell him.'

'Tell him what? We'll say we're just training the horses.'

'Think, Ainsel! He knows that we always train the horses on deck, so why should we suddenly be skulking about down here? Don't give her a reason to gossip. She'll spread lies. She'll do it on purpose.'

'Here,' hissed Ainsel. He slid back the tin panel over the tack box and pushed her inside. The box was not tall and she'd have to crouch. 'Sorry,' he whispered, and replaced the panel.

'Come in.' He was pleased that his voice sounded steady – but then he realised he was only half clothed. He scrambled around the damp deck for his shirt. 'Ah – I was just changing. And I know you saw it all when we were kids, but we should save something for our wedding night.'

North climbed into the coracle, and the gods of land and sea must have been looking out for Ainsel, because he even managed to grin at her. She smiled back, but it wavered.

'I have to talk to you, Ainsel. It's about the other night. Our dive.'

'I'm listening,' he said.

North hesitated, frowning at the deck of the coracle. Ainsel followed her gaze: sponges, pooled water, an upturned bucket.

'Right. I spilled the water. While I was getting changed.' He bent over to collect up the sponges, dropping them into the bucket. Although it was impossible, he felt a sudden stab of worry that North would see Avalon's fingerprints on the sponges. To him, the scent and touch and sight of Avalon permeated the entire boat.

'Were you grooming them?' North nodded at Lady's damp mane. 'I'll help you.'

Ainsel forced his face into a smile and handed North a brush. Perhaps he could have explained why Avalon was in his coracle: to check the horses, to discuss their act. But he would not be able to explain why Avalon was hiding in the tack box. No matter how much North trusted him, he knew she trusted his father more – and if she saw Avalon here then she'd tell him, she'd run right out there and tell him in front of the whole crew. Jarrow would find out about his son and wife eventually. But not yet. Not before Ainsel had what he wanted.

His heart thudded in his throat. He hoped that North could not see the vibrations above his collarbone. With a dry cloth he patted at Lady's mane.

North ran the brush down Lord's withers, snowing dust on to the deck. 'I've been thinking a lot about that place,' she said. 'The flooded city.'

'Yes. The landlockers know about it, but they won't go down there. And the damplings don't care.'

162

'I've been thinking for a while now, ever since we were at the grace-yard to Rest Whitby – I was talking to the gracekeeper there – why are our choices land or sea?'

Ainsel resisted the urge to roll his eyes. 'Because that's what the world is, North.'

'But couldn't there be a compromise?' North blew into Lord's ears so that he flicked them back and forth.

'A boat is a compromise.' Ainsel kept his arms close to his body so that his hands wouldn't shake. It took everything in him not to glance over at the tack box.

'No, I don't mean that. I mean a way that people could live in that city under the sea. Don't you think that could be possible?'

'Like the weird baby born to that landlocker? It was a sea monster with legs!' Ainsel pushed out a laugh. 'It sounds like Bero has been filling your brain with silly stories. That woman buried her baby alive, just as it should be.'

'Ainsel, I'm serious.' She looked up at him, her fingers lost in Lord's silver mane. 'Couldn't there be something? A baby born that could live in the sea or on the land. Would it be so bad? Wouldn't it be – don't you think that's the way forward for us all? A new world. A new start.'

Ainsel untangled North's fingers from the horse's mane, letting the ribbons fall to the damp deck. He led her over to the bunk and sat her down.

'Oh, North.' He patted her knee in a soothing manner. 'I see what this is about. You're scared about the wedding, aren't you?'

'No, Ainsel. I – I thought maybe you were trying to tell me some-thing. With the dive. I thought you were showing me that the world has changed before, and that it could change again.'

Ainsel sighed. Of course he'd been telling her something. And, of course, she hadn't understood. He'd been showing her that he was a lord of the land, and she'd seen some nonsense about sea monsters.

'What happens now?' said North. Her voice wavered as if she was trying to breathe underwater. 'What happens when you speak to Jarrow, and we don't get married?'

This was not the time for weakness. Avalon could hear every word and Ainsel had to be strong. He had to show her that he had a plan. He could convince North, and Jarrow, and everyone.

'But we are getting married,' he said.

'Don't talk nonsense. When are you going to tell him?'

'I'm not, North. We'll get married, and we'll get our house, and we'll live happily ever after. That's the only ending.'

North gave an irritated snort. She paced the deck, tapping her fingers along Ainsel's possessions as if making sure they were real. Loose paint flaked off an orange float strapped to the wall.

'Ainsel, I don't understand you. Neither of us wanted this. Why have you suddenly changed your mind?' She paused at the tack box and Ainsel turned to stone. Coloured lights crept across his vision and he remembered to breathe.

'We can't do this,' said North. 'I can't.'

Ainsel felt his temper stretching, stretching, until it threatened to snap. 'I don't care what you can and can't do, North. Avalon's baby will be born soon. We need to be in the house before that.'

'But, that doesn't - what does her baby have to do with it?'

Damn. Damn, damn, damn. Ainsel leaned back against the wall so that he wouldn't collapse.

'The baby. Avalon's baby.' North looked as if she'd swallowed a fishbone. 'It's true then, what everyone was saying - it's not his?'

Ainsel attempted a smile. 'Don't be an idiot, North. Of course it's Jarrow's baby.'

North was still frowning. From the tack box came a heavy silence.

Avalon had heard it all. It was too late to swallow the words back down - he'd have to embrace them.

'The others are all talking about it. They say the baby will be half-horse,' said North.

Ainsel threw back his head and crowed. North was an idiot! She knew nothing at all! Oh, such sweet relief.

'A half-horse baby?' he said. 'Wouldn't that be a sight? That's about as likely as your baby being half-bear.'

North's eyes widened. 'What do you - what baby?'

'Come on, North. We're past the time for silliness and lies.'

'How could you know? Did Avalon tell you?'

'No. I saw for myself.'

She paced from one side of the coracle to the other, touching things, unable to settle. Her voice shook. 'Does everyone else know?'

Ainsel shrugged. 'I don't think so.'

'Does Red Gold - I mean, Jarrow. Does he know?'

'No!' Ainsel snorted. 'He doesn't know anything at all. He'd think it was mine anyway. But we both know it's nothing to do with me. So whose is it? Bero's? Whitby's? Unless - wait, is it my father's? You always were his little favourite.'

North stopped pacing and glared at him. 'Don't be disgusting. It's not your damned father's. And it's not Bero's or Whitby's either. I've never - not with them, not with any of them. It's nothing to do with this circus.'

'Fine, have your little secret. So you bunked up with some grubby dampling. Very impressive. It doesn't even matter, North. We'll say it's mine. We'll be married; no one will care about the dates.'

'But that's - I don't understand. I thought we agreed. And then Jarrow told us about the house. Is that what changed your mind? I know you want that underwater city, Ainsel. I know you want roots. But marrying me, and being a landlocker - it will never work.'

It took everything in Ainsel not to let his eyes stray to the tack box.

So that North couldn't see his face, he stood and resumed grooming Lady's mane.

'It's not like that,' he said. 'I started to feel differently about you. I know we said we didn't want this marriage, but I've thought about and I – I do want it.'

'You're lying.'

'I love you.'

North seemed to waver. 'I know you say you don't care. But you will care when the baby comes, Ainsel. How could you not care? How can you marry me when you know –' She gestured at herself.

He focused on the grooming, turning his back to North. She had to leave. She had to leave now.

'I will marry you because I love you, North. I want us to have a life together. Because I love you.'

'You don't love me, Ainsel. I know you don't.'

He closed his eyes, remembering to breathe, picturing Avalon, seeing them as husband and wife, taking strength from his future. He threw down his grooming brush and turned to North. He grasped her hands tight and looked into her eyes. Her hands were cold, and they shook. But he was strong and he would not blink.

'I do, North.'

She pulled away and stood with her hands clasped over her belly, as if it was a treasure Ainsel had threatened to steal. 'You don't! I know you don't, you just –'

'I love you.'

'But you –'

'I. Love. You.'

Ainsel kept his jaw tight and his gaze unblinking. It did not take long for North to look away. While she wasn't looking, he allowed himself a triumphant smile. He had won this one, as he would win them all.

'I love you,' he said. 'I love you. I love you. I love you.'

He stood his ground, ready to profess love until his tongue bled. Finally North turned and scrambled out of the coracle.

He waited for twenty heartbeats before opening the tack box. Avalon climbed out, her face red as blood, and walked straight past him.

'Wait!' he whispered, as loud as he dared. 'Avalon, my love, please!' But she swayed up the ladder and disappeared back to the *Excalibur*, leaving his words to drift into the night.

14
Callanish

D ays and nights passed on Flitch's boat, and every dream
Callanish had was of the bear-girl. Every night when she
closed her eyes, she saw the same memory: the warmth of
the coracle, the comfort of the bear-girl's hand, the bear's heart beating
strong and steady against their palms. Only two people had ever seen
Callanish's bare hands: her mother, and North. Her mother's reaction
was to sew a pair of silk gloves and instruct her to wear them at all
times, for ever. North's reaction was to grip her hand tighter.

When Callanish woke each morning, she felt sad. Not for having
dreamed, but for the dream ending.

'Little fish,' Flitch would coo to her every morning as he consulted
his compass and his sextant. 'Did you dream of me?'

'No,' she would reply, because it was true, and also because she
tried to use as few syllables as possible when speaking to him.

And so Callanish kept her mind busy with thoughts of the bear-
girl, and the bear, and the sea-made baby. She pulled bones from tiny
fish and thought about the way that North had looked ready to punch
her when she'd mentioned the baby. She checked over Flitch's star
charts and thought of the way they'd leaned their heads on the wall of
her house, sharing secrets in the silvery night. She watched Flitch
barter for food with other damplings and thought of North's neat

pirouette as she leapt between the coracles. She stitched up a tear in the cutter's sail and thought of the way North had caught her when she fell.

She still didn't know what it meant that soon a child would be born that was... what? Callanish's own kind? A distant sister? Webbed and scorned and hidden for ever? For her whole life, her mother had refused to discuss Callanish's hands and feet. *Put on your gloves and your slippers, Callanish, and don't ever take them off. Don't ever let them see.*

She'd thought it was the revenge of the gods, proof that she did not belong, that she was half-monster. But North loved her baby. She would not have desired a monster, and she would not now love a monster's child. Perhaps there was nothing wrong with Callanish at all.

These thoughts were a good distraction; she'd spent two weeks with Flitch and had not felt the urge to drown him. Mornings were the time when she liked him least. His clothing sat in rumples and peaks, the way a grace ruffled its feathers when it was displeased. His breath was sour and his belly was empty – and so was Callanish's, so perhaps neither of them liked each other in the morning. The days swept by faster than the clouds. Callanish and Flitch sailed, ate, did repairs, bartered with the other boats. The sun dipped into the sea, throwing blood and honey across the sky. Flitch busied himself with settling the cutter for the night while Callanish prepared their dinner. It was not easy to gut the tiny fish while wearing gloves, and Callanish had to wash them a dozen times a day. Flitch had never asked her about them, though she'd often caught him eyeing the fishgut-speckled silk, and for that she was grateful.

In the evenings, Callanish suspected, Flitch liked having her as a travel companion, though he'd never admit it. Together they ate poached fish and fried seaweed, and Callanish loved it so much that she resolved never to eat anything else.

'Aren't you supposed to eat landlocker food?' Flitch had asked her on their third night at sea.

'Do you have any?' she'd asked through a mouthful of sardine; in answer, Flitch only shrugged. 'I thought not. You're not supposed to share quarters with a landlocker, but I don't see much of an option there either. Who's to know what we do or say or eat out here? And anyway, I like dampling food.'

Evenings were the time when she disliked him least. Their bellies were less empty, their eyes were heavy, and they could look off the boat's stern and see all the ocean they had covered that day. For Callanish, too, the evenings meant that she could look forward to her dream.

One evening, their bellies fish-full and their feet warmed by the seal-fat lamp, Flitch seemed to take more care than usual in dropping his lobster creels into the water. Callanish did not comment; she'd noticed that his store-chest was almost empty, and it was tricky to barter with other ships when you had nothing.

'I think we'll get some good lobster tonight,' she said, though she didn't think that at all. She knew that she would have to pay dearly for this passage, and finding fault with Flitch would increase her payment. In response, he only grunted.

She busied herself with scraping the last of the flesh from the bones of their dinner, dropping it into the soup pot for tomorrow. If the creels were empty, then she and Flitch could work carvings out of the bones. She didn't think there would be much call for such trivialities among damplings, but what did she know about their desires? Perhaps they wanted nothing more than tiny animals made out of the skeletons of other animals.

Flitch dropped the last of the creels, then leaned his head on the stern and rubbed his palms over his scratchy-looking scalp.

'Little fish,' he said. 'Do you see a problem here?'

Callanish turned a full circle, observing. The lamp enclosed them in a pool of golden light between the black of the sea and the star-spattered sky. A breeze stroked her cheeks and waves swayed the boat. She'd scrubbed her gloves back to white. Half a dozen ropes were slung over the sides, holding the creels safe in the depths. All around them she could see the distant glows of other boats. She thought of her dream: the bear-girl, the growing child, the steady beat of a heart under her naked hand.

'We don't have any problems. Not yet.' She moved her feet closer to the warmth of the lamp.

'My hair,' he said. 'It's too long.' He retrieved something from the cabin; Callanish heard a clatter. 'Messengers need shaved heads, so that people know what they are. It's our sign, so that we don't have to wear bells when we go ashore, like the other damplings.'

She shifted her position, propping a blanket behind the small of her back. 'Enjoy your shave,' she said. 'There's water in the filter. I'll watch that the lamp doesn't go out.'

'No.' He held a razor, a bone bowl, and a strip of fabric out to her. 'I want you to do it.'

She leaned closer to him in the lamp's yolky glow. 'You'd trust me with a blade near your throat?'

'You can't sail this boat without me,' he replied. 'And you'd be lonely.'

'I don't get lonely.'

She took the razor and the fabric. He went to fill the bowl from the filter.

There was a bench nailed across the cutter's stern; this was a seat when Flitch sat when there was no wind, and a worktop when Callanish gutted fish and rinsed seaweed for dinner, and a step when they needed to reach up and adjust a sail. Callanish took it as a seat now. Flitch knelt on the deck before her, his elbows on her knees.

'Open up, little fish,' he said, bowing his head towards her lap.

Callanish held the razor up as a warning, but let him spread her knees and crawl closer towards her. He rested his chin on his hands, his forearms pressed to her thighs, his head bowed.

She scooped a palmful of oil and spread it across his scalp from temples to nape, then rinsed her glove in the water. The curve of his head was vulnerable, tender. She wielded her razor.

As she moved the blade she thought of the barbs of a feather, and made her movements match that shape. After every five short, light strokes she wiped the razor on a scrap of cloth, leaving a half-moon of amber oil studded with hairs. The tracks left by her razor were as smooth as a fish's belly.

'What are you thinking about, little fish?' asked Flitch.

'North.' Callanish blinked away thoughts of bears and of home. She tried to concentrate only on the blade, the oil, the pale arcs of Flitch's newly revealed skin. 'The far north. I've never been. Have you?'

'I can go anywhere I like.'

'But have you? All the way?'

'No one can go all the way to the far north. Your sails would freeze and shatter. Your filter would clog and your eyes would ice over so you couldn't blink.'

'So you can't go anywhere you like.'

'I *can*.' He pulled away, ready for a fight, and Callanish tugged his head back to its place. He settled. 'I can go anywhere I like,' he said, and his voice sulked. 'But I don't want to go to the far north. So I don't.'

'That's a shame,' she said lightly. 'I'd like to hear about it.'

'Why didn't you just say that? Little fish, you never ask what you really want to know. I haven't been, but I've heard stories. Messengers have the best stories.'

The razor feathered, scraped, feathered in her grasp. 'So tell me,' she said.

'In the north there are chunks of ice as high as towers, higher than the mast of the biggest ship you've ever seen. And the sound – it cracks and groans like it's got a beast inside, something angry and roaring to get out.'

'Like a bear?' asked Callanish, with a smile.

'I haven't heard a bear. But listen: whole ships can get encased inside the ice, squeezed flat between two bergs, and then years later they reappear. The crew are all ghosts, and when they're set free they can come on your boat and haunt you for ever. You go mad with the light and the sound and the frozen fingers of the ghosts tapping at your eyes.'

Callanish remembered her childhood winters: the men beating the ice near the shore to break it up so that the dampling boats could come and go; jars of paint and buckets of milk freezing to splintered stars; a sealskin hat pressed soft over her ears.

'Flat ghosts,' she said.

'What?'

'You said the boats get flattened in the ice. So the ghosts must be flat too.'

'Little fish, would you be quiet for a moment and let me tell the story? You're always like this. Always picking holes in things. If you're not careful, it'll all come unravelled.'

Flitch's head was shaved from the nape to the ears. She tilted his chin up so that she could do the rest.

'I'm sorry,' she said. 'Tell me what else you've seen.'

'I've seen everything you can imagine, and some things you can't. I've seen a sunken city with a horse's head bigger than your house. I've seen an underwater bell that chimes during storms.'

Callanish knew that these things were not real, and at that moment she pitied Flitch. It would be cruel to contradict him. And she was nearly finished with her task, so she might as well let him go on. She slid the razor across his scalp for five strokes and wiped it on the cloth. The rhythm soothed her.

She saw her mother in the future, old and starving, left to rot inside the crumbling walls of her house. She saw her mother now, fingers numb from cold, stroking the grace-feather and not understanding its meaning. She saw her mother then, approaching her with the knife, blade glinting white in the northern sun, trying to set her free.

'Did you hear what I said?' he asked.

'I'm listening,' said Callanish, and it was not a lie because she would listen to the next part. She scraped the blade for the last time, still half dreaming, then wiped Flitch's scalp with the clean side of the cloth.

'I said I can fix it.'

'Fix what?' she asked.

'You.'

Flitch straightened his back and leaned in to Callanish, on his knees, on the deck. He took the razor out of her hand, placing it on the bench. He raised his hands as if to cup her face, as if to caress her cheek, as if to hold her steady for a kiss. Instead he slid his fingers behind her ears. He stroked her scars; the fat ragged lines like gills.

'Little fish,' he said, and she could not breathe.

In the morning, Fitch pulled up the lobster creels. Dawn spread slabs of yellow-pink cloud across the sky. Callanish shivered as she drained water from the filter, put it on the lamp to boil, spooned coffee into bone cups. She watched Flitch from under her eyebrows. Each creel contained an enormous grey lobster, but when he went to take them out, they crumbled in his grasp.

'Squid,' he murmured, more to himself than to Callanish. 'They get in the cages. They suck out the flesh and leave the shell behind.'

He opened the creels and tipped the corpses into the sea.

That night, Flitch and Callanish sat facing one another across the glowing lamp. It had not been a good day. Soon after midday a mist had drifted down around them, swallowing the wind and wrapping the boat in a damp blanket. Callanish reached for the lamp, ready to light it, but Flitch snatched it from her hands.

'It's a waste,' he said, 'and it won't make a difference anyway. The mist is too thick. The light will just reflect it back at us. We'll have to wait it out.'

And so they had spent the day inching forward through the murky sea, sails barely fluttering, Flitch with his hands white on the wheel, Callanish with her shoulders aching as she hunched over the compass. It was almost a relief when the day gave up and brought on the night. There was no sunset, just the grey mist deepening to blue.

Finally Callanish was allowed to light the lamp, to put away the compass and take out a handful of dried fish and salt-jewelled seaweed, to say goodbye to the day when she had barely had a chance to greet it.

They ate their dinner in the cloudy embrace of the mist, unable to see past the boat's edge in any direction. Afterwards, Flitch bent into the cabin and popped up again holding a bottle. He poured a finger-width into two cups and handed one to Callanish. She held it over the side of the boat, ready to tip it out.

'This stuff isn't safe,' she said.

'What are you scared of, little fish? What could possibly scare you in the big bad ocean? You've got gills. You can swim away from danger.'

'I've seen what happens when people drink too much of this. They lose control. Remember Odell? He could barely keep his graces alive, never mind himself.'

Flitch shrugged, drained his cup, refilled it. 'He drinks to forget his loneliness. We drink to bring it on more sweetly.'

'I thought you didn't get lonely.'

'I don't. Not now.'

Callanish pulled her hand back and drained her cup. It burned on the way down; she gritted her teeth and took deep, salty breaths to stop it rising up again. She held out her empty cup to Flitch's bottle, and then it was no longer empty.

'I'm going to leave soon,' she said.

'I know. But you'll come back.'

'Come back where? You're nowhere, Flitch.'

'I'm everywhere. But if we want to get to where you want to be, to your island, we can't go like this.' He swept his hands around the edges of their circle of light, out towards the choking walls of the mist. 'We're blind and slow. But I can get us a ride on a bigger ship: a military vessel or a revival cruise. I can make it better, little fish. I can fix this.'

'I don't need you to fix me. Just –' Callanish tapped the rim of her cup against a creel-rope. 'Just share your drink and your food. It's all I need.'

'From me?'

'From anyone.'

'I don't think that's true.' Flitch leaned forward and pulled her hand away from where she'd been rubbing at her scars. They felt raw, itchy, as if they were still healing. 'I think you need more than that. I think you need me.'

Callanish threw the contents of her cup into the sea. The stuff muddied her thoughts. It wasn't worth the risk of the sea's call. It made her conversations with Flitch emotional when they should be practical; heavy with sediment when they should be transparent.

'What I need,' she said, 'is to have my message delivered properly. The way you should have done it. The way I paid you to do. This, all of this –' she swooped her hands at the mist, then pointed at Flitch, 'is because of you. If you'd done it right in the first place, if you'd seen her, really seen her, then I wouldn't be here. If I could rely on you. If I could rely on anyone, then I . . .'

Restless, she stood up, only to sit back down. There was nowhere to

177

go. She wanted to pace, to think, to mark out the tinny slats of her porch with her bare feet, to focus her eyes on the distant touch of sky and sea. But there was only the mist and the boat and the weight of Flitch's steady gaze.

He watched her, tapping his teeth against the rim of his cup. He waited until she'd settled on the bench beside him before speaking. 'Why do you want to go there?'

'Because –' Callanish's voice felt thicker than the mist. She swallowed, and it hurt. 'I have to know.'

He touched a fingertip to the scar behind her ear. 'Isn't this your answer?'

She knocked his arm away, sliding along the bench so he couldn't reach her. 'No,' she said. 'That's nothing.'

'Doesn't seem like nothing to me.'

'And what would you know, Flitch? What would you know about anything?'

She could smell the alcohol on his tongue, but his hands and his gaze were steady. 'I know you,' he said.

'You don't! You don't know the first thing about me.'

Flitch shrugged and refilled Callanish's cup, holding it out to her. 'Okay, little fish. You're right, maybe I don't. But I could.'

He was wrong. She was sure of it. But he seemed sure too, so how could she say that her conviction was stronger than his? She'd seen that look of certainty before, and she had suffered for it.

Callanish remembered that morning: pulling her gloves and slippers off once again, letting her bare feet almost touch the sea, the final snapping of her mother's temper. *You want the sea so much?* she'd said, voice eerily calm. *Then I shall give you the sea.*

Her mother had come towards her with the knife, her belly fat with child. *You're half fish already*, she'd whispered, her voice as calm as a lullaby.

And then the blade slinking behind her ears, so sharp it felt like nothing as her skin split. Soon her mother would have a real baby; why would she need her half-fish monster? Callanish barely even cried. It was such a small crime.

Callanish had had options then, after the cutting. She could have chosen confession, and seen her mother rot on a prison boat, seen her baby sister born in a cell. She could have chosen revenge, and carved out matching gills for her mother. She could have chosen forgiveness, and lived there with her family for ever. But instead she'd ignored her feelings; tamped them down into the soil until the whole house was unsteady, until she was ripe for mistakes, until she did something she could never undo and then years later had to run halfway across the world to a tin hut surrounded by dying birds.

'Do you think it's a punishment?' she whispered. 'To be a grace-keeper. To grieve every day.'

'I don't know. Is it?'

'I had a sister,' she said. 'She was three heartbeats old. My mother, Veryan, she wanted to give birth in the copse. At the World Tree. She needed me to help, and I tried to help. But I didn't know what to do. I ran away. I left them alone. I could have got help, but I just hid. And my sister never got past three heartbeats.'

Callanish was not sure whether she was speaking aloud, or only inside her head. 'My father – he didn't want to be the father of a dead child. His heart broke and he died. They died, both of them, because of me.'

She took the bottle from Flitch's hand. What did it matter if she got so drunk she fell into the water? The sea had caused her problems, and it could solve them all. 'This life is a punishment,' she said, 'and I deserve it.'

15
Veryan

Veryan remembered everything. Spring was the bestest and most important time to the gods, and as the most loved child on the island - she had never been told this officially, but she knew it, and never hesitated to inform her older sister, as long as their mother couldn't hear - she was due to lead the procession. She had not led it last year, but that was because she was only nine. Now she was nineteen, and the procession was for her marriage. But no, a year later from nine made her ten, so she wouldn't be married for a while yet. She remembered now. She remembered everything.

Veryan filled the kettle and lifted it on to the cooker. Her hands shook. She looked down at them and they seemed strange to her: the skin softer, the joints stiffer, the hands of an old woman. But they could not be hers, because she was nineteen. No, she was nine. She was ten.

She was sitting beside her mother and they were making oak-leaf masks. They had a good store of leaves: she and her sisters had been out every morning, shuffle-crouching through the copse, filling their skirts with fallen leaves. They started each school day with aching backs, but it was vital not to straighten up while in the copse, for danger of knocking or - gods! - breaking a branch. It wasn't the island's punishment they feared; the gods had more power than any man, and did not look kindly on such sins. But she and her sisters were good girls. They had nothing to fear.

Veryan lit the fire under the kettle. Her shaking hand swayed into the flame, but she felt no pain. She dipped her finger into the kettle of cold water to soothe it, simply from habit. It would not do to have blistered fingers when she had the oak-leaf masks to sew. She looked around her house, but could not see any leaves. Her mother and her sisters were missing too. But her back ached, so she must have been gathering leaves in the copse, so it must be almost time for the procession. She was going to lead it this year, because it was her wedding.

Her mother peered over at her sewing, then eased the leaves from her hands to straighten her stitches. She was good at sewing, but not as good as her mother. The gods could be angered by anything, even shoddy stitches. It was best to be careful. And everyone would see her mask when she was leading. She wanted it to be perfect. She'd collected the largest leaves she dared. Only the island elders were allowed the king leaves – their masks were one enormous leaf, while everyone else had to stitch together lots of smaller leaves. She could never be an elder, but perhaps she could be an elder's wife one day, depending on her husband, and they were allowed masks made of two leaves. One day, she would have a mask like that.

It was time. She was nineteen, she was nine, she was ten – it didn't matter, nothing mattered except that she was leading the procession and it was her wedding day, her very own day. Behind her, the islanders had begun their chant: low and solemn at first.

At Penhill Crags we tear his rags
At Hunter's Thorn we take his horn

The fur cape was warm across her shoulders, the collar tickling her throat. It was lined with silk, the softest thing she'd ever felt. She wished that the fur and silk were sewn to her skin so that she could feel it every day. The candle was heavy but she held it as high as she could, not even flinching when the dollops of wax rolled down her hands. They hardened in creamy lines on her forearms, caking her wrists and itching her elbows.

At Capplebank Stee we break his knee
At Grasshill Beck we snap his neck

She sneaked a glance behind. The line of islanders was lit up like flickering stars. Half of them held a lit branch as high as they could; the other half wielded flutes and tambourines, playing them in rhythm with the chants. She almost stumbled, enchanted by the sight of so much fire. The punishment for burning wood when it wasn't for processions or official business was harsh, though deserved. Wood was holy, and must be burned carefully so that the sparks and smoke were sent up to the gods.

She faced forward and stepped more carefully; the procession wasn't even halfway around the island yet, and already her shoulders ached, and her hands felt raw, and her vision was narrowed by the oak-leaf mask. But it was her wedding, and she would not flinch. She lifted her candle and resumed the chant.

At Wadham's End he cannot fend
At Grassgill End he'll meet his end

In the days of the great-great-greats, the land stretched out so far you could have walked it for weeks without a sniff of sea. That was the time of true processions: long gleeful snakes of people stretched across valleys and hills. Then the land shrank, and shrank, and shrank, until now everyone must march in circles, around the island and spiralling in to link hands and surround the copse at the centre. By then their chant would not be low and solemn any more, but gleeful and loud, the words called at the tops of their voices to echo among the trees.

At Wadham's End he cannot fend
At Grassgill End he'll meet his end
GODS, HEAR US.

Their island might be small, but the gods knew the distance they covered in their hearts, and that was what mattered. The islanders showed their obedience. After their deaths, they would all have a seat at the table of the great forest feast.

The kettle was shrieking. Veryan creaked to her feet and moved the boiling water off the flame. She tipped tea leaves into a bone cup and added water, and she only spilled a little bit so her hands couldn't be that shaky after all. Perhaps she was tired after the exertions of the procession, or excited to begin it. It had either just finished or was just about to begin, she remembered that. She sat back and waited for her tea to cool.

For the procession, the island was completely dark. There were no lights in any of the buildings and no lights at the dock. Damplings kept their distance during processions. It was safer for everyone. Damplings had wickedness deep within their bones, so deep it couldn't be scraped or burned or cursed out, no matter how much the great-great-greats had tried. Given half a chance, damplings would steal landlocker babies, everyone knew that. They envy us: our traditions, our food sources, the power of our gods. Everyone dreams of a house on land, but most damplings will never have one. And that's as it should be; they wouldn't know the traditions, and might not perform the proper appeasements. They might break a branch, and then where would they be? Where would we all be?

Around the copse, hands linked, the islanders increased their chant. Tambourines clashed and flutes shrilled. The rest of the song's words were abandoned in favour of the final line, called over and over, rising to a shriek - and then it died. Her time had come. She was the most loved child, the most beautiful woman, the island's bride. She had been chosen for this. She raised her candle, her forearms caked in wax, her blonde hair gleaming across her fur cape. She made her voice as loud as the wind in a storm.

So here's a thought your teeth should clench
All greenness comes to withering.

The islanders picked up her lines, chorusing as she led them along the narrow path and into the heart of the copse. They pulled their arms in then, candles and burning branches tucked in to their bodies so that there was no chance of the trees catching fire. Tomorrow, everyone would wake to welts and burns on their chests and faces, but they'd be glad of it. To be burned at a procession, to carry marks earned by protecting the sacred trees, was an honour.

Veryan had drunk her tea too soon and burned her tongue. She wrapped her hands around the cup, knowing it was too hot and not caring. It was an honour to have burns. Heat cleansed. That reminded her - she got up to check her coal store, but sat back down. If she did not have enough, then what? There was so little left to trade. She had sealskins, and her father had told her just this morning that they could keep even a giant warm through the winter. Not that she remembered winter; perhaps it was something that people feared, though it never occurred. Veryan did not find it strange that her memories consisted only of spring and summer.

All greenness comes to withering
All greenness comes to withering

185

The copse seemed to answer the islanders' chant: it was green, and withered too. Their steps stirred up scents: leaf-mulch, overripe berries, the tang of new green leaves. They held their flames close.

At the heart of the copse grew the World Tree, centre of the whole archipelago. For the wedding, it had been set all about with the banquet tables and benches carved from the oldest and holiest oak. There was a place set for each one of the islanders, from the oldest to the youngest. The platters were of oak wood, as were the knives, and each place had a single item, covering the bounty of the whole world. She glanced around the table as the islanders took their places, setting their burning branches in bone-carved holsters around the edge of the clearing.

She took her place at the end of the table, her platter laid with an entire roasted rabbit, and gazed at the feast in the glow of the flames: bone tubs of honey and mustard and rock salt; salads of nasturtium and nettle; bread as white as snow, made from fine-milled wheat and with a sugar-crunchy crust; more bread as brown as earth, peppered with seeds; turkeys roasted with butter and garlic, their combs fried crispy. In these days of lack, not all the items that grew on the earth could be found. Pomegranate, banana, lemon: these things could not be stored for long enough to trade to a northern archipelago. But the gods did not care for trade routes. Their punishments could be harsh. As a compromise, the missing items were still there in spirit, carved from sacred oak wood and placed on platters.

No one would go hungry that night, even those with totems on their plates: their island had good rich soil and could sustain many crops and animals. They had bread and wine, pears and apples, roasted potatoes and spit-fired pig, enough to fill the bellies of the whole island.

Veryan sipped her tea. It tasted of nothing, but she did not mind. Her tongue tingled with the memory of tastes. It was just yesterday that she'd eaten that rabbit, after all – or if not yesterday, then she was anticipating a taste to come the following night. She rubbed the tight joints of her knuckles.

After the islanders' bellies were full, the sacrifice could begin. The youngest islander had been born only a few weeks before – she suspected that the child's mother, married at last year's procession, had conceived in a well-timed way so that the child would have this honour. Perhaps she would try the same thing, so her child could be honoured too. One by one, the islanders passed their platters along, forming a tall oak tower in the centre of the main table. It reached higher than their heads, but it did not waver: oak was strong like that, which was why it was the finest of trees, which was why this was the finest of islands.

The child's mother clambered on to the table and placed her baby on the platter: a symbolic meal offered to the gods. The islanders lit fresh branches from the final sparks of the old ones, forming a circle around the tables with the raised child at the centre. Up rose the islanders' voices, inverting their earlier chant as they stamped and cheered around the banquet tables.

All withering grows to green
All withering grows to green

The child wailed at the noise and the lights, but only because he did not understand the great honour. In time, he would be proud. The damplings told stories about the islanders killing babies to appease their gods: a tiny life traded to protect hundreds more. But that had never happened, not that she remembered – and she remembered everything. It was just nasty talk among the damplings. And they were nasty, the damplings: full of spite and wickedness, and it couldn't be burned out of them. Even the islander children knew it: they invented little chants and taunts, daring one another to cross the blackshore and grab handfuls of seaweed to fling at the boats. It was all in fun, of course – just the play of youth – but those nasty damplings did make such a fuss about it, feeling so sorry for themselves. She tried to pity the damplings. It came from a lack of heritage, of family. How could anyone feel steady without good land under their feet?

The procession had marched itself to bed and the island was asleep. She was nineteen – the perfect age for a bride. The island council had chosen her husband, and they had chosen well. Now all that remained was their wedding night. Making love was making life and that was her duty, she knew, though it was never spoken.

Her husband was green-eyed and strong-boned with hair the colour of oak leaves. She waited for him at the edge of the copse. Her underwear was scented with lilac. His cheeks were red from the spiced wine and he came to her with the passion and honesty of a lit candle. Afterwards her skin was raw, parallel scrapes down her thighs and back, and she thought of the lines left by the melting wax. She would be proud of her burns. They were a mark of duty, of worship. Her husband kissed them before heading back to the feast. She stayed in the cool dark of the woods, praying to the gods that she would conceive soon, so that her child could be honoured at next year's procession. She could not concentrate; her scrapes ached.

She wandered alone across the island to the shore, looking for seaweed to soothe her skin. Damplings were disgusting, but some of their old folk remedies did work. There it was, spreading in lines across the blackshore: damp from the water, slimy and repulsive. But her scrapes burned. She bent to gather an armful of seaweed and her feet slid on the wet sand. She landed on her back in the blackshore's embrace. Her skin sighed at its coolness. She stayed.

She fell into sleep. Then: a slow pull out, reality seeping into her dreams. A mouth pressing against hers, cold as the sea. Was this her husband, come back to love her again? She felt the weight of a body on her own. She raised her hips. In the dim light of the stars, she saw the silvery gleam of scales.

Veryan's tea was cold, but she drank it anyway. There was a draught coming from somewhere, wrapping itself around her throat; she pulled her shawl tighter and hunched her shoulders. She could still feel the squeaking strands of grass that he'd plucked from the ground and braided into her hair. She could smell the sharp green scent of the grass, and of him. She inhaled: no grass, only dust and damp wool and cinders from the fire. From her sleeve she pulled a feather, its iridescence faded, its barbs tatty from touching. She stroked it against her cheek.

She was going to have a child. She would not see her baby for a while, but already she could imagine her: a tiny baby girl, fingers curled like daisies before dawn, skin petal-soft and scented with milk. She would name the baby Callanish, after the old sacred land.

Callanish, came a whisper.

Veryan slid out of her chair in silence, as if to catch the speaker unawares. She looked all around the house: the hay-mattress bed, the chest of sealskins, the big tin bath, the almost-empty pantry. Nothing.

Callanish, hissed the voice again. She realised now that it came from outside. She tucked the feather back into her sleeve and pulled open her front door. Outside, two of her neighbours were deep in whispered conversation over the front gate. When they saw her they straightened up, looking guilty.

'Are you speaking of my child?' asked Veryan.

'No, Veryan.' One of the neighbours – Veryan could not think of her name – attempted a smile. 'You have no child, remember?'

She remembered, of course she did. She would remember the neighbour's name, too, if she'd known it, so she must never have known it. And she had meant her one-day child, the glory of her future – that should have been obvious. But she did not need to tell this strange, gossipy neighbour that. She wouldn't understand.

Veryan did not bother with a response. She went back inside and sat at the table. She went to sip her tea, but the cup was empty. She tipped it to read the leaves. In all their clusters, the leaves only made one shape: a baby. There was her proof. There was the promise of a child. Her baby, her Callanish, would be blessed by the gods. She would inhabit all possible worlds. She would do anything and everything, and she would always be happy.

Veryan remembered the scent of woodsmoke, the enchantments of flutes and tambourines, the softness of a fur cape, the tall pile of wooden platters, the crinkle of the oak-leaf mask against her cheek. She remembered feasts and flames and weddings. She remembered everything.

16
Avalon

Avalon's time was approaching. She felt it like a lit coal in her chest. This was love: a white-hot burn, bright enough to obscure everything else.

She'd been awake for hours when Jarrow snored out of his dreams. Just like every morning, she pretended to be asleep. It was difficult to contain her smile. She lived for the mornings: the moment when her husband loved her unobserved. The warm weight of his hand on the swell of their child, the comfort of his fingers on her lips. When she was awake, he loved her with distraction. There was always a coracle to be fixed, a whining performer to be fed. Always, always a problem to be solved. But just then, just for that wakening moment, her sleeping face was his whole world. She kept her breath steady, filling her lungs with the scent of his hands.

She held herself still until he had clambered out of the bunk and up on to the deck of the *Excalibur*. Only then did she let her mouth slide into a smile. Jarrow's saltwater smell, his bear-broad shoulders, the glitter caught beneath his skin: all of it quickened her heart. When she was sure he had gone, she allowed herself to stretch her limbs, cat-sleek.

She slipped out of the bunk. Her baby nestled low inside her, and she took a moment to rest her hands on him. This was why. Her husband, her child: for them, it would all be worth it.

Above her, on the deck, she heard Jarrow's heavy tread. It was too late to slip back into bed and enjoy his touch again.

'Queen of mine!' he crowed, his voice filling the tiny cabin. 'You have surfaced. But calm yourself, my sweet. I have plans to winkle a cup of special tea from our fire-breather and bring it to you in bed.'

Avalon wanted nothing more than to luxuriate in their bed, sipping tea and feeling her child grow. But she had something more important to do.

'My king,' she purred, reaching out her slender arm to her husband. 'You are kind to take such care of me. But perhaps I could convince you to take care of me in a different way?' She pulled Jarrow closer, wrapping her hands around his, using them to slide the hem of her nightdress up her thighs. She leaned into him to whisper in his ear: 'A wife needs her husband.'

Avalon had loved Jarrow from the moment she met him. Fiercely, fully, she loved him. She dreamed of growing old with him, the two of them with their feet firmly on land and their arms around their children. She would never let the flame sputter out, no matter what it took. But everyone knew the danger of flames on a boat.

Jarrow smiled at her, but she knew that he wasn't really seeing her. His mind was on coracles and circuses.

'Alas, my queen. I wish I could. The day is upon us, though, and I have duties that I must –'

'I understand,' she interrupted, biting back a sigh.

This was love observed. This was love at sea. If they had a home, a steady home on steady ground, then Jarrow could love her unobserved all day. He could look at her and truly see her.

She pulled her nightdress back down. 'Before you begin your day, would you help me to the mess boat? Our son is restless this morning, and I must feed him. This life at sea is not good for him. The unsteadiness. The constant movement. A child needs somewhere to plant his feet and stand tall.'

Jarrow did not reply, but simply waited while she continued dressing and washing. As she scooped water over her body, she peeked over her shoulder to see if he watched. His eyes were distant, looking at nothing.

He had barely touched her since she had fallen pregnant. And – she could be honest in her own mind, if nowhere else – there had not been much touching before her pregnancy either. In the first years of their marriage, their passion could set a boat aflame. But grief can dampen any fire. All those babies, lost before their first breath.

She straightened her dress, pinned up her hair, and leaned girlishly on her husband's arm as they emerged from the *Excalibur*'s cabin. She didn't need his help, but she knew he liked to look after her. In truth, Avalon had never felt healthier. Her son nourished her as she nourished him, and each day she felt her strength grow.

Strength was good. Strength was important, because this was an important time. She needed to get it right. For the baby, and for her husband. She knew what they needed – she only had to work out how to get it.

After Jarrow had deposited Avalon at the head of the mess boat's long bench with a cup of nettle tea and a rough-lipped kiss, she sat. She watched. She waited. A plan would reveal itself as long as she was ready for it.

She saw the twittering, glittery nonsenses from the beauty boat descend in a clumped trio, flirting aggressively with the fire-breather before taking their seats at the far end of the bench. How they managed to lever any food into their mouths while spewing all that gossip from them, Avalon didn't know. She averted her eyes, sipping her tea with dignity.

She saw the clowns slump through one by one, exchanging winks with the fire-breather and swallowing their breakfast in fast, furtive spoonfuls. They were planning rebellion, no doubt. Avalon had told Jarrow a thousand times that the clowns weren't to be trusted, but he would never listen. He never doubted his crewmembers' loyalty. Avalon, on the other hand, never doubted anyone's deviousness, and that was why she was always a step ahead.

She saw Ainsel drop effortlessly into the mess boat, ignoring the slats bolted to the coracle's inner wall. He sauntered to the serving hatch. He must have seen Avalon – perhaps his whole louche show was for her benefit. She sipped her tea and made sure that she didn't look at him, but also that she didn't obviously avoid looking at him.

She prodded at her guilt, but it did not give. She could not regret her nights with Ainsel. The logic leading up to it had been clear. All those babies with their unbeating hearts. All those nights that she and Jarrow could not stand to love one another. This baby was a Stirling, and it was alive. Those were the only important things.

She would never know how close Jarrow had come to giving up on their marriage. But it did not matter. Now she had a baby, and he would never give up on her. Ainsel had served his purpose, and Avalon was grateful. But Jarrow's old family had had their time, and now it was her turn. Hers and her baby's. Ainsel would be fine; he would be the ringmaster. He was a man, and men should make their own way in the world. Let him earn his own home, as Jarrow had.

Lost in thought, Avalon had not noticed Ainsel approaching her at the head of the table. The sway of his steps at the corner of her eye snapped her awake. She saw him dare a glance at the glorious moon of her belly. She saw a smile spread slow across his face. She saw him move to sit beside her. She turned her face away from him. He hesitated.

Luckily the bear-girl clumped in, and Ainsel took the chance to turn away from Avalon and bow low to North. He climbed the mess boat's ladder one-handed, gripping his breakfast bowl, off to eat alone with the horses.

North accepted two breakfast bowls from Bero, but ate neither. One seemed a reasonable portion, but the other was heaped with crab stew and topped with several wedges of knobbly brown pitta, the stack so high it was in danger of toppling. For her dirty great bear, no doubt. Avalon and Ainsel's horses needed a special diet of seaweed and oils, but the bear required no such consideration. It ate the same food as the rest of the crew, and did not seem fussy. Avalon did begrudge the scale of its portions, though; such a vast amount of food would be much appreciated if spread out among them. They never stopped muttering about their empty bellies. Avalon never complained about food, even though she should have the biggest portions. For the baby.

All morning, none of the *Excalibur*'s crew spoke to Avalon. That was as it should be. They might pretend that they ignored her out of disdain, but Avalon knew it was because they were afraid of her. The clowns, the glamours, the fire-breather, the acrobat – and that irritating little bear-girl most of all. Why Jarrow seemed to like the wretched urchin so much, Avalon couldn't imagine. Well, so much the better that the crew would soon have the circus all to themselves. They were too interwoven, tangled together like seaweed around an anchor. They were dragging Jarrow down, clotting him up, and if she could just –

The bear-girl. If she didn't marry Ainsel, then they could not provide a Stirling child. It wouldn't be easy for Jarrow to set up another match for his son – it was too much of a gamble to choose a dampling stranger from another boat. No child meant that Ainsel's claim on the house would be useless. Avalon's baby would be the only Stirling.

She had been holding on to North's secret, waiting for the right

moment to reveal it to her husband – but why complicate things? A
smile spread across Avalon's face. She lifted her cup of cold tea to hide it.

Now that Avalon knew she would soon be leaving the circus, she
almost felt nostalgic for it. She enjoyed her steady afternoon progress
from the mess boat to the *Excalibur*, her careful hold of the salt-
crusted chains between the coracles.

Here was the clowns' coracle, where she'd made them fear and
respect her. Here was the beauty boat, where she'd crept at mealtimes
to steal perfumed oils to wear in bed with Jarrow. Here was North's
coracle, where – no, nothing good had ever happened there. Here was
Ainsel's coracle, where she'd spent hours alone grooming Lord and
Lady when Ainsel was off being preened by the glamours.

And here was the *Excalibur*, where she had first seen Jarrow all
those years ago. She paused on the deck and lost herself in the
memory. She loathed circuses, and had only come that night to keep
her sister company. Any excuse for an evening away from the cabin of
their family's fruit-trading clipper; any reason to avoid yet another
evening sorting good apples from bad. The damplings' section of the
big top had been crowded and sweaty. But all that had faded to
nothing when the ringmaster stepped on stage. His broad shoulders,
his glittered cheeks, the boom of his voice so strong it vibrated through
her ribs. She felt a flame burst to life in her chest. The show was dull
– all the performers trying too hard to shock with their genderplay,
their costumes ragged and their eyes desperate. But that didn't matter.
The ringmaster was all that mattered.

Later, after the show, she unhitched the rowing boat and sculled
from her clipper to the circus schooner. She climbed the anchor chain
to the boat's deck, letting the rowing boat drift free behind her. She
would not need it again.

Tap-a-tap on the cabin door. And there: the ringmaster, bear-broad, haloed by the seal-fat lamp.

'And who are you?' he asked.

She remembered the name painted on the boat's side: EXCALIBUR. She thought fast.

'Avalon,' she said. 'My name is Avalon.'

She'd spent the day sorting fruit. She knew that her skin smelled apple-sweet and looked as white as just-sliced apple flesh.

'I would like to come into your cabin,' she said.

She stayed still, letting the air carry her scent to the ringmaster. It did not take long. She saw herself then, reflected in his eyes, and she liked what she saw. He lifted her in his arms and carried her into his cabin. And there she had stayed.

Now, post-performance, Avalon readied herself in her marital bed. She had held North's secret inside for weeks. She could taste it now, hard and honeyed under her tongue.

She watched, her smile steady as Jarrow washed and undressed. He slid into the bunk beside her. She snowed kisses on his face, but he seemed distracted. Of course he was. His mind was over-full of repairs and rehearsals and every unimportant thing in the world.

Avalon leaned across as if to kiss her husband again, then sat back with a sigh. 'Sweet husband, I must speak to you.'

'Yes, my queen. Any time.' Jarrow's smile was honest, but his eyes were unfocused.

'You know how much I love and value our crew – but there is something I must tell you. It's not right the way the crew keep things from you.' Avalon paused and bit her lip, trying to look as if the truth was being reluctantly squeezed from her. 'Our sweet north child – she will soon have her own child.'

Well, she certainly had Jarrow's attention now. He sat up on the edge of the bunk.

'I am sorry, my love. I think I misheard you,' he said, his throat tight.

'Alas, Jarrow, you heard me perfectly.' She tried to put a slight wobble in her voice, the threat of tears. 'North – our bear-girl, Ainsel's bride-to-be – she is pregnant.'

'I see.' Jarrow sat, hands on thighs, head lowered, motionless. He held the pose for so long that Avalon glanced at the rise and fall of his chest, to make sure. A thousand accusations against North rose up in her throat. She swallowed them all down. She waited.

Finally, Jarrow spoke.

'Thank you for telling me. But everything is fine. The child will not come before the wedding. Nothing needs to change.'

Anger flared in Avalon. She inched in closer to her husband, keeping her voice light.

'Sweet husband. I do not think that you understand. North is pregnant, and she can't marry Ainsel.'

'It's Ainsel's baby.'

'Jarrow. Please listen. I have tried to be delicate, but –' Avalon resisted the urge to scream. 'But you are not hearing me. North has been with another man – many men, for all we know. She is having a baby, and it is not Ainsel's.'

'The baby is a Stirling,' said Jarrow.

'But it isn't!' Avalon could not help the shrillness in her voice. 'It isn't his! The baby is a bastard, a filthy nothing child, and it doesn't deserve the home that should belong –'

'Enough, Avalon. I won't have this. That child is Ainsel's, and he will raise it with North in their house, and the Stirlings will be restored. I thank you for telling me. But nothing has to change. Everything is the same. Everything is fine.'

Avalon wanted to pout, to cry, to slap Jarrow in his stubborn face. The thought of the bear-girl raising that bastard child on land, flouncing about in a mockery of the life that Avalon should be living – it made her sick. But it would never happen. Not while Avalon's heart still beat.

She slid her slim arm around her husband. He simply needed time to absorb what she had said. Soon he would come around to her way of thinking.

If this plan did not work, no matter – she had already begun thinking of another. And if that one did not work either – well, if she had to tear down the whole world to build a new one with her husband and child, then she would.

'My husband,' she cooed. 'My wise, wise husband. I am sure that you are correct. But let's not speak of others. We are the only ones here. We are the only ones who matter. Us, and our child.'

She pulled him back on the bunk, pressing kisses along his hairline. She took hold of his hands and slid them along her hips. She was ready to love him. Gently but firmly, Jarrow pushed her away.

'Alas, my queen, I cannot. It's not a good idea.'

'Oh, but it's a very good idea indeed. Look, I'll show you how good it is.'

'Avalon!' Jarrow pushed her aside and stood abruptly, thudding his skull on the overhead. 'Enough, please!'

Avalon could not respond. Nightdress rucked, hair tousled, legs at awkward angles, she stared at her husband.

'My queen. Let me explain.' Jarrow sat back on the bunk, reaching for her hands. 'I fear for our baby. So many of our children have been lost.'

Avalon tipped back her head and laughed in relief. 'Oh, Jarrow! This one is different, I can feel it. You can't harm him.'

'I just think – can we be safe? I don't know what I would do if I lost this one too. I need you both kept safe.'

'Of course, my love. How wise you are.'

Avalon felt the flame inside her flare, then fade. She collected the feelings, squeezed them small, held them in her fist so that she could examine them. The rough edges of a plan began to smooth together.

'Thank you, sweet husband,' she murmured. 'You always know the right thing to do.'

There were many ways to be unsafe at sea. Storms could drown you, sharks could bite you, pirates could attack you. You could starve or die of thirst. Your own crew could turn on you. And the dangers of a circus at sea were even greater: twisted limbs, animal attacks, falls from a great height.

So many dangers. So many reasons to choose land over sea. Avalon rested her hand on the swell of her son and smiled. If Jarrow would not leave the circus for love, then he would leave it for fear.

17

North

North woke shivering. Her bear's arms weighed heavy around her, but she shrank further into them for warmth. She had dreamed of bells chiming under the sea, of ghosts as translucent and choking as chalk dust, of linked hands with webbed fingers. In the coracle, Melia and the bear were still snoring. The air was so cold it ached. Last night, North had tied her canvas tight to keep out the reek of earth – but she could feel that it was past dawn, and the sun should have warmed her coracle by now.

She slipped out of her bear's grasp and stretched up to pull back the canvas. Dew plipped on to her shoulders and scalp as she peered out. Even from inside the coracle she could see what was causing the chill: the massive bulk of the revival boat, casting its shadow across the *Excalibur*'s tiny convoy. The boat's crew had left their painted banners unfurled, blaring out redemption to any passing sinners. In the shade, the Virgin's blue eyes and blue robe were as dark as a bruise.

This was their fourth morning in its shadow. It was following the circus from island to island – or perhaps the circus was following it. North hoped that Red Gold had a plan to shake the revivalists off. It was affecting the size of the circus's crowd, which affected the size of their payment, which affected the size of their dinners. It was bad enough that her own belly was empty, but she couldn't stand to hear the rumbles of her bear's stomach. She'd never seen a revival show, but from the music and stamping coming from the ship – and the dazed, dreamy looks in the landlockers' eyes when they exited – it was not dissimilar to the circus.

It made sense, she supposed. Landlockers visited the circus to escape, to believe in something magical, something powerful: something bigger than their own tiny muck of land. As far as she could tell, religion held the same appeal. As she slipped back into her bunk, North wondered if the revivalists had a bear too.

North woke hours later with the sun in her face and bells ringing in her ears. She was glad to see that the revival boat had moved on. Melia was already up and out of the coracle, so North washed, dressed, and went to the mess boat to get breakfast, which was dinner's leftovers: a few salted white beans, crisped chicken skin and half a slice of toasted rye bread. Melia was not in the mess boat, and in her early-morning fug North forgot to ask Bero whether she'd already had breakfast.

North and her bear ate their food and washed their faces. More specifically, North washed herself, and then the bear sat still while North washed his cheeks and snout, which were speckled with smears of bean and grease from the chicken.

It was then, with her damp hands rubbing at the bear's fur, that she felt her baby kick again. Her guts shifted and she gripped her fists, trying to swallow her excitement. She breathed slow and hard through her nose until the feeling passed, but she couldn't help the grin spreading across her face. She finished the washing, feeling her baby wriggle along with her bear.

The baby was fine. The bear was fine. And if they were fine, so was North.

North settled her bear back in his bunk before setting off in search of Melia. She'd need to be quick; her bear could not be left alone for long, and there was always the danger of nosy landlocker children climbing aboard. It had not happened yet – their fear of crossing the blackshore saw to that – but still North worried. Her bear could pose no harm to the children. He was tame and good and safe. But perhaps he was not.

She'd already tried the mess boat, and she could see that the *Excalibur*'s deck was empty. Melia wouldn't be in Ainsel's coracle, so that left the glamours' boat. She tapped on the hull before pulling back the canvas and dropping inside.

The Island of Maidens smelled of honey-spiced perfume and dusty fabric, with something rotting-sweet underneath. North inhaled: she couldn't identify the smell, but it made her think of the inside of her bear's mouth when he yawned, or the mess boat on warm nights. The coracle was bigger than North's, but felt smaller due to the clothing rail that stretched like a spine through its length, strung with dozens of circus costumes.

'Cyan?' called North into the mass of feathers and velvet. 'Teal? Mauve? I'm looking for Melia, is she in here?'

She ventured deeper into the coracle, pushing aside swathes of leather and cotton. Her steps were tiny; the soles of her feet were hard enough for stray beads or sewing needles, but she feared stepping on whatever was making that raw, meaty smell. Sequins gleamed back at her like hundreds of fish-eyes. Strings of beads bumped her head and bright hairpieces tickled her shoulders as she passed. She recognised the white dress from her funeral waltz; she'd given it to Cyan for repairs, as her bear's claws had nicked a seam during the last performance.

Her hip thudded against something solid: a table, bolted to the deck. It was dark among the dusty embrace of the costumes. She squinted down at the table, and discovered the source of the smell:

fish guts, scooped-out mussel shells, inedible animal parts. Whatever Bero could not fashion into a meal, the glamours ground up for dyes. North had never been squeamish, but now her stomach roiled like a stormy sea. She clutched at her middle and turned to fight her way out of the coracle.

'North!' cawed Cyan. 'It's an honour. Do you need...' She lifted one of North's golden braids and examined it. 'Yes, I suppose you do. Come on in and we shall prepare some lovely new dyes for you.' Cyan folded an arm around North's shoulders and led her further into the coracle, ducking and bending expertly around the swathes of hanging fabric.

Teal and Mauve were arrayed on a bunk as if they were about to perform a maypole: bodies draped in pink and orange silks, limbs stretched, eyes languid. Now that North thought about it, the glamours always seemed ready to perform at a moment's notice. She wished she could develop the same skill in her bear – not that he'd satisfy a crowd of clams, his broad furry body wrapped in ribbons, gyrating around a maypole. That thought tweaked a smile, lessening the roil in her belly.

Cyan kept up a constant monologue, puttering around the coracle. 'Teal has been experimenting with the leftover bits from the chicken hearts – not much colour in them, mind, but they do mix up so nicely with the razor-clam shells. Oh, watch yourself! There's sharp edges on those sleeves, we're making them for your crucifixion so you don't need to carry the blades, isn't that clever? All Mauve's idea, you know how the thinking goes, our Mauve was always so good at sharp things, and are you all right? You look a bit sick. Tell me if you're sick. I won't be having sick in here, the smell of it, I can't stomach it. Here, you sit down next to Mauve and I'll make you some herbal tea. Bero's just brought a kettle over, he's such a darling, though Teal thinks he was trying to get a peep at us in our undones!'

Cyan's giggle and hair-toss seemed more threatening than flirtatious. North managed a weak smile as she reached for the tea.

'I was looking for Melia,' she said. 'I thought she might be in here, but...' She peered into the mass of costumes, but knew it was pointless.

'She's not here,' said Teal with a sigh.

'She's not here at all,' added Mauve, with a little wink at Teal. They giggled together, and how did the glamours make laughing and hair-tossing look like they wanted to start a fight?

'What do you mean?' asked North. 'Where is she?'

Mauve and Teal shrugged in unison, a tandem dance. 'Oh, somewhere. We're all somewhere, wouldn't you say?'

North had had enough. She drained her tea in one go, forcing herself not to wince at her scalded tongue. 'Thank you for the tea, Cyan.' She began elbowing her way back through the storm of fabric, calling over her shoulder: 'I'll come by later to collect my costume.' She suspected that her words were swallowed by the layers of velvet and silk, but it did not matter. What mattered was getting out of the coracle and seeing the sky, and breathing clean air, and finding Melia.

North hunched over the edge of the glamours' coracle and clenched her teeth until her nausea passed. When she straightened, she saw that she was being observed. Avalon stood at the stern of the *Excalibur*, back straight, belly pressed out, as proud and round as a mermaid carved on a galleon.

'Feeling seasick, north child?' she called across the line of coracles.

North did not answer. She waited, but there was no movement from the taut canvases of the other coracles. Without breaking Avalon's gaze, without cradling her inferior bump, she began her steady progress across the chains towards the schooner. Avalon's eyes flickered, but she did not flinch, and she did not retreat – not even when Red Gold came up behind her, wrapping one arm over her belly and hailing North with the other.

North stepped from the Island of Maidens to her own coracle, to Ainsel's coracle, and on to the deck of the *Excalibur*. She did not want Red Gold to recognise her standoff with Avalon, but neither would she be the first to break their gaze.

After a heartbeat, Avalon tilted her head up and smiled at her husband. 'Are we not lucky, my king? A visit from our darling future daughter-in-law. I shall leave you two alone.' She darted a kiss at Jarrow's raw cheek, then perched on a pile of blankets along the boat's port side. She took a long look at North's midriff, eyebrows raised, before resting her chin on her hands and gazing out at the bustling port of the island. North's cheeks felt as burning red as the ringmaster's.

'It's Melia,' said North abruptly.

'Ah, yes,' sighed Red Gold, draping a heavy arm around her shoulder and leading her belowdecks. 'I'm glad that you feel it's time we discussed Melia, my little north child. Do you feel she will be ready for a new act tomorrow night? Or shall we wait until the night after? I shall bow to your knowledge and judgement, my dear.' And he did bow, forehead almost touching his knees, arms spread wide like bird-wings.

'Tea?' cooed Red Gold, straightening. 'Avalon made some. She will insist on me drinking this peppermint nonsense. For my stresses, she says.'

North shook her head; her tongue still burned from the glamours' tea.

'I'm worried about Melia. She's gone.'

Red Gold sighed and poured the tea. The act was oddly dainty, the teapot absurdly small in his meaty hands. 'I know, sweet child. She hasn't been the same since we lost Whitby, has she? At times I fear we will never have her back.'

North's head spun from the dust and guts in the glamours' boat. She felt as if she'd slept too long and missed a whole day during which the world had changed. 'Is she – did you put her somewhere? To heal?'

'What on oceans are you talking about, North? Melia is with you.'

'She's not! That's what I'm trying to tell you. She's not with me and she's not on the mess boat and she's not with the glamours, so where is she?'

In the sea, hissed a voice in North's head, *in the sea with Whitby*, but she would not listen to the voice.

'Hush now,' said Red Gold, leading her to a bench that was once upholstered in velvet but was now mostly patches. 'Calm yourself. It's not good for you, in your condition.'

North gaped. She was tired and she was confused and that was what Red Gold meant, it must be; he must see the shadows under her eyes and the shake in her hands.

He swallowed the contents of his dainty cup in one go, then turned to North and patted her hand. It was absurd, the whole thing was absurd, and she needed to find Melia, and she needed to get back to her bear, and it was taking all her self-control not to vomit her breakfast right into the ringmaster's lap.

'I know about the baby,' he said.

North forgot how to breathe. Red Gold frowned down at her. For a moment, North thought he was going to loom towards her and press a cracked, bloody hand to her forehead to check her temperature.

'I was referring to your future joy. Yours and Ainsel's. My own first grandchild.'

'Ainsel. And me. And my ...' She locked her fingers over her belly – whether to hide or highlight it, she wasn't sure.

'It is Ainsel's, yes?'

'It – well, I ...'

Red Gold's voice was deep and low, burring through the cabin.

'Because if it is not Ainsel's,' he said, 'then that means it is someone else's, and that makes it a bastard. You are free to do whatever you like, love whomever you like, sleep with whomever you like. I do not own you. But I do own the *Excalibur*, and any coracle that is lashed to her. Any bastard baby that lives inside you cannot live in your coracle, because that coracle belongs to me. Do you understand, my north child?'

North's body fell cold and still. Red Gold's voice vibrated through her bones. 'Yes, Jarrow. I understand.'

'Then it is fortunate indeed that your child is my grandchild, is it not?'

'Yes, Jarrow. Of course it's Ainsel's. I didn't mean to – well, we didn't...'

'No matter, no matter. Ah, but perhaps I should not call you our north child any more? Clearly you are a woman now.' He chuckled as if he'd made a joke. 'My Ainsel is a fine-looking boy, don't think I don't know. You're young, you're in love – well, it's not as if you're the first couple who couldn't wait until their wedding night!'

There was a storm in North's ears, blowing in rhythm with her heartbeat. She took a breath.

'Are you well, my north child? Is the pregnancy tiring you out? Is the baby addling your brains?' His expression was pure concern.

North ached a smile across her face. 'I am quite well, Jarrow, thank you. But I should go and lie down, just to be safe. To protect my – Ainsel's – baby.'

Red Gold went to speak, but his words were drowned out by a louder sound: the long, low blast of a horn. North's guts twisted and the baby kicked a drumbeat on her ribs. The military were boarding.

A *thud-tink* – Red Gold's cup tumbled to the deck and broke. He was casting anxious glances at the hatch – but North knew that there was no need. If anyone could smarm the charmless military men, it was Avalon.

The schooner swayed in its moorings as the military boarded. One, two – five men in all, judging by the sound of their boots. Only the military would be stupid enough to wear boots on board; clearly the thud of heavy feet was more important than having a decent grip on the deck.

'Dampling!' commanded a voice. 'On deck!'

Two strides, and Red Gold was out of the cabin. North followed him reluctantly. It was better to come to attention before you were commanded, but that didn't mean it was pleasant. As she walked she hunched her shoulders to hide her bump. She wasn't sure why; even the military couldn't command her not to be pregnant. But if there was anything she didn't want to have to discuss with them, it was the state of her womb. With the military it was best to be as bland as possible. North tried to imagine herself as a thin shell full of seawater and fluff.

On the *Excalibur*'s deck, the military men were lined up along the stern, as stiff and grumpy as crows in their starched black uniforms. Avalon simpered at their side, hands folded on her round belly, her smile beatific. North strained her ears in the direction of her coracle, willing her bear to stay silent. If he woke to find her still gone he might be upset. Growls and gleaming teeth would not impress the military, and there was nothing to stop them taking the bear away from her.

She tried to breathe steadily. Her bear was safe.

The military captain paced the deck, prodding the off-kilter wheel, scraping a fingernail of paint off the flaking mast, tapping at the wooden hull where it was rotting. He seemed much taller and straighter than the other men, but North wasn't sure if this was an optical illusion. Maybe he selected short, awkward men to enhance his own bearing. His actions were so studied, so exaggerated, that he seemed a parody of himself: North peered at him to make sure that it wasn't Cash or Dosh trying out a particularly convincing outfit for the clown military show. Panicked laughter tickled in North's throat, and she swallowed it down hard.

The captain lifted the folded sail from its cubby. From a distance, in the darkness, the sail made a lushly exotic big top, but up close the silk was spattered with wrinkled pocks and different coloured threads where tears had been darned. In the circus, nothing should be seen close up.

'What is this, dampling?'

North glanced at Red Gold; he was frowning at the captain, unsure how to answer. The truth seemed cheeky, but anything except the truth was unacceptable.

'A sail?' said the ringmaster.

'Are you asking me or telling me?'

'It's a sail. And it's also our big top – or it will be, if you fine gentlemen allow us to perform this evening.'

The captain thudded across the deck. He stopped short of Red Gold; he probably wasn't used to being the smaller man in a conflict, but the ringmaster dwarfed everyone.

'Is that disrespect, dampling?'

The military captain stood as steady as an anchor, as if the deck of the boat was the crest of a hill. But behind him the other military men swayed with the motion of the boat, fidgeting with the weapons holstered at their belts: knives, clubs, a cleaver that looked more suited to hacking meat than subduing damplings. They were not subtle in their intimidation.

Red Gold gave up his attempt at boisterous charm and bowed his head like a chastised child.

'No, sir. It's the mainsail, sir.'

North saw Avalon avert her eyes from the ringmaster and shift uncomfortably in her beatific pose. Her pride seemed to have been knocked, and something in this knocked North too. She bowed her head so that Red Gold would not see the hot rush of shame that heated her cheeks: shame for her shabby home, shame for her cowed captain and his faithless wife, shame for all of their silences.

Then she remembered Callanish during the Resting: the calm hands, the steady voice. The gracekeeper didn't bow her head, and neither would North. She lifted her chin and straightened her back. Soon the military would tire of them, and she would settle her bear, and she would find Melia, and they would all perform, and then they would eat and drink as if this had never happened. They just had to grit their teeth until then.

'You know why we've boarded, dampling,' sighed the captain. 'You may as well give it up.'

North felt a flutter, the thrust of a fledgling foot. She locked her fingers over her belly as if to still it. There was a movement in the corner of her eye. She glanced up and was surprised to see that Avalon was mirroring her action.

For a moment, North and Avalon looked at each other, mother to mother. North knew that Avalon's heart was coal and that the flames would catch them all; but at that moment her own chest felt full of fire too.

The military captain strode over to Avalon and laid his heavy arm across her shoulders. After a moment he patted her belly in an avuncular way, directing an expression bump-wards that was half sneer and half grimace. Avalon simpered a smile up at him, but North could see the tension in her arms, the twitch of a muscle in her cheek. He squeezed Avalon's shoulder and addressed Red Gold.

'It seems you have a lot to lose here, dampling, so let's not play games. Captain to captain. For you are a captain' - he cast his eyes around the scrubbed and peeling deck of the *Excalibur* - 'of a sort. There's been a report of activity from your convoy. What have you to say about that?'

Red Gold kept his eyes down. 'Nothing, sir.'

'Nothing, is it?' He motioned to his line of military men; one of them produced a roll of fabric. The captain let go of Avalon, then unrolled the fabric and consulted the rows of neatly printed numbers.

'So, dampling. You're confirming that if my men were to check your convoy, we would find – let's see – thirteen crewmembers?'

He glanced up. Seeing Red Gold's expression of panic, he made a point of frowning down at the fabric again. 'Shall I name them for you?'

'We did lose one crewmember. There was a storm, sir.'

'Was it a recent storm, hmm? The past few nights, perhaps?'

'No, sir.'

'And yet you did not update the military records. You have no documentation whatsoever.'

'No, sir. Sorry, sir.'

'Is that not part of the Resting procedure, dampling? Is it not – and correct me if I'm wrong, though I rarely am – is it not impossible to conduct a Resting at a graceyard without the proper documentation?'

Without looking, the captain passed the fabric back to one of his men. He stepped towards Red Gold – careful, still, not to get too close.

'You're right, sir, but we didn't ...' The ringmaster trailed off. He glanced up at Avalon, but her expression stayed blank.

'Didn't have the documentation, or didn't conduct a proper Resting? Think carefully on your answer, dampling. Someone is in serious trouble here, and I suspect it is you.'

'I ... sir, we ...'

'And we have not even begun to discuss this morning's transgression, have we? Let me explain. Before it left port this morning, the revival boat *Stella Maris* submitted a report. This report states that the *Stella Maris*'s crew has increased by one. This one new member claims she is from the *Excalibur* – which, you may have noticed, is this very convoy. The problem, captain' – and he made the word sound like a curse – 'the problem is that there was no report from you about your crew reducing. Do you see how we must be sure of these numbers? People cannot be allowed to slip through the cracks in the deck. Before you make me promises, I suggest you check your own boats.'

'I don't... I haven't checked today, sir.'

'Oh, dampling. Here I am, presented with a captain who cannot even control his own crew – well, it would be irresponsible of me to allow such a man to retain ownership of a convoy, would it not?'

From the harbour, chains clanked and birds shrieked and ships scraped into their moorings; from the other boats, waves slapped and damplings called and fishing lines squealed. But on the *Excalibur*, they all choked on silence.

Underneath it all, North heard the low vibrations of her bear beginning to growl. It took everything in her not to glance over at her coracle. She did not dare look up to see if Red Gold could hear it too.

'Shall we –' Red Gold coughed the waver from his throat. 'Shall we go belowdecks, sir? I believe I have the proper documentation there.'

'Ah, now there's a good dampling. I knew you had it all along.'

The two captains disappeared, and North did not need to hear the clink of coins to know that Red Gold was saving the *Excalibur* once more. The bribe took only moments, but it would take the circus many months to save up for another visit from the military.

Realising that there would be no need to wield their weapons, the military men had lost interest in the *Excalibur*. Without orders from their captain they didn't dare to disembark and head for their own boat, but they turned their gaze to the island instead of fixing it on North and Avalon.

Avalon swayed over to North; North gripped the handles on the gunwale to steady herself for the onslaught.

'Are you well, north child?' said Avalon in an undertone. 'Is the baby well?'

North tried to hide her surprise. 'Yes, thank you, Avalon. And yours?'

Avalon sighed. 'Weathering the storm. It's a tough one. Half ring-master, after all.'

'You don't need to weather anything now. The storm is over,' whispered North. From her coracle came no growls, no bumps or roars. She felt the sun's warmth on her shoulders; saw its bright glints catching in her eyelashes. 'Look around you, Avalon. It's over.'

With a thud of boots and an out-of-tune whistle, the captain emerged from belowdecks.

'Did you think the storm had passed, little urchin?' crooned Avalon into North's ear. 'We're in the eye. And just you wait until we emerge. It will be glorious.'

North pulled back from Avalon, her hip bumping hard against the gunwale. The convoy was small, but she could still stay as far away from Avalon as possible.

The captain nodded to his men, who filed messily off on to their own boat, hands on their weapons. One or two glanced back, all the better to remember Avalon, who had a conventional sort of beauty, North supposed. One of the men glanced over at North and she stared at the deck, trying to be invisible.

The captain stepped on to his boat and turned around, one foot still on the *Excalibur*, straddling the boats. It was an awkward pose but he'd chosen it now, and it would be weak to fidget.

'I hope I won't have to see you again, dampling.'

'No, sir. Yes, sir,' muttered Red Gold, louder than he must have meant.

The captain paused, one foot still on the deck.

The *Excalibur* teetered.

'I'll be watching,' said the captain.

And then his boot left the schooner, and the military boat sailed on to the next convoy, and without all those booted feet the *Excalibur* felt light, light enough to float up to the clouds. Relief made North giddy.

Avalon turned her back to North and pressed her body into Red Gold's arms, stretching up to whisper something in his ear.

That beast, North heard, and something about danger. Before she could separate more words from the rapid crooning, Avalon turned and went back into the *Excalibur*'s cabin. Red Gold was left staring at nothing. He didn't seem to know what to do with his arms now that his wife was not in them.

North wanted to thank him but her tongue would not form the words. Her coracle bobbed in the swell of the military's boat, silent now. She needed to return to it but she hesitated, afraid of what she knew would be missing from it.

'It was Melia, wasn't it?' she asked Red Gold. 'On the revival boat. She's gone.'

He did not reply. North had so many questions that they tangled in her mouth and she said nothing at all. If Ainsel would not ask his father to call off the wedding, she had no choice but to get married. Angering the ringmaster meant she would be kicked off the *Excalibur*, with no food, no shelter, no payment to buy her way on to a new boat, and no bear to perform with even if she made it to another circus. All she could do now was go back to her coracle and begin the routines of another day: feeding, washing, dressing, performing.

She stepped off the boat's stern and on to the tow-chain, but Red Gold's hand on her ankle stopped her. She glanced up at him, surprised. He seemed surprised too, as he pulled back his hand and placed it on the stern.

'I'm sorry,' he said. 'I'm sorry, North. I didn't know about Melia. That she was planning to leave us. There are coins missing from my cabin. She must have bought her way on board.' Even though his hand was steady on the stern, North could see how it shook. 'It's over. There's no use in weeping for those who have chosen to leave. Now go and tend to your bear. He will be fractious.'

The schooner caught in the swell of a retreating boat and North wobbled on the chain, one foot slipping off to dip into the water. To her shock, Red Gold seized her by the shoulders and lifted her on to the *Excalibur*'s deck.

'Damn it, North!' he snapped. 'Be careful. Don't you think I've lost too much in this ocean already?'

Surprise stole North's words, but Red Gold did not seem to notice; after depositing her on the deck, he turned away from her to look out towards the island.

'When will he be tame?'

North froze. 'He is tame.'

'Don't lie to me. We both heard the growls.'

'I... he was confused. I left him alone for too long. It's my fault, not his.' North tried to keep the pleading note out of her voice. 'You know he's safe, Jarrow. He's never hurt anyone.'

Red Gold sighed. 'Oh, my sweet north child. He is a beast, and he will always be wild.' He turned to North, reaching his meaty hands out to her. 'The bear can never be tame. But you can.' He took her hands in his. 'You'll soon wonder how you ever lived at sea,' he said. 'You'll learn to sleep on land. You'll learn to love the steadiness of earth, the lullaby of trees in the wind. You'll watch the afternoon swing a bar of sunlight up the wall, and you'll wonder how you ever lived on a deck that never stays still. Your world will become rock and shell and trees. You'll love it, North. You will make it your home.'

Inside North, the baby woke. It wriggled, it shifted; it turned a somersault in the ocean of her insides.

'Yes, I will,' said North to Jarrow. 'I will make my home.'

18
Flitch

When Flitch first let the gracekeeper girl on to his boat, the moon was full. The days had slipped by, and when the moon rolled its round white eye around again, he knew something had to change – so he'd shown her that he knew about her scars. That she was his little fish. But when the sun replaced the moon the next morning, things slipped back, just like the other days. They bartered, they cooked, they sailed. Tonight the moon's eye would roll around again. Two months was enough to eat up all the unsaid things between two people, but for the two of them the silence remained. She would not let him beneath her skin.

Luckily for Flitch, he was a good observer. She'd had her blood twice, he knew it – though he was man enough not to let her know that he knew. Flitch was like that. He was a good man, a proper man, no matter what people said about messengers. The other messengers were like that, but he was not. Well, he had been like that at times, but the ocean was vast, and good at keeping secrets.

Anyone could see that he was a good man by the way he had been treating Callanish. Even after she'd taken him into her bed on their very first meeting. Anyone else would have thought that was an invitation to more. Anyone else would have expected it, would have made her – well, would not have been a man, like he had been. He had been good to her. She'd better know it. And when the time came, she'd better show it.

Despite the mist and the silence and the squid eating their lobster, Flitch did not lose heart. He was a messenger, after all. He'd had tougher times than this, and he'd have tougher ones in the future. This was nothing.

But a gracekeeper and a messenger were from different worlds. Flitch hadn't seen it at first. He'd watched Callanish gut mackerel, stitch up the sail, drink as fast as he could fill her cup – and he'd thought that she could handle it. He'd thought there was a shark's heart inside her. But it was all a shell. Slowly, slowly, he watched the softness creep into her. He'd said that he would get her to her island, and he would – but at their current pace she would soften and crumble like dry sand before they even sighted the coast.

'We need to hitch a lift,' he announced over their breakfast of boiled seaweed and fried baby squid – well, if the squid were going to eat his lobster, then he would eat their young in return.

The squid was tough, and Callanish chewed and swallowed carefully before speaking. 'On a military tanker?'

'Don't be daft, little fish. A pretty little landlocker like you, among all those brutes? Think what might happen! It would never be allowed. It's improper.'

'And you'd know about that, I suppose, Mr Propriety.'

Flitch raised his eyebrows. 'Whatever can you mean?'

'You must have heard what people say about messengers.'

'That we'll do anything for a few flecks of gold?' He poked his tongue out at her, displaying a half-chewed sucker. 'It's true. But experience means knowledge, little fish, and I have experienced many military tankers. That's not the way for us.'

'Then what? A medic boat? They're big but they don't go far, or fast.'

'Don't worry your pretty little head. You leave the thinking to me.'

Callanish did not start on a new piece of squid. Instead she glared at Flitch until he gave in.

'A revival boat, little fish. That's where we need to go.'

'And how will we do that? I haven't seen one since we left the grace-yard. Should we send up a prayer to the lady in the blue robes? Say to her, *pretty please come and collect us?*'

'Don't try to be smart. It doesn't suit you.'

Callanish's eyes darted to the canvas bag containing Flitch's razor – then she seemed to think better of it, and returned to her breakfast. Flitch grinned; maybe there was a bit of shark in her after all.

'You may not have seen one,' he said, 'but I have. That's why I'm in charge around here, and not you. Because I know how to use my eyes.'

He reached behind the bench and handed Callanish his telescope. She scowled at it for a moment before raising it to her eye. She was still suspicious – what cheek! After all he'd done for her. Still, in the end she'd show her appreciation. Flitch knew that he was not the only one who needed company.

'Which way?' she asked.

'North.' He waited for her to shift and focus. 'See it?'

'It's far.'

'Have faith, little fish! I find you the perfect ship, going in the perfect direction, and you tell me it's too far?'

Callanish shrugged, but she did not put down the telescope. She kept it trained in the direction of the revival boat, transfixed. 'I'll help you sail,' she said. 'When you're tired. Or I can do the lobster creels.'

'You won't need to. It won't take us long to catch up. Until then you can cook my meals and look pretty, like you've been doing all along. And if you want to be wearing less while you do it, all the better.'

Flitch thought he'd gone too far then. Callanish jerked back the telescope and he felt a quick heat of fear that she was planning to jam it into his eye. He held up his hands. 'Keep your temper, little fish. If that goes in the sea, you'll be the one who has to dive in after it.'

She handed the telescope back to him a bit more roughly than was necessary. 'Fine, Flitch. Whatever you say. Just get me to the island.'

It took them less than a day to catch up with the revival ship. Its size lent it speed, but it chose to move slowly. All the better to pick up new converts along the way, thought Flitch – though he and his grace-keeper girl wouldn't be signing up to anything, oh no sir. But messengers knew the way of all types of boat, and if he had to raise his eyes to the sky and chant some holy-holies to earn his passage, then he would do it with gusto.

Soon they were almost close enough to hail the enormous ship. Flitch lifted Callanish up on to his shoulder so that she could tie the beacon to the top of the mast. The wet silk of her gloves made it hard for her to knot the rope, and she still refused to go bare-handed. It was ridiculous – did she really think that he didn't know about her webbed fingers by now? He supposed that if the landlockers saw, they'd probably burn her alive or tie her screaming to some sacred tree, or cut out her heart and eat it on a slice of bread. Flitch didn't mind it so much. It was repulsive, but he'd seen worse, and he had excellent self-control. Not only did he resist slipping a hand up her dress, he didn't even sneak a glance. For that, he should certainly get some credit. Besides, he'd seen the contents of her underwear before, and was blessed with vivid powers of recall.

Flitch steadied the cutter as Callanish busied herself with wrapping and stowing anything moveable on deck. It was tricky: the revival ship's wake was strong and erratic, and it took all of Flitch's strength to keep the cutter steady. If he hadn't been a messenger then the skin would have scraped off his knuckles and the muscles would be burning in his back. But he was a messenger, so he felt none of it. He kept his breathing slow and steady so that Callanish would not hear his struggle.

Callanish sat in the boat's bow, gaping up at the approaching wall of the revival boat's hull. She seemed not to be concentrating as she leaned over and dipped her fingers into the sea to clean her gloves – usually she would use the water in the filter, and Flitch was about to tell her to stop, because when the saltwater dried it would make the fabric rough on her poor soft skin, and she struggled enough with the knots, so he didn't want her to be completely useless to him. But before he could, she lifted her hand and gazed at it in disgust. The glove was slickened dark with oil and filth.

'What is that?' she asked, rubbing her hands in the remains of the filtered water to clean them. As they drew closer to the revival boat, the bumps and thocks against the side of the cutter increased. He didn't need to look to know what it was: frayed ends of rope, the hollow bones of birds, dirty sponges, scraps of fabric sewn with beads. All the big boats left filth in their wake.

Flitch shrugged and kept the boat steady. 'Debris. Those revival boats are clean as fishbones, because they throw all their muck out behind them.'

'But what about everyone else? What about their boats?' Hands clean, she took her place back in the bow. The closer the cutter got to the revival ship, the denser the filth became. Now they could see the name *Stella Maris*, painted in enormous gold letters on the gleaming white hull. As they neared, Callanish pressed her nose into her shoulder, but Flitch didn't need a reprieve from the smell because he was a proper man and he could take it. He could take anything.

'What about them?' said Flitch. 'Little fish, the folk in that boat are too high up to care.'

'But it's not right! Everyone else scavenges and reuses until their things fall apart. Everything can be used for something. It's not right. If they don't need it, they should share it.'

'Ah, so you're angry because they're rich? Because they don't have to scratch around for every single thing they eat or touch or use? You have a lot to learn, little fish. There's no use in the poor hating the rich. There's more to the world than landlockers versus damplings. And we all know what side of the balance you're from.'

'I don't need to learn that,' she snapped. 'Don't pretend you know me, Flitch.'

Flitch knew a lot more about Callanish than she thought, but now was not the time to point that out. Her blood was due, after all, and girls could get uppity when the moon turned. Instead he kept sailing, pulling in level with the stately pace of the revival ship until they acknowledged his beacon.

They did not have to float in filth for much longer. With a clank-flosh, a chain was thrown over the side, just missing the cutter's deck. The revival ship was too tall for Flitch to see who'd performed the clumsy throw, so his withering look was wasted. Quickly he furled the sails. He instructed Callanish to grab the mast, then fastened the chains to the cutter. He held tight to Callanish as the cutter jolted, and they were hoisted into the sky.

Flitch was pleased that he managed to appear unimpressed by the revival ship. He wouldn't have bothered, but Callanish was there, and she was clearly unnerved. The more uncomfortable she seemed, the more important it was for him to be calm and confident. It was his duty to be the man in the situation.

Revival ships are always big, but this one was a beast: big enough to house a dozen blue whales, with seven decks and all its windows intact and every surface gleaming white as bone. As he watched, a blue-robed revivalist slid from the upper deck window with a rope around her waist. She steadied her feet on the boat's side, then reached for the cloth and bucket attached to her waist and began to scrub it as if the ship was caked in filth. It looked clean enough to Flitch – but then, maybe religion made you see dirt where no one else could.

'I need to speak to your captain,' he announced to the trio of scrunch-faced, blue-robed revivalists who'd hauled up the cutter. Two of them were occupied with lashing the cutter to the deck, but the other abandoned his work to peer down his nose at Flitch.

'You will speak to the crew manager.'

Flitch had no idea what a crew manager was, or where he could find one – but Callanish was standing right next to him, so he kept his expression steady.

'Fine by me. Where do you keep him?'

'Deck three. Port side, cabin nine. And, messenger?' The revivalist laid a commanding hand on Flitch's shoulder. 'Show your respect. Your wife is uncovered.'

Flitch's face jerked into a sneer. Before the revivalist noticed, he managed to slide it into a wheedling smile. 'Of course, sir. Whatever you say, sir. I'll sort that out right now, sir.'

It was cheeky, but the revivalist seemed placated. He was clearly a fool, but he had the cutter now, and Flitch could go nowhere without it. He and Callanish would both have to fit in with the holy-holies if they wanted to get to the island.

He put his arm around Callanish and pulled her into the shadow of the upper deck.

'You're indecent,' he said.

She pushed him away. 'I am not!'

'Little fish, it's been too long. Look at yourself. Is that how you want the revivalists to see you? Is that how you dressed at your graceyard?'

Callanish, still frowning, looked down at herself. When she'd first come on to his cutter, her dress was grey, long and loose; now it was faded and torn, the bottom hem ripped above her knees, the fabric so thin it was almost transparent in places. When she raised her head, she looked shocked.

'Flitch, I didn't know. I didn't think about it – I didn't see. What can I do?'

Flitch shrugged. 'Makes no matter to me. But if we want the revivalists to play nice, we'll have to be what they want us to be.'

'And what's that?'

'Don't you know anything? Revivalists want women to show true faith. So what would that mean to you?'

'Stop being awkward, Flitch. On my island we worshipped the World Tree, all right? And I don't see any trees on this damned ship, so if you could stop being a pain and tell me what I'm supposed to do then we can –'

'Calm, calm, little fish.' He put his hands on Callanish's shoulders, pressing down when she tried to shrug him off. 'I'm sorry. I won't tease you again.'

'Yes, you will. You know you will.' Her muscles were still tensed, but he saw a smile ghost across her face.

'You're right. I will. But for now...' He ran back to the cutter and retrieved his spare blanket from the hold. 'For now, wear this.'

Callanish took the blanket, unsure. After a moment she draped it over her head like a shawl, then gave him a questioning glance. He tipped his head back to let his laugh go.

'Little fish, you crack me up! No one's asking you to be the Holy Virgin. Here, this is what I meant.'

He pulled the blanket off her head and wrapped it around her chest, folding and knotting the corners at her shoulders. It hung down to her ankles, covering her body in a mass of fabric.

'There,' he said. 'You look terrible. The revivalists will love it. Now let's go and find this man before they decide we're too grubby and throw us off the stern.'

The more Flitch saw of the revival ship, the harder it was to appear nonchalant in front of Callanish. The ship was so huge that he was sure the sun had crossed the sky by the time they found deck three. It was impossible to know for sure, though, as the gangways were windowless. After years spent almost entirely on his cutter, Flitch got anxious when he could not see the sky.

From the outside, the door to cabin nine looked like all the others: shiny metal panelling, with a shiny metal number bolted above the shiny metal handle. All metal was salvaged, but this looked brand new. Or at least, how Flitch imagined it would look brand new. It must have been hammered and sandpapered and polished and polished and polished. After wandering down dozens of scrubbed-shining gangways, Flitch's eyes ached. On every gangway they'd had to step over at least one revival-ist with a cloth and bucket, scrubbing at the already spotless walls. Flitch knocked on the door to cabin nine and waited to be summoned.

'Yes.' It was not a question, but still Flitch answered by turning the handle and holding the door open for Callanish. He thought that the crew manager, being a revivalist, would identify with a bit of old-style chivalry.

He didn't know what he'd expected of the crew manager, but it was not what he got: a pale-lipped woman with black hair in thick spiral curls. She wore the blue of all revivalists, but instead of robes she had on a modest knee-length dress.

The room was all bone white and shiny silver, as thoroughly scrubbed as the rest of the ship. A deep shelf ran at head height all around the edge of the room, with objects placed on it at regular intervals. Flitch tried to take it all in at once: the gleaming gold orbs, the tiny glass vials, the stacks of silver coins, the candlesticks studded with red and purple gems. He reminded himself to breathe.

'You must be new,' said the woman. 'Welcome home.'

Flitch couldn't see Callanish's face, but her body language was enough. She was terrified, humbled, excited. He'd forgotten how small her world was. Had she even met a revivalist before? Did she understand what the woman meant by the welcome?

'Thank you,' he said, silently willing Callanish to trust him. 'We appreciate your kindness.'

The woman nodded, motioning Flitch and Callanish on to the bench in front of her desk. A glint amid her hair: jewels, set in shiny metal, dangled from her earlobes. Up until that moment, Flitch had forgotten how it felt to covet. He blinked the gleam out of his eyes.

'I regret that we cannot remain as permanent members,' he said. 'But we have heard much about your generosity and were hopeful that you could help us. We wish to get to the North-West 22 archipelago.'

The woman raised her eyebrows and opened a drawer in her desk. Flitch stretched his spine, peering over the far lip of the desk. She spotted the movement and stopped him with a frown, but not before he'd seen that she was consulting a map. He sat back and smiled at her in a manner both humble and charming.

Flitch knew that if he could get under her desk and under her dress, he could get under her skin – and then she would do whatever he asked. It was the best way to get what you wanted from a woman. Not so easy with Callanish shadowing his every move, though. Still, his manners were pretty enough to get him through. And a bit of flirting never hurt.

'Some nice shiny stuff you've got here,' he said. 'If you weren't all such good people, I'd suspect it was stolen.' He held back a wink, but allowed her a cheeky grin.

'We do not steal. We liberate.'

'If these are holy objects, shouldn't they be in a holy place? A sacred copse, but – well, on a boat?' asked Callanish. Flitch cursed himself for not telling her to stay quiet.

The crew manager looked up from her map and regarded them with an expression of long-suffering patience. 'Everywhere on the revival ship is a holy place. Everywhere must be fit for worship and everything must be sacred.'

Flitch resisted the urge to ask whether the revivalists' shit was sacred too.

'Of course,' he soothed. 'That makes perfect sense. And if I were in your position, I'm sure –'

The woman slammed her drawer shut. 'You are not in my position, and you never will be. I am not asking why a messenger is travelling with a landlocker. I am not asking why she is not on her home island. I am not asking about the nature of this ... relationship. You may thank God's grace for that. We are travelling towards the North-West archipelago. You may stay on board until then.'

Flitch forced out a smile. He wasn't sure what she would want in return for letting them tag along. Sex? Money? Faith? Flitch was pretty good with the first, but he'd long run out of the other two. Still, he would try to make her believe that he could believe.

'Thank you,' he said. 'We had heard of your generosity, but the glory you have shown is –'

'You are here to be saved, and salvation comes from work. Go to the next gangway. You will be issued with cleaning materials. You will have noticed as you came aboard what happens to dirt on this ship. Mind you keep clean.'

'Right,' said Flitch. 'Thank you. Shall we just ... ?'

But she had already dismissed them.

19
Callanish

That night, the revivalists put on a show. Callanish accepted Flitch's offer to sit with him in the dampling section and watch, but now the show was starting she found it hard to make her eyes focus. Still, it was a distraction. She'd scrub, she'd gut fish, she'd watch a revival show: anything to make the days go by faster, so she would be at her island quickly. And, at the same time, she'd do anything to make the days feel dull and endless, so that she would never arrive at her island.

WELCOME, WELCOME, TO EACH AND EVERY ONE OF GOD'S CHILDREN, boomed the preacher from the stage, his voice caramel-rich and too heavy to echo, filling the enormous space at the heart of the revival ship. Earlier that day they'd used this as a dining room, but now the tables and chairs had been cleared to leave an empty deck that was quickly filled with revivalists, damplings who'd docked nearby, and the brave landlockers who dared to cross the blackshore. To one side stretched a stage, dominated by a huge banner of the blue-robed Virgin.

At first the sheer number of people in the room had panicked Callanish; it was more people than she'd seen in one place in her entire life. She tried to count, but lost track in the triple figures. Flitch was restless beside her, and the room was warm with mingled breath.

THIS EVENING WE WILL SHOW YOU GOD'S LOVE, continued the preacher, his voice intimate now, AND WE WILL TEACH YOU, AS WE HOPE YOU WILL TEACH US, and whatever that was supposed to mean, Callanish didn't know. The preacher was dressed in the same blue as all the revivalists, but the fabric of his suit seemed richer and denser than the usual rough cotton – and was that a fresh flower in his button-hole? No, it couldn't be. Callanish scrunched up her eyes to see better. She had not seen a fresh flower since she left her island. Except, now that she thought about it, hadn't she seen one... where? In someone's hair, thick and treacle-dark hair, and there was some bad feeling attached to that – the memory loomed up, the pregnant woman from the circus, with her imperious face and scent of pollen, but even as the memory solidified it began to fade away again to be replaced with something else, something good. The bear. The bear-girl. The beat of a heart.

AND SO OUR TALE BEGINS, said the preacher, his voice returned to its boom, WITH THE SORRIEST OF GOD'S CHILDREN IN THE SORRIEST OF SITUATIONS, AND PERHAPS – his voice dropped again, bedroom-soft – PERHAPS YOU WILL SEE A LITTLE OF YOURSELF IN THE STORY.

Lost in thought, Callanish had missed the set-up, but she soon found her place: the preacher was bemoaning the fate of the forsaken sinner, who was represented by a woman in glittery scraps and painted red lips, balanced on a perch so high she could almost touch the ceiling.

OBSERVE THE FRAGILITY OF THE SINNER'S FOUNDATIONS, said the preacher with a dramatic gesture at the sinner's perch, FOR WITHOUT GOD'S LOVE SHE IS UNSTEADY WHEREVER SHE STANDS.

Throughout these proclamations the preacher was pacing the stage, raising his hands skywards, and ALAS! he proclaimed, PITY THE POOR SINNER, and to Callanish's surprise the crowd all bewailed 'Alas!' and – most surprising of all – Flitch joined in with them. She turned, eyebrows raised, to find him winking back at her while crowing 'Alas! Oh, alas!' and shaking his fists gleefully at the ceiling. Callanish suppressed a smile, not wanting the crowd to think she was mocking them.

When the crowd had reached sufficient volume, all the lights fell to black, leaving only a spotlight trained on the preacher. He pointed his finger and swept it around the room, his voice booming over the crowd's wailing, YOU WILL SEE, MY CHILDREN, THAT A BEDROCK OF SIN IS NO BEDROCK AT ALL.

On his last word the spotlight swooped up to the forsaken sinner, in time to show the crowd how she twisted, turned, and slipped off her perch – dropped down, down, down – and as the crowd readied themselves for the crack of bone, the bright reveal of blood, the sinner straightened her arms, letting the ropes looped around her wrists catch her and she jolted to a halt – her muscles juddering, her body suspended at head height above the hard wooden stage.

THIS IS GOD'S LOVE, announced the preacher, his tones honeyed once more, FOR GOD'S LOVE WILL ALWAYS CATCH US BEFORE WE FALL. The sinner – now presumably saved – unlooped her arms from the rope and landed neatly before the preacher.

BUT WE MUST ALWAYS, continued the preacher, and Callanish wasn't listening because there was something familiar about that sinner. She leaned across Flitch the better to see the stage, but she must have been blocking his view for he pushed her back. She turned, frowning, trying to explain, and he must not have been able to hear her now that the preacher was rhapsodising WE MUST ALWAYS HOLD ON TO OUR FAITH AS WE WOULD HOLD ON TO A ROPE, and Callanish was trying to tell Flitch that she knew the sinner, she knew her from somewhere but she didn't know where. He wasn't listening, too distracted by the now-saved sinner who, despite having oddly large arms and shoulders for a woman, was still dressed in a sinner's glittery scraps, which Flitch would surely think was more important than anything Callanish had to say.

BUT WE MUST NEVER – and here the preacher's voice took on a forbidding edge – WE MUST NEVER CLING TO UNHOLY THINGS, and he took hold of the sinner's dress and, in one swift movement, tore it off.

The crowd gasped, shrieked, couldn't decide whether to cover their eyes or lean forward for a better view. But underneath the glittery scraps the sinner was clothed in a flesh-coloured bodysuit, and it seemed to Callanish that she might as well be naked, except that technically no skin was on show, and she had an enormous flaming heart painted on her chest, from her collarbone right down to her breasts. Callanish wasn't sure what the heart meant, but the crowd seemed to know, as they all leapt to their feet and clapped and cheered. The sinner swooned into the preacher's arms, making the tears painted on her cheeks sparkle.

As he held her, the preacher was saying THE KNOTS OF OUR LOVE FOR GOD WILL HOLD FAST THROUGH ANY STORM, and Callanish shouted into Flitch's ear: 'I know her.'

'Who?' he mouthed back.

'The sinner. But she's not a sinner, she's an acrobat in a circus.'

She could hardly hear herself over the burr of the preacher and the praise-shrieking of the crowd, but Flitch must have heard. He tipped back his head and laughed right up at the ceiling.

'Clever, clever, little fish!' He leaned in close and shouted into Callanish's ear, intimate despite the crowd. 'But don't let the revivalists hear you call it a circus. They won't take kindly to that.'

Callanish shook her head, mouthing, 'No, I didn't mean –'

It didn't matter. The show had reached its climax and the crowd had rushed the stage, frantic to touch the saved sinner, to be blessed by the preacher. Callanish hunched over in her seat, trying not to let any of the passing limbs hit her.

For the revivalists, the show had been a success. By the next morning, their crew would be even larger – but soon Callanish would not be a part of it.

Callanish spent the rest of her time on the revival boat – fifty-nine window-washings, twenty-one deck-scrubbings, ninety-two sheet-rinsings – trying to be alone with the acrobat. At first she'd hoped that the acrobat's presence meant that the whole circus was on board, but she soon realised that was impossible. If the revivalists had a bear, the revival show would have a bear.

Her task was not easy. Even at night Callanish was surrounded by revivalists; as she and Flitch weren't married, the crew manager had forbidden them to share a cabin, eliciting a barely suppressed snigger from Flitch and a not-at-all-suppressed grimace from Callanish. Instead she was assigned to a narrow bunk among many rows of identical bunks, each occupied by a blue-robed revivalist, their eyes glassy with bliss and their conversation breathy and excited. This suited Callanish, as she was not interested in eye contact or deep discussion.

She attended the revival show each night, but watching the acrobat tumble and swoon did not bring them any closer. During the day, she'd catch glimpses of her reflected in the passageways' polished floors as she trailed after the preacher, but Callanish clung to her mop and stayed silent. The acrobat had clearly confessed her past on the circus boat, or the preacher would not have known to cast her as the tumbling sinner – but still, Callanish did not want to mention it in front of anyone else. She dug through her memory, trying to retrieve the acrobat's name, but North and the bear loomed so large in her mind that they blotted out all the other circus folk.

With each passing day, the air grew colder and the sky paler. The boat was edging further north, and Callanish knew they would soon arrive at her home archipelago. She needed to ask the acrobat about the bear-girl before that happened. Rather than wait for an opportunity that might never come, she resolved to make one.

The next night, she slipped into the revival show as late as she dared, to get the perfect seat: at the back, on the edge. She moved slowly and kept her head bowed so that her neighbour wouldn't notice her. She waited until the crowd's wails of ALAS for the poor sinner reached a crescendo, and she slipped away - not through the door she'd entered by, but through the back. This passageway was windowless and gleaming like all the others, though Callanish was sure it was not one she'd polished.

She waited.

She heard the shrieks, the wails of joy, the staggered silences that meant the acrobat's fall, her unrobing, her swoon.

Still she waited.

The door opened, making the last of the applause blare into the passageway, and the acrobat appeared.

'Hello, my sister,' she said.

'Hello - sister.' Callanish's tongue tripped over the word. The acrobat smiled and turned to walk away. 'Wait. Please. I want to ask you - to tell you - I know you.'

'That is good, my sister. We are all friends here.' The acrobat rested a hand on Callanish's wrist - to soothe, Callanish thought, but then realised it was in defence - she had grabbed the acrobat's muscled shoulder. She eased her grip.

'I mean I know you, the real you. Not this you.'

The acrobat frowned.

'Sorry,' mumbled Callanish. 'I - sorry. I'm not making sense. Do you recognise me? We've met before. You visited me to - you came after your . . . I'm a gracekeeper. You were at my graceyard. Do you remember?'

A flicker passed over the acrobat's face – pain, panic – though it was quickly smoothed out. 'It does not matter what came before,' she said. 'It only matters that we repent and live our lives cleanly and correctly. That is the only way that we will reach heaven, where our loved ones await.'

The acrobat peeled Callanish's hand off her shoulder – a little harder than necessary, Callanish thought, though to be fair she was probably coming across like a madwoman – and turned to go.

'I won't ask anything else of you,' Callanish said. 'I'm leaving the ship soon and I may never see you again, so I have to ask now. I need to know how to find the circus. I mean, I might want – I might need to find it again. Do you know where the circus is now?'

The acrobat tightened her jaw. 'Once the devil has touched you, you'll always carry the scar. You can never get rid of him, not completely. He'll take everything from you.'

'So you know how I can find them?' asked Callanish.

'Sister, trust me when I say that you don't want them. That circus, it's cursed. You can't make that many sparks and not expect one of them to catch. That whole sinning lot is going to burn, you'll see.'

Callanish forced her face into a smile. 'I'll stay safe. My business with the circus is minor. I will return to the revival ship afterwards, of course, to do my true duty. And I may not need the circus at all. But first I must cleanse myself. There are threads in my life as yet untied, and I must atone.'

The acrobat's expression softened. 'I understand. I know all about purgatory. And we all have to cleanse ourselves.'

The noise behind the door had lessened; soon the preacher would extricate himself from his ecstatic children and sweep the acrobat under his arm once more. It was a risk, but Callanish took it: she grasped the acrobat's hands in her own and squeezed. Tears prickled, and that was one thing she did not have to fake.

'Please,' she said. 'You're the only one who can help me.'

After a moment, the acrobat squeezed back. 'I'd say you're in luck, sister, but there's no luck to be had at that circus. They've been behind us this whole time, lurking on the horizon. I fear they want to steal me back. They have not taken enough from me, and now they want the rest.'

Callanish thought it more likely that the ships were simply following the same sailing route, but she didn't point that out. 'The same way the revivalists stole you?' she asked.

'They did not steal me, sister. They saved me. But I am not afraid, for the circus sinners will not come close enough for thieving. They are kept at bay by the glory and power of Our Lady.'

Callanish thought it more likely that the circus folk wanted to avoid to performing on the same island on the same night as the revivalists, but she didn't point that out either. 'So tomorrow,' she said, 'when we go ashore at North-West 22, if I wait there then they'll come, and –'

'But we won't go ashore there.'

'What? Why?'

'They're pagans, my sister. Tree-worshippers. The preacher says that we have gained family from every island, in every archipelago, but never that one. They are irredeemable sinners. It would be a waste and a danger.'

The passageway was windowless, white-scrubbed, lined with door after door after door, but Callanish saw none of it: all she could see was the expanse of ocean between herself and her island.

'So all I have to do,' she murmured, more to herself than to the acrobat, 'is get from the ship to the island.' She began to wander away down the passageway, then rushed back to grip the acrobat's hands in thanks. 'From here to there!' she said. 'That's all I need. And then I'll know. And if I need to, I'll wait. For the circus, and the bear, and my – I'll wait.' She released the acrobat before wandering away in the other direction, head bowed.

'I hope someone saves you, my sister,' called the acrobat after her. 'Even if they have to steal you first.'

But Callanish barely heard. In her mind, she was already home.

The next morning Callanish woke before dawn. The room was restless with the sounds of sleep, but that was not why she woke. She could smell oak leaves. She inhaled so deeply she felt the muted clicking of her vertebrae. Eyes bleary, she slid from her bed. Through the door, down the passageways, up on to the deck, and still she could not breathe in deeply enough, and still she could be dreaming. Out of habit she checked her hands; she felt the silk gloves, and knew she was awake. In dreams her hands were always bare. In dreams she slipped into the sea and felt it soothe her tired, air-parched skin.

The night's cold hit her with a slap. She crossed her arms over her chest, hunching so that her blue nightgown covered her knees. From the deck of the boat, she saw her home island: the answer to her question. The scent of oak trees enveloped her.

She wanted to turn the ship around and sail to her empty graceyard without looking back. She sat cross-legged on the deck, back pressed hard against the wall, and watched her distant island.

Clouds thickened overhead. Through the gaps, the blackness smudged to grey, to pale blue, to the first pinkish wisps of dawn, and the oak-tree scent was as soft and comforting as a feather bed, and the air grew heavy around her, and perhaps she dozed off, because she snapped awake to the warm weight of an arm around her shoulders.

'Good morning, little fish. I see you've made it home.'

She shrugged off Flitch's arm and stood, feeling her joints crack. The first heavy raindrop plipped on to the deck.

'Not yet, Flitch. I won't really be there until my feet touch the land.'

'Don't be a silly fishy! You're so close. Can't you smell the trees? Can't you smell your mother?'

Callanish clenched her jaw and breathed hard before she could speak. 'You said you'd bring me home, and you did, and I am grateful. Thank you, Flitch. But I have to go now.'

Flitch smiled and turned his palms to the sky. 'In this terrible weather? We can't take the cutter out in this. We'll have to wait for the rain to stop. But whatever can we do to entertain ourselves until –' A raindrop hit his upturned palm and he frowned at it, rubbing his hand on his leg as if it had hurt. 'Until the rain stops? Speaking of which, we haven't agreed on a payment for my services.'

'I only have a few coins,' said Callanish. 'Nothing to trade. But you can have the coins, all of them. I'll get them right now.'

'Oh little fish, we always have something worth trading. You paid me before, didn't you? I'm sure there are plenty of coins left in that soft little purse of yours.' He leaned closer to her, rain heavy on his eyelashes. 'How about you make a partial payment now, hmm? Then when we rescue my cutter, maybe we can renegotiate terms.'

The rain grew heavier, thudding on Callanish's shoulders, and she saw it was not water now but ice, breaking apart as it ricocheted off her and smacked the deck.

'Seven coins is all I have, hidden in my pillow, and you can help yourself to every single one of them. But I'm not your little fish, Flitch.' She put her hand along his jaw. She felt his teeth clench, and resisted the urge to pull her hand away and punch him instead. His cheek was rough with stubble, his skin cool and damp from the hail. 'I don't want you. I want my mother, and I want the bear, and I want –'

A sudden thud, a shock of pain, and they stared as an acorn-sized hailstone skidded across the deck. Blood trickled from Flitch's head on to Callanish's hand, warm on her fingers even through the gloves. Disgust leapt in her and she took a step back. Flitch raised both hands to his head, his fingers coming away bloody.

'What did ... ?' he murmured. 'What hit me?'

Callanish pulled off her gloves and pressed them to the cut on his head, linking his hands together over the compress before letting go. She walked away from him, towards the edge. He could see her webbed fingers now. For all it mattered, the whole of the revival boat could see them. They could curse her and damn her and throw her into the sea, and it would not matter at all, because that had always been where she would end up. Below her, waves sucked at the boat, hungry for her. She had travelled halfway around the world and ended up exactly where she started.

The hail drummed on the deck, scudding messily, turning the polished metal white. The noise of it blocked all thought. Callanish concentrated on staying still, her feet slippery on the ice. She put her hands on the guardrail, Flitch's gaze weighing heavy on her back.

'Are you going to swim home, little fish? Those landlockers won't rescue you if you drown.'

One step, two steps. Her silk slippers were sodden and she slid out of them. She flexed her feet, stretching the webbing between her toes, feeling the chill of the guardrail against her bare soles.

'You can't swim that far! No one can!' Panic grated in Flitch's voice. 'Come back, Callanish. I need you. I won't call you little fish. I'll take you ashore, and I'll wait for you, and then I'll take you wherever else you want to go. You don't have to pay me anything. Just stay with me.'

Callanish paused, perched on top of the guardrail. The island was so close. Two hours of swimming; maybe three. Maybe more. But what choice did she have? She inhaled the scent of oak leaves. She jumped.

For two heartbeats she couldn't breathe. Couldn't think. Could only feel the way the wind caught her and seemed to hold her, to lift her –

'No!' Flitch was shouting after her, or maybe it was 'Go!' – she couldn't tell because the wind stole everything, all the sound, all the feeling, and she was an acrobat, falling from the heights of her sin, clad in scraps of nothing, with no need of a rope because the wind was safe, was holding her, would never let her fall, and –

The sea. She was in the sea. The water held her but it was cold, cold. Too cold to breathe and don't breathe, Callanish, don't breathe because you'll only breathe water and that's called drowning. The sky was down – the sky was up – she kicked out, fought back, and she would have to give up because she couldn't, she couldn't – but the harder she fought to hold her breath, the harder grew the pressure from her scars, as if they were trying to open, to let her breathe water – but that couldn't be, surely they weren't really gills, just scars on her flesh from her mother's knife, and that was not how it worked, you couldn't just cut yourself open and expect to find gills under your – then her scars strained, and she knew she couldn't breathe underwater but still she was, she was breathing.

She was not drowning. The knowledge that she wasn't drowning calmed her panic and she could think. The sea cocooned her in darkness so she couldn't see – but there, look, there were the silvery pocks of the hail falling on to the water, and so there was the surface. She kicked towards it. The webs between her fingers and toes caught the water, displacing it easily. She pushed once, twice – and there was the sky, and her lungs stretched, and she could breathe air.

On the deck the hail thudded, shattered, tore open skin – but here in the sea it scattered on the water gently, like snow on snow. Hailstones tickled her limbs as they sank past. Her whole life she had been afraid of the sea, terrified that it wanted to swallow her whole. And now here she was, and it held her. She felt something that she had not felt since that night in the circus coracle, her bare hand linked with North's. She felt at home.

Behind her, on the deck of the scrubbed and strange revival boat, Flitch raged and bled and called her name. But Callanish did not look back. She took a deep breath and swam for shore.

20
Avalon

'Help! Jarrow, help me!'

Was the canvas cover pulled back too far? Was it obvious that she had not really been in the coracle? Should she lever herself inside more – but that filthy beast might take a swipe at her feet, and she wasn't sure she could get her feet on the slats, and it was tricky enough to manoeuvre when she was this big, and what if she accidentally knocked her son?

'Jarrow, please! Help!'

She steadied her feet against the coracle's entrance and opened her mouth wide, ready to scream to the full stretch of her lungs, but as she pulled in a breath she heard the thud of feet and the roar of her husband calling her name. She felt a flash of annoyance that he had not appeared at the exact moment she called for him. What could he possibly be doing that was more important than saving the precious lives of his wife and baby?

'Jarrow, Ainsel, North – someone, please! Help me!'

There were still so many things that could go wrong. North could find the razor blade on the deck of her coracle. Avalon had planned to throw it into the sea after she'd cut her arm, but the sight of a dampling watching her from a medic boat anchored nearby had distracted her. In that moment of panic, she'd dropped the blade. There was no time to go after it, even if she dared to take her son anywhere near that nasty, violent animal. But it was fine. Even if North found it, what would she say? Who would ever believe her?

'I can't get away! I think it's coming! Please help!'

Avalon held in her scream and let out some whimpers instead, tearing her dress a little more. She bent her body at an awkward angle across the canvas, just as the top of Jarrow's head appeared on the *Excalibur*'s deck. And there on his face she saw panic, and fear, and love, and it was all for her. She felt affection kick in her belly. Soon they would have their home, and it would all be worth it.

'Jarrow!' she gasped. 'Save me. The bear – it's trying to kill me.'

21
Callanish

Callanish was on the island. She was shiver-soaked, frantic, tired to the marrow of her bones: but she was on the island.

By the time she managed to pull herself ashore, dawn was stretching out across the horizon. The island was awakening. But most of the windows in the nearby stilt-homes were still dark, so Callanish allowed herself a moment to lie on the wooden slats of the dock.

She stretched her limbs, and it hurt. She blinked her eyes, and it hurt. She breathed, and it hurt. Her lungs throbbed with the air of the island, heavy with smells: leaves, earth, rain, wood, animals, grass, strangers, family. She kept breathing until it stopped hurting.

Over the lip of the hill a landlocker approached. Callanish stood with her bare toes scrunched together and her hands behind her back to hide the webbing. She was ready with reasons. She had been thrown off her ship, her papers had been stolen, she had to leave her grace-yard because… because…

But she knew that none of it would matter, because now the landlocker could see her face.

For a dampling it would be impossible to get on to the island. Stowing away on a revival boat, pretending to be a trader or a butcher: all pointless. They'd never get past the blackshore. But this was Callanish's birth island. This is where she'd come from. The angles and planes of her face, a mirror of her mother's, marked her out. Every landlocker here knew the face of every other landlocker here – including that of Veryan Sand.

'You,' said the landlocker to Callanish, and though she had never seen him before, she knew his face.

'Yes,' she said. 'Hello.' She smiled, pretending that her clothes were not damp and her eyes were not bloodshot and her hands were not clenched into fists. 'I have come home to visit my mother. I am going there right now. Goodbye.'

She took a step. Her pulse throbbed at the base of her tongue and she tasted metal in her mouth. But she took another step, and another and another, and she was past the landlocker who was a stranger and not a stranger, and she was off the gangway and on the path leading up between the stilt-homes, and no one had stopped her. The stilt-homes seemed so flimsy, the salvaged metal walls tarnished, their spindly legs constantly sucked and battered by the waves. Their roofs were planted with short-rooted vegetables – lettuce and cabbage, radish and pepper – and the remaining leaves shuddered in the breeze from the sea.

As she walked further towards the island's centre, the reclaimed land under her feet grew so steady that she felt dizzy. She carried on past the reclaimed homes, their wooden walls thin as fabric, their proportions larger and their roofs lower for maximum contact with the ground. Landlockers could buy these houses even if they weren't native islanders, so she didn't know who would be living in them now. If they were new to the island, they might not recognise her. There might be questions. Her steps quickened, and she walked as fast as she could without tripping into a run.

Memories of her childhood home loomed up, faded as old paper: soaking in a herb-scented bath, her mouth watering for pepper-pumpkin soup, the song of the wind in the trees – then the shush of her mother's footsteps, the burn of her mother's knife...

She had slowed almost to a stop, bare toes dragging in the dirt. It was fine. She was fine. This island was supposed to be her home, and what could be safer than home? She picked up her feet and kept walking.

After all, she'd visited her mother before. Not for a while, true, but she must have visited since – no. There was no use in lying to herself. She had not returned to the island since the day she left for her grace-yard.

Houses and fences and face-framing windows flickered past as she walked. Finally the sun had made its way over the horizon, and Callanish was at her mother's gate. Her house was on old land – the most valuable of all, reserved for native islanders. The ground held her feet so steady she thought she might fall. She stood with her hand on the latch.

There were no flowers in her mother's garden. There was no smoke from her mother's chimney. There were no lights in her mother's window. Callanish swung the gate, walked up the path, and opened the front door.

'Mother,' she said. 'I've come home.'

Callanish knew that she should wait in the doorway until she was invited in. She knew that she should greet her mother warmly, should accept a cup of tea, should provide chatty updates on the noble and horrible business of gracekeeping. But she had come this far, and she could wait no longer.

'Mother?' she called again into the house. 'It's me. It's Callanish. Can I come in?'

Still no answer. She went in anyway.

'Mother? Are you ...' She trailed off. The house was too small for hiding. Callanish saw immediately that her mother was not asleep in her straw-mattress bed, or fetching food from the pantry, or soaking in the huge tin bath. She was not pulling vegetables from the tiny garden pressed up against the back wall of the house. There was nowhere else that she could be.

Callanish slumped on the bed, too cold even to shiver. The sea's chill was deep in her bones, and she knew that the earth would never get warm enough to chase it out. In the centre of the kitchen table sat a grace-feather; from her perch on the bed, Callanish could see how its green-blue colours had faded and its barbs were clumped and bent from repeated handling. The sight of it made tears clot at the base of her throat. Her mother knew her, and her mother remembered her, and her mother forgave her. So where was she?

To slow her thoughts, she ran her hand over the wood of the bed frame, pressed her bare feet on the wooden floorboards, inhaled the scent of oak leaves from the trees at the...

And then she knew where her mother was. She stood up and ran towards the woods at the centre of the island.

22
North

T hings were serious. The *Excalibur*'s crew huddled around the mess-boat table, but there were no dinner plates and no cups of fire. Everyone kept their gaze lowered – except for Jarrow. He looked at North. She kept her eyes down, the same as everyone else, but she could not help her expression. If her outside was anything like her inside, it was shifting between fear and anger.

'Thank you,' Jarrow said, 'for your time. You know why I have asked you here. You heard the cries of my poor wife – you heard the bear try to – you heard it.'

North bit back her protests.

'I do not blame North for this,' continued Jarrow. 'As the bear's trainer, she did more than could have been expected. Her bear performed beautifully every night, and we all know that her dance is of huge appeal to the landlockers. I wouldn't say that it's the only thing keeping the Circus Excalibur going, but it's certainly –'

Avalon flinched and sucked in a breath, tucking her bandaged left arm close to her body as if she'd had a flash of pain. North resisted the urge to launch herself across the table and snap Avalon's arm right off her body.

'But,' said Jarrow, 'a beast is still a beast.'

He rested his heavy hand on his wife's shoulder and she tilted her tear-blurred face up to him.

'We cannot let this incident pass,' he said. 'There must be consequences.'

'No! You can't!' North was shocked at her own outburst. 'That is, I – Jarrow, please. He didn't really – he didn't mean to hurt Avalon. And why was she even in my –'

'Yes, North?' asked Jarrow with raised eyebrows. 'Are you asking why the mistress of this circus cannot go wherever she chooses, whenever she chooses?'

'No. Nothing. I just – he's never hurt anyone before, Jarrow. You know that.'

'He is a beast. And he will always be wild. I cannot risk anyone else being harmed.' Jarrow squeezed Avalon's shoulder, as if seeking strength. 'Tonight he will stay in your coracle. Chain him tightly. Tie his mouth shut. Drug him if you can.'

North clenched her hands white on the tabletop. 'Yes,' she said.

'And as you will not be able to perform with your bear, you will be a part of the maypole instead. We must all earn our dinner.'

North glanced up at him. She couldn't, he knew she couldn't, her bump was far too big now to be bandaged down.

'Jarrow, please. I can't. I'm – it won't …' North trailed off. She hunched her body, trying to make Red Gold aware of her bump without pointing it out to the rest of the crew.

'No excuses. You will do what I say. And after the maypole you can join the clown military. That will be the main act tonight, and tomorrow night, and every night until I say otherwise.'

'Ah –' Cash coughed from the end of the table. 'Ah, boss. You said we weren't to do the military act in this archipelago. You said it would make the clams nervous. You said the military like to lurk around here. You said it might be dangerous. Remember? We haven't prepped, boss, not at all.'

'Then do your prep now. You have the whole day. Everyone will help you. Everyone will do what I say. No questions. In fact –' And here Jarrow glared around the room at each person in turn. 'The next person to question an order will have a reduction in their rations. Another question means another reduction, and three questions means no food at all.'

The reaction of the crew was immediate and negative: backs straightened, eyebrows lowered, jaws clenched. Even through her grief, North felt a bright burst of surprise. The crew often went against orders – the clowns in particular – but there had never been food restrictions before. There was little enough as it was.

'You have your orders, crew. Go, now, and work on your acts. All the things you wanted to do that I said you could not – now you will do them. Tonight, we must upend this island. We must.' Jarrow raised his hands, as if to rest his head in them, then restrained himself. 'Do you understand? We must shock. My wife is injured and Melia is not coming back – that means we're down a horse-performer and we have no acrobats. And without the bear to please the crowd, this is the only way we will eat tonight. Now go.'

He slumped at the head of the table. The crew filed out of the mess boat to prepare for that night's performance.

23
Callanish

The trees were dense, but Callanish barely slowed as she crossed from the fields to the woods. Beneath the oak canopy dead leaves carpeted the ground, hiding sharp twigs and dents in the earth. Within ten steps Callanish's bare feet were scratched to bleeding, her ankles jolted and throbbing. Branches clawed at her hair, grabbing fingerfuls from the roots; she glanced back, distracted by the blonde strands gleaming among the leaves. At least, she thought as she ran, she would be able to find her way out again: all she had to do was follow the stolen parts of her body.

Thwick went a twig under her foot, and *soosh* went the fallen leaves, and *cwit* went a branch as it snapped off against her shoulder – and oh, the fear of the gods was rising up in her now. She hesitated, but it was too late. She couldn't put the branch back on, so she might as well keep going. She picked up her feet and kept running. The trees were still ripping out her hair and the ground was still tearing at her feet but she was almost at the World Tree.

'Mother!' she called, and the trees threw her voice right back. As she ran she bunched up her hair and tucked it into the neck of her dress. It wasn't enough, so she raised her arms over her head to protect it, surrendering her skin to the sharpness of the branches. They stabbed, and they snapped, and the gods were angry with her: already she felt a constellation of splinters in her forearms.

'Mother!' she called again - and with a gasp she broke through to the clearing, and there she was: her mother, Veryan Sand, standing naked and barefoot in the woods with her arms stretched around the wide, rough trunk of the World Tree. She turned and looked at Callanish. Dew from the leaves glittered a silver fishing net on her hair.

'Hello,' she said. 'I'm going to have a baby. Are you here to help me?'

Callanish knew what she would see, but could not help glancing down at her mother's belly. It was pale and puckered and completely flat.

'Mother.' It was all that she could think to say.

Veryan's face split into a grin. 'Yes!' she said. 'I will be a mother. But not yet. First I must have this baby. And you must help me. It'll come at any moment now, so we must be ready.'

'Mother, it's me.' Callanish took a step forward. 'It's Callanish.'

Veryan stepped forward too, clasping her daughter's hands.

'Oh, that's a beautiful name. Don't tell anyone, but -' she lowered her voice to a whisper, leaning in, conspiratorial - 'that's what I plan to call my baby. Callanish Sand. Lovely, don't you think? My baby is going to be blessed by the gods. That's why I am having her here, you see. At the World Tree. So that my baby will be blessed. So that she will always be happy.' She turned away and stroked the tree's bark, crooning a lullaby under her breath.

Callanish pulled off her dress and put it over her mother's head, rubbing Veryan's arms to warm them. She shivered in her thin slip, trying to hide her shock at her mother's chicken-bone limbs, her distant eyes, her twitching fingers. It took all her self-control not to snatch her mother's hands away when she rested them maternally on her belly.

'It's not your time yet, Veryan. I'll take you home now.'

'But you'll bring me back here later?' Veryan allowed herself to be led away from the tree, though she cast longing glances back as she walked. 'You'll bring me back when the baby is coming? I know it won't be long now. I need to do right for my child. For my Callanish.'

'Yes. I'm sorry, I should have said that. I'll bring you back, and I'm sorry, and I'll do whatever you need, and I'm sorry. I'm sorry.'

24
Dosh

The clowns had waited a long time to sate their hunger. But when it happened, they wanted it to be in the right way, for the right reasons – and Dosh knew that this was not the right way. They'd never liked the north-west archipelagos. The clams were too busy worshipping tree gods and bowing to the military to appreciate the circus. Why go somewhere you weren't wanted? With Cash in charge, rebellion would be as indiscriminate as rain. Dosh preferred to choose battles. Better to save your revolution for where it had a chance to take hold.

'Maybe we shouldn't do the act tonight,' Dosh said, leaning in to examine Dough's face. They were painting the outlines of teeth on one another's faces, to make it look as if the flesh of their cheeks had been cut away.

'No choice,' said Dough, trying not to move too much under Dosh's brush. Dough always spoke as if only a set number of words had been allocated for the day. It was annoying, but not as annoying as Cash – who, of course, had started talking over the end of Dough's short sentence.

'We want to,' Cash said, 'and we have to, and so we will. Red Gold said that without the bear and the acrobats and that horse-whore we had to shock the clams. Every night before this it's been maypoles and flirting with the glamours and chucking paper money at angry clams. Safe and boring. Finally, we have our chance.' Cash had finished the pre-show prep, and sprawled out on a bunk, long limbs twisted at unlikely angles, checking that the tight military coat allowed the proper sensuousness of movement.

'What's been happening so far with our safe and boring act? Are you satisfied? Is your belly full? When the clams are bored, we go hungry. Red Gold told us to do the military act. For once, he's right.'

Cash was definitely bored, and it made Dosh nervous. For Cash, boredom led to restlessness, and restlessness led to danger.

'And let's not even mention our poor beds,' went on Cash with a theatrical sigh. 'Just as empty as our bellies.'

The curtains around their bunks hadn't been shut for weeks. Northern girls were more cautious about going with the clowns. They said the circus was all surface and lies, which was obviously true, though only northern girls seemed to think that was a bad thing. They had religion in their blood where circus folk had glitter, Cash always said, and nothing closes a clam girl's legs faster than fear of gods.

Clam girls were hard to seduce, but there were always a few who wanted a secret taste of rebellion. Once or twice, Dosh had enticed one behindcurtains post-act, eyelids smeared black and limbs speckled with paint and blood. The clam girl had shared a drink in the mess boat and then giggled her way back to the coracle, joining Dosh behind the bunk curtains before sneaking back to her island before dawn. But not lately. Angering the gods wasn't worth a boring clown.

'It's just,' said Dosh, reluctant to give up so easily, 'it seems risky. We saw a military boat a few days ago, and the northern archipelagos don't like circus folk.'

Dough chimed in. 'Don't like the military more.'

Cash scoffed. 'The military are still landlockers. Under their uniforms they're just clams. They're all on the same side, as long as it's against us.' Cash leapt from the bed, pacing the narrow coracle. Dosh and Dough stopped buttoning up their bloodstained coats to watch.

'Red Gold put us in charge tonight. He knows how tonight will go – no bear dance, so no applause, so no food. Well, boo-bloody-hoo. Is a wild animal really the best performer in this whole circus? Our whole lives, our ringmaster trains us for subversion – and then shies away from our suggestions when they get a bit too daring for him. *Good* suggestions, I might add – ones that would have got food in our bellies.'

'Cash, don't be so hard. He's kept us off the prison boat, hasn't he? Maybe he was right to –'

'Shut up, Dosh. Red Gold's lost his nerve. He's hiding away in his cabin, petting his horse-whore, buying her flowers so she'll keep pretending she carries his child. He should be the Lord of Misrule, tearing apart the world and leaving the clams to put it back together. But he's forgotten who he is. He doesn't know what to do any more – that's why he made us the ringmasters tonight. He fears those military masqueraders. He fears the prison boat.' Cash paced, outfit tight over flexing limbs. 'Well, we don't fear anything! What's the point of living life under a booted heel? It's worth the risk, I say. Tonight . . .' A slow smile spread across Cash's face, matching the painted-on teeth. 'Tonight we go all out.'

Dosh knew that whatever new tweak Cash wanted to put on the military act, the others would go along with it. They had to. And more than that – Dosh wanted to. He would not be frightened by the clomp of boots on the deck. They'd chosen their battle, and this was it.

25
Callanish

Callanish fed her mother, bathed her mother, put her mother to bed. She tweezed splinters from her mother's feet and stroked her mother's hair until she fell asleep.

It was still morning, but the day's light was pale and watery. Callanish left a candle burning beside the bed in case Veryan woke. Her mother's clothes were far too big – they had all been sewn with roomy hips and a pouch in the belly, to accommodate a growing bump – but she pulled them on anyway: boots, a dress, a fur over-vest. She could not chase out the chill. After a moment's thought, she pulled on a pair of her mother's leather gloves. They had been made for her mother's hands, and they pressed uncomfortably on Callanish's webbed fingers.

She clicked the front door shut behind her and crossed the tiny front garden, leaning her elbows on the gate to rest her head in her hands. Compared to the stillness of the graceyard, the island was a riot of sound and movement – but compared to the constant wind and waves and motion and chatter on Flitch's boat, it was as calm as death. She stood with her eyes shut, steadying herself on the motionless land. Her mother did not know her. She was not forgiven.

'Callanish?' The voice was tentative. Callanish jolted upright, muscles protesting. 'I thought it was you. Did you find your mother?'

The woman was familiar. Pale lips, awkward shoulders, wood-brown hair wrapped in a long braid. Her hands were chapped red, and she smelled of bread and musty fur.

'Mrs Farrow?' guessed Callanish, her brain still catching up. But her memory stumbled: this couldn't be Mrs Farrow, because Mrs Farrow had looked like this when Callanish was a child, and now she looked exactly the same, and how could –

The woman smiled. 'Mrs Farrow was my mother. My parents both passed so I have the house. I'm Mrs Rye now.'

'I remember. From when we were little. You're – it's Jenny, isn't it?'

The smile stayed. 'Mrs Rye will do. You found your mother, then?'

'Did you know she was there? Why didn't you bring her back? She was freezing.'

The smile disappeared. 'She's always there. Every morning, every evening. You'd know that if you'd ever come home.'

'I'm sorry, Mrs Rye. I didn't mean –'

'Me and the other neighbours, we've done right by her. We've spent weeks of our lives bringing Veryan back from the woods. Islanders look after one another.'

'I know. But I'm here now, and I'm going to take care of her.'

'Ah. So you're staying.' Mrs Rye tucked her hands in the pockets of her sealskin over-vest and looked satisfied.

'No, I – I don't think I can stay. On the island . . . it's not the place for me . . . and – I'll have to go back to the graceyard. But I can look after her there.'

'You want to take Veryan with you? Away from her home, to your island of dead damplings? Disgusting. We've heard all about what happens out on the water. Those people living out on the sea, they're already infecting the good folk of the islands.'

Mrs Rye's voice was getting louder, and curtains were twitching in the other houses. Callanish was sure that the islanders had been watching her from the moment she knocked on her mother's door. They would have all seen her stumbling back from the woods, wearing only her underclothes, carrying her mother as best she could. And behind those curtains they'd stayed. If they'd seen her hands and feet, then they'd seen them. It was too late now to hide. She was too big to be buried like a baby.

'We should have known,' went on Mrs Rye. 'As soon as you sent that dirty great feather, we knew you'd turn up here sooner or later. We should have guessed that it wasn't enough that you abandoned your home to go to that - that horrible place. But how can you even think of taking Veryan? She led the spring procession more than once - as the spring bride, even, and you can thank that for your own life. There's not many here can claim that honour. This island is her home. And you want to make her serve damplings for the rest of her days? To touch their dead bodies and say heathen prayers over them. Tell me, is that what your mother had planned for you?'

'There's no other way. I have to earn a living, and the graceyard is the only work I know. I have to take her back with me.'

'You have to let her live here, so that she can die here. What would you do when she passes? Tip her into the sea with the damplings? She belongs on this ground - in this ground. She should be burned on sacred wood and scattered at the World Tree - where she was born, where she was married. It's the natural order. Her body should nourish the good earth after she dies.'

'She's not going to die! Why are you saying that? She won't die. She's fine.' Callanish had held more dead bodies than she could count. She knew that people died every day - dozens, hundreds of them. But not her mother. Never her mother.

Mrs Rye took a long time to reply. 'You left, and you forgot all about us. But we remember. We remember what happened in this house.'

Callanish felt a shiver from deep in her bones to the top of her scalp. 'I know, and that's why I'm here. I came to say sorry. To make it right with her.' She tightened her jaw. She would not let a single tear fall, not in front of Mrs Rye.

'I know I haven't visited, but I tried to make it right. I sent her a feather from one of the graces, to show her that I remembered her. But you – you already knew that. Did she show you? Did she know what it meant?'

'What were you thinking, sending her that? What good could it have done?'

'So she did know? She does know, still?'

'Oh, Callanish. Your mother doesn't know anything at all.'

'You're wrong. She's ill, and you're being cruel.'

'She doesn't know you, child. She's been this same way for a long time. We looked after her when you wouldn't, and that's what she knows: her home, and her neighbours, and her island. Why change that now? What good could it do?'

'She's my mother. And she doesn't –' Callanish swallowed hard. 'She doesn't know me.'

'That is sad. But the world is full of sadness.'

Callanish glared at every one of the twitching curtains, refusing to blink. 'What do you want? You're angry that I didn't come back, and now you're angry that I'm here. Tell me. What do you want me to do?'

Mrs Rye pushed open the gate, forcing Callanish to take a step back, then walked into Veryan's garden. Shock replaced grief. All landlockers were fierce about their own tiny patch of earth, and in all her childhood Callanish had never seen an islander trespass on another's ground. Mrs Rye took hold of Callanish's arms and leaned in to hiss in her face.

'Leave. Leave, and don't look back. She's better without you.'

Callanish pulled away, but the garden was too small for retreat.

'But I'm her daughter. She needs to know who I am. It's better that she knows.'

'Better for who?'

Without waiting for an answer, Mrs Rye turned and went into her own house. Callanish stood, silent and alone in the garden, still trying to steady herself.

She stayed at her mother's house, living off the neighbours' thin-wearing charity, letting the days blur. Every night she sat and watched over her mother, every morning she made breakfast for her mother, every afternoon she weeded and planted the back garden with her mother, every evening she fell asleep upright in her wooden chair and had to run into the woods to the World Tree and bring back her mother. Did she know? Did she know that the tree was where she'd lost a child? Did she know that this soil held the tiny bones?

At times it seemed that Veryan remembered. She'd call out her daughter's name in her sleep, but when Callanish woke her, she smiled glassily and patted her hand. It took Callanish longer than it should have to realise that her mother dreamed not of her, but of the daughter she was yet to have. She wished that she could be that daughter, blessed and happy and at home. But if she stayed, it was only a matter of time until the islanders saw her hands and feet. She couldn't stand to wear those gloves and slippers for the rest of her life. North had seen her hands – and instead of flinching away, she had pulled her closer. Callanish was tired of hiding. But when the islanders knew what she really was – what her mother had given birth to – would they still look after Veryan? Would she even be allowed to stay on the island?

When Callanish did manage to slip into sleep, Mrs Rye's words spun in her head: *she's better without you*. Within an hour of waking she'd convinced herself that the neighbour was wrong. How could a lie be better than the truth? But the next night sleep would blind her again, and there were the words.

Every time Veryan passed the table, she picked up the feather. She'd stare at it, stroke its soft barbs over her cheek, then put it carefully back down. One day she stared at it for longer than usual, then held it out to her daughter.

'What is this?' she asked.

'It's a grace feather. See how its colours shift from green to blue, like the sea? It means remembrance. It shows that no distance, no amount of water between two people, will make them forget. Someone gave it to say that they remembered you.'

'Oh, that's nice. But they didn't need to. I remember everything.'

Callanish didn't know how to reply, so she didn't. Veryan put the feather back and carried on pottering around the house.

The next day, she picked it up again, asking 'What is this?', and the conversation was repeated. The day after, she picked up the feather, but did not ask anything. Instead she stared at Callanish, heavy and slow. Then she put the feather in the chest of sealskins and shut the lid. She did not speak for the rest of the day.

Callanish had sailed across the world to her mother's house knowing that she would receive one of two answers: yes, she was forgiven; or no, she was not forgiven. Now she had her answer, and it was neither. She was not forgiven, but she was not unforgiven.

She did not need Mrs Rye's voice echoing in her dreams to know that the words were true. The longer Callanish stayed, the closer her mother came to remembering – and remembering would bring her nothing but sadness.

It did not take long to make the arrangements with Mrs Rye. The neighbours had already been looking after Veryan, and Callanish promised to send coins and copper when she could. Mrs Rye was kind enough not to tell Callanish that she was doing the right thing.

Afterwards, she stood at the gate to her mother's garden, but did not go inside. Dusk was creeping in, though the stars had not yet appeared. A chill shivered through her. Inside the house a lamp had been lit, casting a honey-warm glow. Through the window, Callanish saw her mother, singing to herself as she rolled two boiled eggs on the counter to crack their shells. On the table sat a block of butter, a white loaf, and a small pot of honey. She would have a good supper.

As she pushed open the gate, it squealed. Her mother's head snapped up at the sound. Callanish dropped to her knees and crawled underneath the window. The grass was damp and the wall scraped her back as she pressed against it.

Veryan's silhouette spread out into the garden, blue-black in the honeyed light. Callanish kept looking at the shape until it slipped away: back into her house, back to her supper, back to her life.

'Goodbye,' she whispered to the space where her mother's shadow had been.

26
Dough

Another night. Another show.

Bero coaxed music from the wind-up gramophone, Ainsel turned flips on horseback, North wound ribbons around the glamours' bodies for the maypole. The air smelled of damp fabric and strange spices and a hundred unfamiliar bodies.

Beneath it all, Dough imagined Red Gold and his wife hiding in the *Excalibur*'s cabin. The stage was the ship's deck, so they would be able to hear every word – a thought both enticing and nerve-racking. Since Avalon's injury, Red Gold had stayed belowdecks during every performance. In his absence, the clowns had free rein – and every night, they pushed their act further.

Dough lurked with Cash and Dosh in the seawater-rough embrace of the curtains, striding on stage between acts to rile the crowd. Red Gold's usual style was old-fashioned: booming commandments and enticements that echoed between the clams' ears, the tent lit up bright as stars with dozens of seal-fat lamps. Safe scares glittered with a fat dollop of magic.

The clowns favoured a more sinister approach: dressed in floor-length capes, the hoods pulled low, they slinked across the stage to hiss warnings in the faces of the closest clams, the tent dim with shadows cast by a handful of lamps. The capes were creepy, which they liked, but they also served to hide their costumes and make-up. The clowns didn't want to lessen the clams' shock and delight when they were finally revealed. That night, the circus was an altogether darker place. When on stage, the circus performers could see nothing at all of the crowd. The clams might all have up and left, but for the scent of their skin and the sound of their applause.

As well as sharing ringmaster duties, Dough also danced the maypole with the glamours and Bero, all of them sporting masks made of fake flowers; helped with costume changes; and watched Ainsel's horses while he primped his hair. Dosh was glad to keep busy so as to avoid speaking to North. The sadness on her face was so distracting, and nothing would make her feel better.

'Ready?' hissed Dosh.

Dough jolted awake. 'Now?'

'You were dreaming. Get ready. We're on.'

There was no announcement for the military act. After the last flare of Bero's fire-breathing act had faded, the stage was left empty and dark. The clams waited.

Then the gramophone squealed into life: a military march, loud and aggressive. This was something new. The clams waited.

Behindcurtains the three clowns stamped to the beat in their metal-soled boots until the striped silk shuddered with the sound. When the clams' excitement and fear was so thick they could taste it, the clowns marched on stage.

In the centre of the stage they marched in place, arms straight, chins held high to let the lights hit their painted skulls. The clams were silent in their darkness. The march got louder, the clowns stamped harder. Dough felt the deck judder under their heels – if they kept this up, the whole ship would topple. What would Red Gold make of it, hunched down in his cabin with his unfaithful wife, feeling the walls shake?

Just in time, the military march slowed, the notes drawing out, part sinister and part sensual. The clowns calmed their dance too, keeping time with the slower beat, easing their stamp into a slide. They let their hips sway under their tight-buttoned coats, twisting their painted skulls into smiles. Their arms stretched towards the darkness of the crowd, fingers spread, beckoning. Each move was aggressively sexual, confronting the audience.

Dough felt good – and it was clear the other clowns felt good too. This was how they were supposed to be. This was their purpose. What's the use of a clown who doesn't subvert? What do they bring to the crowd? Everyone has sadness, and rage, and frustration – and so everyone needs a clown.

Cash gave a subtle nod to Bero offstage and the march slowed again. The clowns switched from aggressive sexuality to coy submission, straightening their legs and bending at the waist, undoing their top buttons to flash a glimpse of the bare skin beneath their coats. Legs wide, they tugged at the fastenings of their trousers, inching them down to show the pale skin of their lower bellies – revealing more and more, but not yet enough for the clams to know, to be sure…

This was the crowd's cue. Usually some of them, having seen the clown military before, knew to bring projectiles with them: spoilt food, broken tools, handfuls of seaweed from the blackshore. In their rage and frustration they'd hurl these things at the clowns – at the military, in their minds. The objects hit, and it hurt, and the clowns bled. And the more they bled, the more the clams screamed and raged and threw. That was good. Scapegoats must always bleed.

Dough knew that clowns made perfect scapegoats, because what's scarier than a clown? They stand for money and hunger, sex and rage, loss and loneliness, displacement and death. They stand for everything, and they stand for nothing.

The clowns owned the stage: three painted, half-nude skeletons, baiting a hundred people to attack them. Dough waited for the shock of impact, the thud of objects on flesh.

But something was wrong. The clams stayed in their seats with their mouths shut. Under the sluggish throb of the military march, Dosh heard nothing. No shouts, no taunts, no scrape and rustle of objects ready to be thrown.

'ENOUGH!' came a shout from the crowd. In the shadows, Dough thought a clam stood up – but was that the gleam of buttons on a military coat? Was that the shine of a metal club?

The music stopped. The clowns stood on the stage, frozen in mock-sexy poses, staring into the breathing dark.

'You are under arrest. Landlockers, stay in your seats. Damplings, drop any weapons. If you are armed, you will suffer for it.'

'We don't have any weapons!' called Cash into the darkness. 'We're just circus performers! We –'

Dough nudged for silence a moment too late. A dozen more shadows stood in the crowd. As they approached the stage, the military boots weren't loud enough to shake the *Excalibur's* striped silks, but they were no less scary for that.

The clowns straightened, trying to fasten their costumes without looking as if they were hiding weapons. They didn't fear the military, but they didn't enjoy a beating.

'Present your captain. Who is in charge here?'

Dough stepped forward without hesitation. 'I am. I take full responsibility.'

From behindcurtains came a clatter, a muffled curse, and Red Gold burst on to the stage with his face as red as blood. He looked at the cluster of real military men on one side of the stage and the painted, half-dressed military clowns on the other side. He understood. But he said nothing.

A hundred landlockers filed from their seats and back on to their island, mouths closed and eyes on the ground. When the tent was empty, the military men rounded up everyone from the Circus Excalibur who'd performed that night. Together, they marched on to the prison boat.

The prison cabin was nowhere near large enough to house the three clowns, the three glamours, Ainsel, and Bero – but there they were, and there they would stay.

'Damn it, Cash, would you *move*?' Teal shifted, hip-wiggling to force a finger-width of space on either side.

'Move where, exactly?' replied Cash, hunching to show that they were all feeling squashed. 'The only way is out. If you want to try and squeeze your admirable mass out of that porthole, feel free.'

Dough admired the restraint: Cash spoke of being in the prison boat as a chance for some revolutionary action, though how much revolution could be enacted from inside a locked cabin, Dough didn't know. Cash usually paced the tiny space and ranted at the military men guarding the cabins, though Dough was sure they didn't listen to a word of it. Still, it kept Cash busy, and that was useful. Now they were penned in, shoulder to shoulder, uncomfortably aware of one another's breathing, getting each other's hair caught in the sweaty remnants of their make-up every time they moved. It was a good thing that Dosh had grown up in a coracle with two others – claustrophobia was an anxiety that no dampling could afford.

'Red Gold will get us out soon,' soothed Cyan.

'Sure as tides he won't,' said Cash with a snort. 'He'll be far too busy making peace between Avalon and North. The three of them, stuck there alone – can you imagine? Such chaos! It'll be magnificent!'

Dough couldn't resist sneaking a glance at Ainsel. They all knew that something was up with him and Avalon – she'd always disliked

North, but since the agreement that Ainsel would marry North and move into a clam house on an island, she'd progressed to hatred. Dosh wasn't sure if it was about Ainsel, or North, or the house, but her hate burned so strong that the source barely mattered. Ainsel's face, though, remained as impassive as ever. He hadn't said a word since they'd been rounded up for the prison boat: he'd simply handed his horse's reins to his father and traipsed after the clowns. It wasn't Ainsel's first time in a locked cabin, but he was usually in better spirits.

'Are the landlockers celebrating that we got arrested?' Mauve was the only one with a view from the porthole, and was making good use of it. 'It's fireworks or something. Bright lights. Maybe that procession that they do, with the candles? The island is so dark, it's hard to tell, but it looks like –'

Cash tried to elbow Mauve out of the way. 'Don't be stupid. The landlockers hate the military more than us. They won't be celebrating. If anything, they'll be mourning the loss of our act. I bet they had pockets full of old vegetables and broken things, ready to pelt us with. They needed to vent just as much as we did.' Cash leaned over Mauve and peered out of the porthole. 'But – what is that?'

One by one, the circus crew wriggled and bent and stretched so that they could look out the porthole. Dough managed a glimpse: a slow gleam of light in the dark. But Dough had been the first into the prison cabin, and had glanced out of the porthole then. The island's location was easy to remember, and the location of the boats around it. The glow came from the circus boats. Dough leaned over for another look, and the light had grown enough to show that it fitted the shape of a coracle.

'What is that?' Dough asked, frowning.

'Fire,' said Bero, his voice low.

'Fire?' shrieked Cyan. 'But it can't – Red Gold wouldn't let – how could –'

Finally, for the first time since he'd boarded the prison boat, Ainsel spoke. 'She didn't wait. I had a plan. It was good. It would have got us a house. I thought I knew what she wanted, but I – but she – she'll do anything, burn anything, destroy everything. She'll tear it all down if that's what it takes.'

Dough lost patience. 'Ainsel, what in oceans are you talking about?'

'Avalon,' he said, and his voice cracked. 'It's Avalon.'

27
Callanish & North

allanish was on the dock the day the striped sails appeared on the horizon. She had been preparing for another night sleeping on the shore, followed by another day hiding among the trees and trying to avoid her mother's window. The islanders had patience with their kin, but that patience would soon snap.

She watched the circus boat dock at the next island. From this distance, she could not make out the identities of the figures – was that the bear-like bulk of the captain? Was that North's dark head peeping from a coracle? It had to be. It had to be. The comings and goings of the island continued around her, steady as breathing, predictable as dawn. She saw none of it.

Night fell, and still she watched. Even from this distance, the circus was magical. The lights beneath the silks lit up the colours, soft as embers. If she strained her ears, she was sure she could hear whispers of music. She lay back on the dock, using her fur over-vest as a pillow, and let the distant circus lull her.

If they were on the next island tonight, then they would be at this island tomorrow. She felt her future rolling out in front of her, blurry of detail but featuring one vital part: North, the bear-girl, the one who would –

She jolted upright, eyes straining against the dark. Why was a prison boat, lights dimmed almost to nothing, being hauled ashore beside the circus? Why had the music stopped? Why were the land-lockers all filing back on to their island?

Callanish waited. Finally, when she had almost given up, a line of people marched across to the prison boat, and she did not need to see their faces to know that it was the circus crew. After a while, the circus boat was hauled off the island and back out into the water, where someone appeared on deck and linked the main boat back up to the coracles. She squinted her eyes: it looked as if two others had come out on to the deck, but it was hard to see shapes in the dark.

Callanish stood on the dock, heart pounding, frantic with helpless-ness. She could try to convince the military to – but no, they wouldn't be convinced by anything. She could barter for – but no, the military already had everything they wanted. She could show her support for the circus by – but no, there was no point, and she might be arrested too.

The circus crew would have to do their time on the prison boat. Depending on the charge, they might not come to this island until next week, or the week after. She sat back down on the dock. She had spent her life waiting. What was another few days? She tried to unclench her fists, to slow her heart.

She'd never been on a prison boat so didn't know what the condi-tions were like. If they'd been mistreated, given meagre food rations, perhaps they would be too weak to perform as soon as they were released. Perhaps they'd think that this archipelago was altogether too dangerous, and skip over the rest of its islands. Perhaps –

Callanish was pulled from her dreaming by a flicker of light from the coracles. It did not look like a seal-fat lamp, nor a clutch of candles. It was bigger than that, wilder. Then she knew.

It was fire. The circus was on fire.

Callanish did not stop to think. She kicked off her shoes, pulled off her gloves, and waded into the sea.

North knew that she shouldn't have crept away to check on her bear during the clown military. Even as she slid silently along the chains to her coracle, she tried to persuade herself to turn back. But then she was climbing up on the canvas and dropping into her coracle, and there was her bear's warm fur, and she knew that she was going nowhere.

At first she had raged at Red Gold's suggestion that she drug her bear. But despite her pleadings, he refused to be chained, refused to lie still on the bunk, refused to let her leave the coracle without opening his jaws wide, ready to roar. Bero provided some secret herb from his kitchen stocks, and finally the bear lay still. And now, while the circus sparkled and thrilled behind her, North lay still too.

She tried to stay awake, but had almost drifted into dreams when the music stopped. She jolted upright. The world shook with the steady tromp of military boots – and she knew that it was not the clowns. She prayed to the gods of the sea for the military to pass her by. Silence fell, broken only by the sway and whisper of the clams leaving the circus for their island homes. The circus was still.

North knew what had happened, though she didn't know how. Through timing and luck, she escaped the prison boat – though as soon as she emerged from her coracle she realised that it was not good luck, but bad. Red Gold and Avalon had clearly just had an argument. He was slump-shouldered and tight-jawed, hefting ropes and stacking equipment; she was sauntering off to the mess boat, chin high, as snooty as it was possible to be when balancing between coracles while heavily pregnant. North tried to duck back down into her coracle, but it was too late.

'North!' called Red Gold. 'Come and help.'

North mumbled some excuse in reply, knowing it was pointless. She checked once more on her dozing bear, then climbed across the coracles to the *Excalibur*.

'What happened?' she asked Red Gold.

'Military,' he replied, his voice low. 'In the crowd. Don't know how. Took the crew. How did you ... ?'

'I was checking on my bear, just quickly. But he's fine. Everything's fine.'

'Is it?'

Red Gold was the strongest man that North had ever known, but now he slumped and strained as if weights were tied to his shoulders.

'Is Avalon ...' she asked.

'Avalon will be fine. She doesn't want the circus, but I've worked too hard and too long to let it go. She just wants a house. We all know she wants a house. And we all know that there's only enough money for one house. That house is for you and Ainsel.'

'Jarrow, I don't want there to be a problem with you and Avalon. It's fine about the house, really it is. Maybe you and Avalon could have it, and Ainsel and I could stay here, with the circus. We'll take good care of it, you know we will, and –'

'Enough, North. I know you mean well, but Ainsel has more important things to do than become a ringmaster. I want Stirlings back on land. Avalon has had everything she wants for too long. I'm not letting her tell me what to do – not about this. It's too important. I'm the captain, and that's that. Now get back to work.'

North bowed her head and busied herself with returning the Excalibur from a circus to a ship. Pulling ropes, storing props, returning the gramophone to its cubby. She kept her gaze on the ship's deck, but let her mind drift out across the sea.

It was only when she glanced across to the coracles that she knew something was wrong.

'Fire!' she tried to shout, her voice constricting in panic. 'Fire, Jarrow!'

Her eyes widened to take it all in. She was blinded by the bright lick of flames already running across the chain that attached the mess boat to the clowns' coracle. Her eyes followed the line, furthest to nearest: Bero's mess boat, clown coracle, Island of Maidens, her own coracle, Ainsel's - and then she saw Avalon, lying on the rumpled canvas of Ainsel's coracle as if in a faint.

In one swift movement, Red Gold emerged from under the silk, roared his wife's name, and took off across the chains to her. His progress was unsteady. His feet slipped on the chains. It made the row of coracles dip and swoon in the water, sending them drifting off.

North saw that the chain attaching Ainsel's coracle to the main boat was still attached, but Ainsel's was not connected to her own boat. The *Excalibur* and Ainsel's coracle were safe from the fire - but the rest of the circus was aflame, already drifting away. And so was her bear.

By the time Callanish had swum out to the nearest circus boat the flames had already taken hold. She scrabbled at the pitted metal shells, unable to find purchase. Her head dipped under and she breathed sea. She opened her eyes, blinking saltwater, and swooped under the coracle to search for a handhold. There: a loose rope. She grabbed it, hauling herself up and out of the water.

She braced herself against the coracle, straightening her legs so that she could peer inside. The metal shell couldn't burn, but through the flames she saw that the coracle was stuffed with fabric: sequins, furs, silks; all the costumes of the circus. If anyone or anything was inside, it was too late. The smell of burning fabric caught in her throat. She dropped back into the water and stretched her arms towards the next coracle.

As she was hauling herself up she heard a shout. On the boat stood North, dream-hazy through the smoke – but she was real, and she was calling to Callanish. She slid back down and swam for the boat, searching the dark water for a rope. She hadn't even made it on to the deck when North fell to her knees, calling over the boat's side.

'We have to help him! He's in my coracle, there! Please, we have to –'

Without waiting for Callanish to reply, North dived into the sea and swam towards a coracle – one that, to Callanish's relief, was not yet burning. She let go of the rope and swam after North.

North did not know why the gracekeeper had suddenly appeared, clambering up the side of the smoking mess boat, but it did not matter. What mattered was getting to her bear before her coracle caught fire.

She kicked and pushed and choked on the water until she reached it, heart throbbing in her ears. The flames reflected off the dark sea, dazzling her. There was the end of the rope.

She could not reach it.

She scrabbled, trying to tip the coracle towards her. Panic rose in her throat – but there was Callanish, swimming smooth as a fish, and with one strong kick her upper body shot out of the water, high enough to grab the rope.

'Come,' she said, reaching down to grab North. Her skin was slick with seawater, her webbed fingers strong around North's wrist. Together they climbed the rope and dropped to the canvas cover, panting against the smoke billowing from the next coracle. Flames licked at the far end of the chain, the metal links reflecting the light greasily.

'We have to unhook the –' North grabbed the connecting chain, then let go with a howl. She clutched her burnt hand to her chest. 'It's too hot. And it's coated with seal fat. That's why the fire is spreading. Avalon, she must have – we must get him out.'

They both dropped down into the coracle. It was dark and hot, and smelled of fur and breath. 'He can't climb up,' said North. 'He's too groggy, I had to drug him, and – he can't. But he's so heavy, and I don't know how...'

'The rope,' said Callanish. 'Where's the ladder?'

North took her hands and placed them on the ladder. Callanish climbed out and threw North the rope they'd used to climb from the water. 'Tie him,' she said.

The bear was too heavy. Callanish knew it, and North must know it too. But still they braced their feet on the canvas. Still they pulled.

'North!' A voice boomed over the crack of flames. The ringmaster balanced on the raised edge of the big boat, a rope in his hands. 'Grab it!'

He threw the rope to North. In the dark and haze and flames, she missed. A shriek sounded – but not from North. Callanish rubbed at her eyes and focused on the figure trying to navigate from a coracle attached to the boat. Callanish recognised her: the ringmaster's wife, black-haired and dressed in blue, her belly swollen to twice the size it had been when Callanish last saw her.

'What are you doing?' shrieked the woman at the ringmaster. 'Are you mad? Leave it! Let it burn!'

He turned his back to the woman and threw the rope again. This time, North caught it.

The rope was rough with saltwater, scraping the skin from North's palms as she pulled her coracle to the *Excalibur*. When they were close enough, Red Gold lashed the rope to the schooner and jumped on to North's coracle. He landed with a thud, and before the coracle had stopped tilting in the water he had the bear's rope looped around his shoulders, and he was heaving, and he was pulling, and North let out a sob of joy when her bear's dark head appeared. With one enormous heave, Red Gold pulled the bear up on to the canvas.

But Avalon had not given up. As Red Gold stepped back on to the *Excalibur*, ready to heave the bear on to the deck, she laid her hands on his arm.

'You made me do this. You know that, don't you, Jarrow?' Her angry tone had lightened to a whine, and North could barely make out the words. 'You wouldn't see the truth. You wouldn't make the choice. So I took away the choice. How can you stay with the circus when there is no circus? Take me home, sweet king.'

Red Gold did not appear to be listening. He lashed the bear's rope and pulled North's coracle closer in, so close the helms thudded. The sound seemed to make something in Avalon snap.

'You can't still want to give her that house. You can't be that stupid.'

Red Gold kept his head down, securing the boats. The flames were flicking at the chain on the other side of North's coracle. The canvas could catch light at any moment.

'It's not Ainsel's baby.' Avalon's voice dropped to a croon. 'North told me. She said she'd got drunk and slept with some nasty dampling – and he paid her, Jarrow, did you know that he paid her? She puts it around everywhere, she's gone through all the clowns and the glamours and the fire-breather too. You have no idea what she's really like, she doesn't even love Ainsel, she just wants a house, she told me, she'd do anything to get a house, she said –'

'Hush now, Avalon.' The ringmaster did not shout. 'Hush,' he said. 'It's finished. It's over.'

As the woman disappeared belowdecks, sobbing, the ringmaster heaved the bear on to the big boat's deck. North and Callanish followed. As soon as their feet touched the deck, the ringmaster loosened North's coracle and pushed it away – just in time, for the flames were reaching for the coracle's canvas top.

Under Callanish's hands the bear's fur felt oily and tangled, almost too hot to touch. He seemed dazed, half asleep. He raised a paw and she grabbed at it, ready to tug him upright. But the paw fell, and the bear's eyes closed.

'Are we safe?' she asked.

'For now,' replied the ringmaster.

North said nothing at all, too busy checking over her bear. Callanish went to ask what she could do, how she could help – and the next thing she knew, the woman was on the deck, throwing herself at North, shrieking something about a house, about a child, about love, and she raised her arm above her head.

In her hand, a gleam of metal.

Her arm fell.

The bear roared.

There was noise, and movement, and light; scuffles and shrieks and the thud of bodies on the deck. And then quiet. North stayed hunched over her bear, protecting him, afraid to move, afraid to look. She counted the slow waves swaying the boat: seventeen, eighteen, nineteen –

'North.' Red Gold spoke low and urgent in her ear. 'I got Avalon into Ainsel's coracle. But you can't stay here.'

'I'll stay. I'll help you.' She spoke into her bear's fur.

From Ainsel's coracle came a thud. North and Red Gold turned their heads towards it. Another thud. The sounds kept coming, steady as heartbeats. Avalon, beating the inside of the coracle.

'No,' Red Gold said. 'You have to go. Take the *Excalibur*.'

'But what about you?'

'We're safe. The fires will burn out. They can't spread across the water.'

From Ainsel's coracle came the panicked whinnies of the horses. Avalon's thuds immediately stopped. North imagined she could hear her soothing Lord and Lady, stroking their manes to the beat of her heart. She patted her bear's fur to the same rhythm. She felt her breathing slow, her fear lessen.

'What about the circus?' she asked Red Gold. 'Without the *Excalibur*, how will you perform?'

'It's too late for that, North. We can't go back to how it was. Our costumes, the coracles – it's all destroyed. I'll pay another boat to tow us to the North-East archipelago. Perhaps I can sell what remains for scrap.'

'Will you buy the house? The one that was for Ainsel and me? Because I'm sorry, Jarrow, but I never wanted it. I know you do. I want you to go there and escape from all this, from the hunger and the storms, and I want –'

'It wasn't about escape. It was about – look, North. The house was a gift. I thought it was the best gift in the world. And yes, I had my own reasons to want you and my son on land. But I thought those reasons could work together.'

She raised her head to look at the coracles. The fires had almost burned out, the empty shells exhaling smoke into the sky.

'You still can be on land, Jarrow. You can live in the house. You and Avalon.'

'No. It will be all of us.'

'The whole crew? In a house? But they can't – they won't want to live on land.'

'They will because I say they will. Working the land pays well. They won't argue with full bellies.'

'But what about Avalon? She won't like –'

'North, be quiet. I will love Avalon until the day I die, but this isn't for her. I need to give you this, for . . .' Red Gold swallowed hard and looked out at the remains of his circus. 'I'm sorry for what happened to your parents. What I let happen. I knew the danger. I knew that bear was a wild beast. And still I let them perform, over and over. I said I'd look after you, but then I – I let you do the same. Every performance with that creature. I knew he'd turn, eventually – it was only fair that he turned on my wife. I'm sorry. I'm sorry that I put you in danger. Not just once, but every night.'

'But I chose to. I wanted to.'

'Is it really a choice when we have no other option? I didn't give you another option. I made you perform, and I was going to make you marry Ainsel. I should have given you a choice then. Get on that boat and get away from here. This is the last thing I can do for you.'

'I can't – I don't know if . . .' North hesitated, emotions stacking up inside her. If she moved, they would topple.

'North, would you please be quiet and do as I say? I'm going to get the money. And when I've done that, I want you to go.'

Red Gold's voice moved away, and North looked up. He was stepping up from the cabin and hefting a sack on to his back. He was climbing on to Ainsel's coracle. He was untying the rope. He was drifting away.

He still spoke, raising his voice so that North could hear him, but he seemed to be speaking to himself. 'We'll be fine in the house. It'll be a tight fit, but we'll manage. A captain doesn't abandon his crew. A house is a boat the same as a boat is a home. Avalon can cook enough for everyone. She's always wanted a house. She'll be happy now. We'll have a house, a house for all of us, clowns and glamours and horses and sons. A family, now and always, a family in a house . . .' And then he had drifted too far away, and North could not hear him any more. So Avalon would get what she'd always wanted – and everything she'd never wanted. The house she loved, crammed floor to ceiling with the circus folk she hated. In time the crew would probably buy their way back on to other circus boats. Then Jarrow and Avalon and Ainsel could live together in the home they all wanted so much, with the baby. The four of them, playing at family, fighting over a shred of ground. It was only a matter of time before the whole thing exploded. North wondered who would be left in the shrapnel, but it all seemed so far away. Her world shrank to the size of her bear's gasping body.

There was a whine of rope, the shush of a sail unfurling. North glanced up: Callanish stood at the wheel.

'Where shall we go?' she asked.

'Away,' said North, and laid her head back on her bear's warm side.

Callanish managed to steer the boat out of the archipelago. She set a course for the darkest patch of sea, figuring that way they'd be least likely to hit any other boats. She heard a gasp and glanced up.

'North, what's wrong?'

'Nothing. Pain. Cramps in my belly, from pulling on the rope. It'll pass in a - oh!' North let out a yelp. The moon emerged from a cloud, lighting her face.

Fear shivered through Callanish. She had seen that look before: her mother, many years ago, staggering to the World Tree, pulling the child Callanish after her. She took a breath and held it, allowing herself to be terrified. Then she let it go, pushing out her fear with her breath. She could be scared later. But not now. Not yet.

She glanced around: distant lights, but no immediate danger. She dropped the anchor and crouched down beside North. It was so quiet that she could hear both their hearts beating. Above them, the stars spread out in glinting layers.

'North, listen to me. It's your baby. It's coming.'

North jerked up, hands clenching in the bear's fur. 'But it's too soon! It hasn't been in there long enough, there should be another month at least, and I'm not – it can't come now. It's not ready. I'm not ready.'

'Babies are like bears,' said Callanish, easing North away from her bear and towards the cabin. 'They don't always do what you want them to. But now, we have some work to do.'

'My bear! Is he okay? Will he go back to sleep?'

As she guided North down into the cabin, Callanish looked back over her shoulder. In the moonlight she saw the gleam of the bear's blood pooled across the deck. She saw that his furry side did not rise. She saw that his eyes were closed.

'Yes,' she said, ducking into the cabin and laying North out on the bunk. 'Yes, he's asleep.'

The days on the boat unfolded, slow and bright.

Every night, Callanish dreamed – not of the sea's endless call, but of her mother. At first she welcomed the dreams, revelling in them, wishing to crawl inside them for ever and never wake. She told North stories of her childhood: the candlelit processions to the World Tree, her mother baking poppyseed bread and slathering it with honey, the pair of them snapping icicles off the window ledges to dip in flower dyes and draw in the snow. The days passed, and her dreams slipped away. She grew glad to wake to North's smile and her baby's hands splaying like starfish.

Every night, North expected to dream of her bear – to wake gasping and frantic, ready to leap into the water so she could be with him again. But she did not. Her sleep was calm and dreamless, rocked by the rhythm of the sea. She told Callanish about her bear: the way his breath turned to snuffles when he was happy, his delight in crisped fish skin, the rough brown pads under his front paws.

Together, the new crew of the *Excalibur* rested. They breathed salt air. They ate fish. They warmed their toes in the sun and shared stories by moonlight. And when the stars came out, they looked up and saw the bear in the constellations.

Slowly, slowly, they moved forwards.

After

'North, what are you doing? Don't put Ursa in the water!'

'Why not?'

'This is a graceyard! The water is full of bodies, rotting. And bones and...'

'Have you ever looked? Actually gone into the water and looked?'

'No. Because, as I said, it's full of bodies and rotting and –'

'I looked. I wasn't about to let my child go somewhere that I hadn't checked first. And you know what's down there? Nothing. There are no bodies any more, Callanish, and the bones are all buried. There are all these flashing shoals of fish, and flowing weeds with purple flowers, and around the chains that anchor the house there are mosses and weeds and all kinds of beautiful things.'

'But the bones are still down there, right at the bottom, under the sand. The fish eat the flesh and the bones sink.'

'So what? Let them be there. The sea is full of secrets, but they're not all out to harm us.'

'But I –'

'Come here, Callanish. Sit with us.'

'Oh, you've got your arms in the water and everything. Hold on to her – no, don't let her go!'

'She's fine. She can swim. And I'm right here. Come and sit with us. Dip your toes in the water.'

'I'll sit. But do I have to put my feet in?'

'Yes, you have to.'

'Okay. For you.'

'There you go! Not so bad, is it?'

'No. I wouldn't go so far as to say I liked it, but…'

'But you like it.'

'I do, North. I like it a lot.'

'And a feather fell from the bear's grace this morning.'

'I suppose that must be what happens when you keep them alive for more than a few weeks. They lose feathers and grow new ones.'

'I suppose so. I'm glad we're keeping this one alive. And we can send the feather to your mother, if you're sure.'

'I'm sure. She liked the other feather I sent. I saw how tatty it was; she must have touched it every single day. I don't know what it made her think, but it must have been a good memory. It only started to cause her pain when I was there to remind her. North, are you and Ursa staying here with me?'

'We can all stay here.'

'For how long?'

'For as long as we like. You can do Restings, and Ursa and I will sit in the house when anyone comes by. I'll catch fish, and cook up seaweed for us. On the *Excalibur* we had seaweed stew, seaweed salad, seaweed puffs, seaweed patties, seaweed fritters, seaweed scones. It's not pretty, but it's versatile. And maybe sometimes you can stay inside with Ursa and I'll do the Restings. Your white dress would fit me fine.'

'Oh, North! You'd be a terrible gracekeeper!'

'I think I'd be good. I'm used to performing, you know. It's not so different really, what we do.'

'But can we do that for ever?'

'Well, when we're ready to go, we can go. All of us.'

'Where?'

'Anywhere. We'll dive for fish and coral and mother-of-pearl, and then we'll trade that. I've seen you swim, Callanish. You can dive deeper and longer than anyone else. You'll be able to find such wonderful things.'

'Where will we live? We don't belong anywhere.'

'You're right, but you're wrong. We don't belong anywhere, because we can belong everywhere.'

'But Ursa. She's different. She –'

'Look around you. Look at us. Is it so bad to be different? To make your own way? We have this place, and we have a boat. We can stay still or we can keep moving. But there are more than two options in the world. In fact, there are more than two worlds. And this baby – *our* baby – she proves that. Ursa is both of us, and she's something else as well. I don't know what these new worlds are yet, but I know that when we discover them, I want us to discover them together.'

'I suppose we've made it this far, haven't we? I just worry.'

'We can't know what's coming with the dawn. Now stop asking questions and come into the water with me.'

North and Callanish slid off the dock and into the water, tilting back their heads to let the sun warm their faces. Around them the sea stretched to the horizon, silver bright, busy with worlds. Between them Ursa swam, stretching out her webbed fingers, floating between earth and sky.

Acknowledgements

Thank You: Cathryn Summerhayes and everyone at WME; Liz Foley, Bethan Jones, Alexis Washam, Jennifer Lambert and everyone at Harvill Secker, Hogarth and HarperCollins Canada; Claire Marchant-Collier, Helen Croney and everyone at Scottish Book Trust; Nick Barley and everyone at Edinburgh International Book Festival; Peggy Hughes; Helen Sedgwick; Katy McAulay; the board and staff at Brownsbank Cottage, Hawthornden Castle and Cove Park; all the Logans, Bennetts, Jinkses, Adairs, and Sopers; and all my long-suffering and inspirational friends.